Any
Minute

Any Minute

A NOVEL

JOYCE MEYER
AND DEBORAH BEDFORD

FaithWords

New York   Boston   Nashville

FaithWords
Hachette Book Group, Inc.
237 Park Avenue
New York, NY 10017

Visit our Web site at www.faithwords.com.
The FaithWords name and logo are trademarks of Hachette Book Group, Inc.

Printed in the United States of America

First Edition: June 2009
10 9 8 7 6 5 4 3 2 1
Library of Congress Cataloging-in-Publication Data

Meyer, Joyce
    Any minute / Joyce Meyer and Deborah Bedford. — 1st ed.
      p. cm.
    ISBN 978-0-446-58253-7 (regular edition) — ISBN 978-0-446-55234-9 (large print edition)
    I. Bedford; Deborah.   II. Title.
    PS3613.E973A85 2009
    813'.6—dc22

                                                    2008054427

*"In everything I did, I showed you that by this kind of
hard work we must help the weak, remembering the words
the Lord Jesus himself said: It is more blessed to give
than to receive."*

—ACTS 20:35

Happiness often sneaks in through a door
you didn't know you left open.

—JOHN BARRYMORE

A woman is like a tea bag—you never know how strong she is until she gets in hot water.

—ELEANOR ROOSEVELT

To the ones who yearn to be happy;
to those who live with hidden shame.

To those who keep trying to find a way home.

‑⟨∽ Chapter One ∾⟩‑

Each morning as Sarah maneuvered her crème brûlée Lincoln MKX up the ramp into Smart Park Tower, the experienced drivers knew they'd best keep out of her way. She scanned her monthly access card and waited, her fingers tapping the steering wheel, for the robotic arm to lift. She made a tire-squealing beeline for the C-level spaces, which gave her direct access to the elevator and the walkway to her office building.

The experienced drivers had learned to practice the list of AAA defensive-driving tips whenever they encountered Sarah Harper. When she was behind the wheel, they put their pride in the backseat and didn't provoke her. They didn't speed up to try to pass or try to hold their own in the climbing lane. Above all else, they fastened their seat belts. Because they all knew Sarah believed life was there for the taking. To say that Sarah was aggressive would have been an understatement.

Sarah wanted the best of everything in life, including the best parking spot.

Newcomers would find themselves whipping around pylons, darting around blind corners, trying to find a way to cut through; it was impossible to get ahead of her. No matter how hard anyone tried, Sarah would take you in that new crossover SUV. She'd downshift the Lincoln going uphill, zip into the spot she wanted, and switch off the engine without even glancing in your direction. She'd check her lipstick in the sun-visor mirror without giving a second glance. If she found a smudge on her lips, she'd touch it up with something called Garnet Burst, blot in a ladylike manner, and tuck the tube inside her purse.

Most annoying of all, the whole time you tested your driving skill against her, she'd be talking nineteen to the dozen, conferring with clients on her cell phone. She'd be setting up the schedule for her day, conversing with colleagues, instructing her assistant, Leo, to send out price memos to everyone on her e-mail list. She'd be mentally comparing currency rates and futures prices and trading strategies, trying to predict a market that had run amok, prices shooting up or tumbling down, terrifying clients who depended on her.

She liked to arrive early.

She liked to stay until the bitter end of the day. You could bet money she'd be the last to turn off the lights in her office at night. She'd be the last to leave the parking lot. She wouldn't depart her office until she had dotted every *i* and crossed every *t*, no matter how late it made her assistant.

This morning, ready to leave the comfort of her vehicle and stroll inside, she would speak one simple command to the SYNC feature in her Lincoln and, just like that, the music would shut off.

She'd tuck her cell phone away, keeping it close enough to hear in case it rang, and remove the keys from the ignition, depositing them inside her Gucci purse. She'd step from the SUV, adjust her blazer, fling her computer case over her shoulder, and lock the doors. That's when you could see for the first time that she'd done all that perilous driving, all that squealing around concrete pillars and speeding up the multistory ramps, in a pair of pretty Prada heels. Name brands and labels were very important to Sarah, and she displayed them any time she had a chance.

Each time Sarah entered her offices in the financial district, you could see someone teasing her about her performance in the Smart Park; they loved to laugh about it on the trading floor. They joked about it as she entered the pit; they pestered her as she hooked up her nest of cables and wires and speakerphones and screens. How did she manage to snag the space with her name engraved on the gold plaque on the curb? Did she ever think of signing up to drive for NASCAR? Who did she think she was, Mario Andretti? And Sarah would shrug all this attention off with a puzzled smile, not understanding exactly why everyone made it such a big deal. She lived life in overdrive, but to her it was normal.

Sarah liked to have everything in her life just so, from the progression of the music selection in her iPod (from the latest pop on the charts to light jazz) to the lineup of roller-ball pens, three black ink and three blue, in the little trough built into her desk drawer. From the baby-soap samples and finger snacks she stored inside the diaper bag (so Kate could be dropped off at the babysitter's at a moment's notice) to the entryway of her house, where she kept Mitchell's shoes, knapsack, galoshes, jacket, and Cubs cap all within easy reach for a little boy darting out the door. From the color-coded Tupperware suppers in the refrigerator (a few of which she prepared ahead on the weekends, others she bought from the grocery or the caterers) to Joe's shirts, ironed and arranged where he could find them by sleeve length in the closet.

Sarah felt that having everything organized was a matter of survival for her, a necessary habit. She felt driven to be a super-mom, as efficient in her home as she was successful at her job. She needed to squeeze everything she could out of her days.

Life was there for the taking, and Sarah Harper was focused on taking all of it she could.

And when you were as busy as Sarah and you had all those plans, things must never be taken out of order. Sarah liked to keep her to-do list as finely tuned as the engine in the Lincoln she drove. This, she had decided, was the way to happiness. Sarah had similar expectations of other people. As a matter of fact, she strongly believed that to live any other way would equate to a wasted life.

This morning as Sarah tossed her dark hair over her shoulder and entered the Roscoe Futures Group offices, an alarm sounded on her personal data assistant, reminding her of an upcoming meeting with one of the firm's senior brokers. At the same time, she was exchanging shoptalk with a client, her cell-phone ear-piece barely jutting from her head: "If you want to do this, we'll have to do it later in the week. You'll have to set up an appointment with Leo." Anyone who didn't realize she had a phone in her ear would have thought she was talking to herself. Added to that, she was thumbing through a report, searching the latest market forecast for any commodity prices that looked like they might rise.

"You get your parking spot again?" a guy from human resources teased her. "Wouldn't want you to start things off wrong. Sort of like getting up on the wrong side of the bed."

"How's it going, Andretti?" someone added. "Ready for another day at the races?"

Sarah ignored the parking-space comments and dropped a box of folders on her assistant's desk. She backed halfway through her own office door and eyed the intern, a small anxious-looking youth named Leo McCall. Leo took care of office duties; he'd gone through at least eleven different interviews to get the internship. Taking him on as an intern meant she could get away with asking him to do anything because he was in training. If luck held out and the market ever came back, he'd also become a commodities trader one day.

Call me in a minute. She pointed to her earpiece and cocked her thumb like the hammer of a gun. *I've got to get off this thing,* she mouthed. "No," she told the earpiece as she disappeared inside her office. "I can't. This evening is out of the question." And for a moment she considered explaining why, that she was meeting the two gentlemen in her life at the Cubs game, that something always got in the way when they tried to have time together, that even though Joe insisted they sit in the bleachers at Wrigley she was really looking forward to it this time.

She swapped her navy blazer for her trading jacket and, still talking on the phone, attached the rat's nest of wires to a microphone that curved under her jaw and referred to the small mirror on her shelf while she twisted her dark curls into some semblance of a bun.

With bobby pins aligned in her teeth, she examined her pale hazel eyes, her narrow oval face, with pessimism. Trading-floor rules required a smooth, contained hairstyle that wouldn't provide a safety hazard around all those miles of cable. She hated to admit how much hair she'd yanked out trying to get untangled at the end of a session.

What is taking Leo so long? She gestured through the glass door, trying to get his attention, but he was busy distributing to-go coffee and didn't see her waving.

Oh well. If she couldn't get off the phone, at least she could check on the baby. Sarah situated herself in her leather chair and briefly noted the photograph of Joe with his heavy brows and his Italian good looks smiling at her. On the other side of the computer sat a snapshot of the kids taken last month, Mitchell, with his new glasses perched atop his nose, grinning at the lens while Kate (with her wisps of hair so much like Sarah's) looked desperate to wriggle from her brother's knee.

Sarah powered up her computer and entered the www.nanny rating.com Web site. She punched in her ID number and waited for the information to load. The nanny site appeared, and Sarah began to scroll through. Sarah had signed up for this service the same day she'd employed Mrs. Pavik. And even though Mrs. Pavik, in her sensation-seeking way, had pitched a fit ("You are *spying* on me with this machine!" "You do not trust me to do the right thing!" "I will let Kate do handstands in her car seat and find out who reports me to you then!"), Sarah wouldn't back down. Every piece of equipment even remotely associated with the baby—the diaper bag, Kate's favorite stuffed bear, the canister of baby wipes—had the same visible placard fastened to it: "How's my nanny doing? E-mail 5384@nannyrating.com." Even the stroller sported a bumper sticker. And even though Mrs. Pavik acted highly insulted by this process, Sarah preferred punching in a password to breaking up her finely tuned schedule.

"Your nanny has three new posts," the screen announced after completing its search. Sarah scrolled down the messages, each of them submitted by a stranger who had happened on Mrs. Pavik and Kate in the park. One of them was from a crackpot who wrote, "This is ridiculous! Get a real relationship with something! Don't use a computer to check on your babysitter!"

Another wrote, "It was a delight to see your baby playing on the slide." Sarah didn't know whether this was meant to be a good post or a bad one. Wasn't playing on a slide dangerous? Yet the writer had chosen the word *delight*. You wouldn't say, "It was a delight to see your baby playing on the freeway." Or, "It was a delight to see your daughter juggling knives." So...maybe let that one go.

The last post proved more beneficial. Finally, someone had given Sarah information she could use. "I don't know if you mind this or not, but I saw Nanny #5384 feed your daughter peanut butter for a snack. Isn't your daughter too young for you to determine whether she has a peanut allergy?"

The phone finally beeped, signaling she had another caller. Through the door she could see Leo holding his phone in his hand. At last, an opportunity to break in! *Took you long enough,* she mouthed to her assistant through the glass. *Where have you been? Why didn't you do this sooner?*

"I need to let you go," she told her long-winded client. "I've got another call I need to take."

There were other things Sarah believed in taking besides the prime parking spot. When she stopped by Starbucks, she helped herself to a great number of sweeteners and stirrers for her desk; you never knew when you might need some Splenda. When she happened upon the cosmetics counter at Macy's, she selected an assortment of disposable applicators and mascara wands for her own use. When she and Joe got the babysitter and had a night out at Ambria in Lincoln Park, she always managed to slip a few of those rose-shaped French chocolates at the hostess stand into her purse. But Sarah's talents for getting the most out of everything became most evident of all when, armed with her cell phone, her laptop in its satchel, her headphones, and her microphone, she tried to make sense of the world's slumping economies on the crowded floor of the Chicago Board of Trade.

Sarah usually arrived at the office by seven o'clock. An hour before trading started, she would leave her desk, plod up the LaSalle Street canyon, and march through the art-deco doors that had guarded the building's hallowed halls ever since the days of the Great Depression. Her Prada heels would click purposefully across the marble tiles. A bell would ring when the elevator reached lobby level and, moments later, she would disappear behind sliding doors of brushed champagne steel.

The quotations board would already be blinking when she arrived on the trading level. Prices would be showing in red, green, yellow—these days mostly red. The pits would be full of frantic, gum-chewing traders ready to buy and sell, trying to lock in prices, making hand signals to show the quantity of their bids.

Sarah thought nothing of jumping into the fray, and according to Tom Roscoe from the brokerage firm, that's when her instincts became extraordinary. In a place where you could lose your shirt just by holding a hand the wrong way, Sarah had an uncanny knack for knowing exactly what to sell and when to buy.

By the time she arrived that morning, she'd already shot Mrs. Pavik an e-mail message about Kate's inappropriate snacking ("No more peanut butter, please," she'd written) and had forgotten about it by the time the market opened. Sarah was quick to correct any error she perceived in her nanny and other people she worked with, but she was not quick to compliment or show appreciation. She wasn't mean-spirited; she was simply busy and very focused on getting what she wanted in life. "Let's get going." She elbowed Leo and pointed toward a number streaming overhead.

Leo followed behind her, frantically scratching observations in his notebook. Sarah's focus darted between the boards and her computer screen. She typed madly on her keyboard for a while before she stopped to wait—crouched, ready.

When the board changed, Sarah acted. "Here we are." She held up her hand with four fingers, her palm faced toward herself. "We're taking!" she hollered as she bounced on her toes. "Taking!" Although buying could be a risk. "All the way!"

There wasn't much time to celebrate before another bargain purchase presented itself. Then another. And, after that, something else looked like a good sell. By the end of the closing bell, Sarah had locked in a favorable price on a good share of crude oil futures as well.

"Great job out there, NASCAR," one of the ninth-floor guys congratulated her.

"Ah," another said, offering a high five as she passed in the hall. "Just another day of healthy risk-taking, I see."

"Yep," she said, pretending to wave a checkered flag.

Leo, who'd returned to his administrative duties sometime between the closing bell and the dismantling of Sarah's many wires and screens and coax cables, leaped from his chair and followed her when she returned to the office, relaying a long list of messages even as her PDA alarm sounded again, reminding her of a meeting with the trading strategists. Sarah's adrenaline was running high, her emotions and thoughts racing as if she was in high gear and could not slow down. She felt excited and was ready to tackle more before the day was over.

"Gary Rothman was wondering if you had any gut instincts about those T-Bonds. He's making his decision tomorrow."

"Why can't he make a decision without me?"

"You know he likes to get your opinion. You know he won't stop bugging you until you give it to him." Sarah made a face as if to say she was aggravated, but Leo knew deep down inside she liked it when other people depended on her. "And Bill Morris's clerk needs your file on the Davis contract."

"I thought I pulled that for him last week."

"Right. It's in the mail. Double-check." Leo hesitated a beat. "Oh yeah. Your husband called to confirm tonight. You can get him on his cell; he's still at the shop."

"Oh, right. Joe."

"He says to remember that you *promised* them."

"I remember." Her tone said she was half deserving of this prompt and this was half none-of-his-business.

"DarCo guy will be in town Thursday. Wants to talk about upgrading software."

"Leo. Hey. In case you haven't noticed, that's why we're paying you the big bucks around here. So you can get rid of people like the DarCo guy."

"This is an unpaid internship," he reminded her.

She ignored his comment.

"Leo McCall takes care of the DarCo guy." He scratched the item off his list with zeal.

"Those plans for tonight?" Sarah announced happily, and any-one could tell that, for the moment, everything felt satisfactory in her world. "Did Joe tell you? I'm meeting him and Mitchell at the Cubs game."

"Oh man." Leo's voice flooded with envy. "Joe got tickets to that? It could be the best game of the year."

Sarah pondered the panoramic view of Chicago, what seemed like miles below their enormous window—the plaid grid of sidewalks and streets, the occasional turquoise patch of a rooftop swimming pool, the elevated train track that sliced the fabric of The Loop like an oversized zipper. One of the pools caught her attention; she liked the idea of installing a pool when the baby got older. Mitchell and Kate would love a pool once Kate got old enough to take lessons. Maybe it was too early to plan, but a pool would ensure her children plenty of friends during the sweltering Illinois summers. After all, having things like swimming pools was what she was working so hard for. *I want my children to have the best of everything,* she thought. Anytime Sarah felt even a twinge of guilt about all the time she spent away from her family, she always convinced herself she was doing it for them.

"Back in Michigan I told my friends that when I lived in Chicago, I'd be close enough to Wrigley to lean out the window and spit on the field," Leo said.

"I thought you lived in Bucktown. With five roommates," she reminded him.

"Back in Michigan, I exaggerated sometimes."

A Midwestern whiz kid come to conquer the city. There would always be an endless supply of them. Sarah smiled.

"I'd give my right kidney to go to that game," Leo said.

"I'll phone the medics for you," she said, teasing. "Let them know they can drive right over and pick it up."

He rolled his eyes at her calling his bluff. "You get the Roscoe corporate seats?" Although the company had cut back, Tom Roscoe had not given up the baseball tickets. Phone in hand, Leo looked ready to call the CEO and make sure everything had been arranged.

She shook her head. "The bleachers."

"You? A Bleacher Bum? What happened with that?"

"It's Joe's deal, for once. He says the bleachers are the best place to experience the people of Wrigley."

"I'd give anything to be in the bleachers. But knowing you, are you sure that's the experience you're looking for?"

A yellow warbler flittered past outside the mammoth window. Sarah wondered absently how such a small bird could find a place to perch this far above the ground. How had something so small flown so high?

Sarah followed up with her husband as she settled herself atop Leo's desk to sort through pages of numerical data. *Can you make sure these add up?* she mouthed as she fluttered two pages in Leo's direction. "Joe," she said after she heard the click. "Joe?" But she'd only gotten the recording.

"See you when I see you," she said after the beep, picturing him with a customer, their heads together beneath the hood of his latest car project.

As fond as Sarah was of conversing with her husband, she was glad to leave a message. She didn't have time for anything else right now. But maybe she ought to add extra information so she wouldn't sound too abrupt.

"It's been another one of those days over here."

She narrowed her eyes conspiratorially at Leo, who shared this madhouse with her and understood. For the hundredth time she couldn't quite believe her luck that she'd gotten an intern this year. Leo McCall, at the top of the Kelley School of Business from IU at Bloomington, who'd ridden his scooter to save gas money and parked it on the sidewalk for each one of those grueling Roscoe interviews. Leo was determined. Sarah liked determined people.

She continued her message to Joe. "Leo's drooling to be in my place. He says it'll be quite the game."

Her intern glanced from the adding machine and gave a thumbs-up sign. With a fortifying nod that said *I'm sticking by you*, Leo returned to the scads of figures, his fingers skittering over the adding-machine keys.

"So don't worry, Joe," she said with added confidence, basking in Leo's enthusiasm. "I promise I won't let anything get in the way of me being there." She needed a night to forget about work and be with her family and let her hair down.

"See you in a few hours then, honey," she said, swinging her leg, absently tapping her heel against the desk. "I might be late, but I'll be there. You know I wouldn't miss this for anything."

⟶⟨ Chapter Two ⟩⟶

Sarah's husband, Joe, would be the first to tell you that nothing much seemed impossible on Chicago's North Side. You could order a Polish dog from any vendor just the way you liked—dragged-through-the-garden, which meant you got the works, sweet-pickle relish, mustard, a dill-pickle spear, sport peppers sliced thin and topped off with tomato—and have all that in hand, sixty seconds max.

You could take the "L" train clear from Skokie to The Loop and it wouldn't cost you more than $2.25 full-class fare.

You could cruise the Chicago River in a tall boat at certain hours of the day while dozens of bridges rose to allow you to pass. You could stand among the skyscrapers downtown in the center of Daley Plaza on Washington Street and know you stood beneath one of the last pieces of artwork Picasso ever created.

But there *was* one particular thing, Joe Harper had to admit, one impossible task, one single feat in Chicago—only one—that couldn't be done.

Try as you might this time of year, you couldn't save a bleacher seat at Wrigley Field. Not in mid-September. Not when the Cubbies were in town playing the Cards. And certainly not when the hopeless Cubs were only a half game out of first place.

"That's saved for my wife," Joe told a portly gentleman who tried to sidle into Sarah's spot carrying one of the aforementioned hot dogs and an overflowing carton of nachos.

"Sorry. This spot's taken," he announced to a girl dragging her boyfriend down the cement steps as if she thought they might be able to fit into Sarah's small space.

"Someone's already sitting here," he told a woman waving a poster that read It's Gonna Happen in his face.

Joe lost count of how many times he thumped the empty bleacher with his hand, "Seat's taken," before he got overruled and everybody starting squeezing in. "Well, dude, *I* sure don't see her," a man in a blue pin-striped shirt insisted as he forced his way in from the aisle. Then he started directing everybody else to where they could sit too. "You got an invisible wife or something? There's plenty of room for us here."

"Look, mister." The lady with the sign shook it at Joe and said, "We're here and she's not. You can't save the cheap seats. You're ruining it for everybody."

"She'll be here any minute," Joe argued, trying to stop the onslaught. "You just have to wait a minute until Sarah gets here." Then, "Besides, it's just this *one seat*. You're trying to fit three people in here."

Joe knew he couldn't hold on to the seat—these Cubs fans had a fighting nature; everybody knew it.

As his mother's space filled in, Mitchell looked disapprovingly at Joe and wailed, "But, *Dad*. There's no place for *Mom* now."

Joe gave a helpless shrug and straightened his son's little eyeglasses. "Guess we'll figure something out when she gets here."

The guy in front made a megaphone of his hands and yelled, "Hey, St. Lou! Let us have a win today, will you?" As he offered

Joe and Mitchell bagged peanuts: "Where *is* your wife, anyway? She sitting in traffic?"

"Guess so." Discouragement took hold of Joe the same way he took hold of a fistful of nuts in the cellophane. Joe had told Sarah to leave the car at the Park & Ride and take the shuttle into Wrigleyville. Maybe she'd ended up coming from The Merc and had taken the Red Line. "Guess so. It happens all the time."

On the field, the first-base coach had sent Derrek Lee to steal second on a wild pitch, and Lou Piniella, "St. Lou" as the peanut man called him, didn't much like the out. He stormed from the dugout and let the ump have it right in front of everybody, one of those dirt-kicking, hat-throwing arguments that ends in ejection. The lady with the sign uttered something foul, and Joe shot her a look as he covered Mitchell's ears with his hands. "Do you mind?"

Joe took chances in the bleachers with a child, and he knew it. He ran the risk of his eight-year-old hearing words that ought to be erased from the annals of human history, never mind introduced to an impressionable boy who might just decide to employ the exotic and enticing new vocabulary in his second-grade classroom. But Joe didn't mind having a few heart-to-heart talks with Mitchell about people who used not-very-nice words whenever Fontenot missed a tag or Theriot struck out—he thought it well worth it.

People in the bleachers came *alive* for baseball. They pursued it completely, from wearing frizzy blue wigs to painting red encircled Cs on their faces to all those It's Gonna Happen signs. They raced through the gate hours early to claim a spot near the field. They hugged absolute strangers whenever the Cubs hit a home run. They offered high fives when an outfielder made a catch in the vines.

Sarah often asked him, "Why put yourself through this with the seats? Why not let me get in line for our company tickets? Or we could spend a little more money and buy our own reserved ones instead." Joe, who loved being a Bleacher Bum, was tempted to come right out and tell her. *Don't you understand? Why show up to the game if you don't want to stop and enjoy the whole experience?*

True to bleacher fashion, Joe had bought Mitchell one of those foam claws, as big as a bed pillow, to wave around on his hand. When Geovany Soto ripped a pitch for a stand-up double, Mitchell mimed a long bear-cub scratch in the air and growled. Joe wanted to grab him off his feet and hug him to pieces; he was so cute wearing his new glasses and that claw.

"How about that swing?" Joe pointed to the replay on the JumboTron. He'd been teaching his son about baseball ever since Mitchell had been old enough to walk. But Mitchell didn't answer. His mind must have gone back to his mother again.

"Dad?" Mitchell held the huge foam paw now pressed pathetically against his chest. "When's she going to *get* here?"

When Joe moved to hug his boy sideways, the hug was only a trap. He tickled Mitchell's ribs, hoping he'd stop asking so many questions. Mitchell giggled and doubled over in self-protection. Which set off a chain reaction of elbowing and shoving and disgruntled looks from the spectators wedged along the same row.

"Hey. We'd better calm down." Joe gripped the boy's shoulder and hauled him up. Their eyes met as Joe set Mitchell's glasses to rights on his nose. Even with Mitchell so young, the two men of the family had an unspoken understanding between them. No matter how hard Sarah tried, she didn't always end up where she was supposed to be. "She'll be here; I know she will," Joe said, sounding doubtful.

"But how long will it take?"

"You know the way your mom drives." Joe shrugged. "How should I know?"

⟋⟍

Tom Roscoe, chief executive officer and president of the futures group that bore his name, gazed out the window of his exquisite new office on the twenty-fourth floor and exhaled with satisfaction. It pleased him greatly, standing this high above Chi-Town. On days like today, when the sun glittered off cars jolting to starts and stops below him, when the street reverberated with noise, horns honking, engines racing, people shouting, it suited him that the frantic activity seemed far below.

Up here in these luxurious quarters, business had no sound. On days when the breeze carried the smog away, he enjoyed broad, sweeping views of the city. Given a rainy day, he preferred having his windows in the clouds. He liked having someone report to him. He made a practice of speaking to the doorman to find out the weather.

No need to worry about what's on the streets below, he philosophized with great pride, *when you never intend to lower yourself that far.*

Tom had good reason today for gloating. He'd been working for months to convince the Cornish brothers, Chicago's great global real-estate financiers, to move their investment assets to his company. Andrew Cornish had phoned this morning to say they might be convinced.

The status of managing such a prestigious account would make him the most influential commodities broker in the Windy City's financial district. Tom could already taste victory like steel on his tongue. The Cornish brothers were stopping by for a casual discussion just as soon as they could get away from their own granite-clad high-rise on the north side of The Loop.

Which meant his stature would skyrocket and the value of his brokerage would soar and he'd have yet another chance to demonstrate the company's worth to his two sons, Jonas and Richard.

Which meant he could someday bequeath his sons a financial enterprise that would set them up for life.

Which he reasoned meant he had no choice but to insist that every employee's schedule stretch to accommodate his demands.

Tom Roscoe needed assistants in the front room to pull files and double-check figures. He needed texts and examples transmitted immediately to his PalmPilot. He expected Rona to carry in the tray with sparkling glasses and tonic water and lime. And maybe she could serve some of those basil tarts she'd spoken about. Yes, that sounded good. Rona could also come up with crusty bread and small squares of cheese.

An hour later, all this quick arrangement left him swiveling his chair to face his guests with a smile. He assured his potential clients that his company stood on firm financial footing, that his brokerage could handle their trading in real time, in only nanoseconds, in places all over the world. He diagrammed his business model for them, showing in full detail how his employees focused on service, support, and integrity. "I tell you both, you won't be sorry if you pursue this."

Andrew Cornish made a great show of stirring the ice in his glass. "And what about this whiz kid of yours we've heard so much about?"

Tom crossed his arms behind his head. "Ah. You've heard about Sarah Harper."

"Hasn't everybody?"

"You want to work with her?"

Their smug, twin smiles told him everything he needed to know.

"She *does* have a mind for strategy. Brilliant moves. Won't back down."

Andrew shot a discreet glance in the direction of his brother. They'd met with a half dozen traders this past quarter, and there was no doubt they'd found what they wanted. Depending on Roscoe's sales spiel, of course. "Can she handle it? What about experience with something of this magnitude?"

"She's certainly got the instinct. Knows right when to take what's coming to her. Makes brilliant split-second decisions, better than I do, actually."

Andrew surveyed his huge manicured thumbnail from three different angles. "May we see numbers to back it up?"

Ah. He'd been right to wield a heavy whip on his staff. "I'll have her assistant bring the spreadsheets." Tom lifted the receiver. He'd almost finished dialing Leo before he got a better idea. "Tell you what, I'll make it even easier than that," he said, hanging up. "Let's get our hands on today's transcript."

The two brothers looked at each other with satisfaction.

"You'd be willing to take her off the other accounts?" Nathan, Andrew's older sibling, slid a pair of spectacles from his pocket and polished them on his sleeve. "We'd want exclusivity."

That's the moment Tom realized how close they were to closing this deal.

"She'd have to agree to it, of course."

He already knew she would. She'd lost the Nielsen account for him last month, which hadn't mattered much. That account had been small potatoes, but because he could use it to put the thumbscrews to her, it meant a lot more now.

Tom made the call to Rona. The three gentlemen made small talk until the requested documents arrived. Rona knocked lightly, opened the door a bit, and handed the pages over to Tom. Tom presented them to the brothers. Nathan steered his spectacles onto his ears and, together, the two men perused the columns. Eventually Nathan Cornish lifted his head and asked, "What do you think, Andy? Would you be willing to write out the check if she agrees?" Then, to Tom, "How about a meeting-of-the-minds over dinner?"

Andrew nodded. "I'd write the check. Absolutely."

Tom Roscoe felt like he might hyperventilate. Everything had happened so fast. "We're on for dinner then." Rona could make the excuses to his family. During the years she'd gotten very good at that.

He didn't let the thought keep him sullen for too long. They'd done it! They'd roped in the most notable financiers in Illinois! Tom could almost picture his company's stock climbing.

"Just give me a minute." He couldn't help it; he was practically leaping up and down. "I'll get your girl on the line."

Sarah raced along the cubicle-lined corridor, tugging off her jacket as she ran. She yanked one sleeve off, then started working on the other. She slalomed a chair that had been abandoned in the aisle after most of Roscoe's employees had departed. By the time she reached the ladies' room, she'd wadded her entire blazer in her hand.

She worked her skirt down over her hips inside the bathroom

stall, which wasn't the easiest thing to accomplish considering the tight space. She lurched out of the stall, balanced on one foot to remove her shoe from the other. By the time she made it to the lavatory mirror, she was fastening her jeans, which meant a sort of chicken dance as she straightened her spine, sucked in her stomach, and drew up her zipper. Precious seconds ticked past as she worked her toes into her sneakers.

Definitely the smartest thing she'd done all day, bringing her Cubs-wear to the office. She hauled the T-shirt over her head and tried not to think of the clock. Everything had taken longer this afternoon than she'd intended.

The last half dozen phone calls, each of which she'd ended with, "I need to let you go. I'm running behind."

Her final session with Leo, where she'd reminded him she needed info on the energy sector in the morning, which meant he'd spend the wee hours doing research.

The time she'd spent tapping her toe behind the young woman at Starbucks who couldn't find enough change to pay for her iced tea. Anytime Sarah's energy started to slump, she managed to get a large coffee with an extra shot of espresso from Starbucks.

"Excuse me," Sarah had insisted, practically pushing the woman aside and moving forward in line. "If you can't pay for that, do you mind letting someone else go ahead? You're holding everyone up."

By the time she'd sent off the T-Bond info for Rothman, the first pitch had already gone out at Wrigley Field. She could still get to the game, but she was glad she'd warned Joe she might be a little late. If traffic wasn't backed up along Lake Shore Drive, she'd still be able to find her seat without missing much.

Sarah employed both thumbs at once, pecking out a text to Roscoe that she'd departed for the night. TR IN IMPORTANT MEET-ING, came the word from Roscoe's secretary, Rona. DOESN'T WANT INTERRUPTIONS. CAN IT WAIT?

YEP, Sarah answered. She smiled at the irony. THANK HEAVENS would have been more appropriate.

She ended up on the marble ledge between the faucet and the soap dispenser, doing her best to tie her shoes. When she hit the door running, she winced at the mucky smell that had picked tonight of all nights to drift in off Lake Michigan. The air was so thick that she could almost see the smog.

The minute Sarah pulled out of the parking structure and headed toward the ballpark, traffic boxed her in. Before she ever left The Loop, she got stuck behind a catering truck whose driver seemed to think he was entitled to two lanes. She veered to the right to pass him, only to zoom up behind a CTA bus dropping off passengers at the curb. She found an opening and darted left again, just in time to screech her tires to avoid hitting a delivery van that swerved out of the alley.

"Come on." She drummed her fingernails against the steering wheel in frustration. She glanced at the clock in the Lincoln. "Come on, come on, come on."

Rush hour had passed, but bumper-to-bumper traffic still clogged the city. Remarkably, Sarah darted to the far left and the lane opened for the next few blocks. The boulevard made a curve toward the waterfront. That's where Sarah saw the boat moving up the river toward the bridge.

No. Not now.

No no no no no.

It was her fault. She never should have cut this so short. Sarah felt the beginnings of a headache as her neck and shoulders tightened from the stress she felt.

The light turned green, and the race was on again. She bolted into the middle lane and made some progress that way. She glanced from the road to the boat in hopes she might be gaining. But by the time she made the corner, the boat had beaten her. The signal flashed red ahead. The barricade began descending.

Tires squealed. Sarah waited, fuming, while she watched the bridge begin its leisurely rise. She counted taillights in front of her and decided at least three more cars could have crossed if only someone had had the guts and the barrier hadn't gone down. The *Windy II*, a sailboat on voyage from Navy Pier, drifted forward as dozens of merry pirate-clad passengers waved from the deck. She watched the stanchions part in front of her to make way for the tall boat to pass along the river. Her nagging headache had grown into a full-blown migraine. She dug inside her purse, searching for aspirin, acetaminophen, anything to dull the pain. She found the plastic bottle and fiddled with the lid. She shook it, frustrated by the childproof cap. Empty. Why was she always running out of these things, anyway? She reminded herself that she needed to go to the doctor for something stronger than over-the-counter pain relievers. She had put it off a long time, but her head was hurting more and more these days.

She kneaded her temples with her fingers. As long as she'd lived, she'd never seen anything move as slowly as this boat.

Sarah fumed. Just to let everyone know how frustrated she felt, she laid on the horn. The guy in the Beamer turned and eyed her like she'd gone out of her mind.

She'd just picked up her cell to text Joe and say she was on her way when yet another call rang through. T Roscoe, announced the screen.

No.

In the hairbreadth of a second, her instincts whispered: *Don't answer it. You're off the clock. Leave well enough alone.*

Sarah could do a great many things, but never this: She hadn't acquired her lofty position by ignoring a ringing phone.

She hooked up her earpiece. "Hey, Tom. What's up?"

Ahead of her the boat began to progress. The haze in the air made the gaping bridge and the sluggish craft appear to shimmer around the edges.

She listened.

"Oh, congratulations, Tom. That's *great* news about Cornish. There'll be a write-up on Bloomberg for sure. . . . Of course it makes sense. It makes sense they talked to all those people and narrowed it down to you. . . . You actually did that? You showed them today's financials?"

He continued talking, and she continued applauding his good fortune until he got to the part where he told her he'd included her in the bargain. Anyone watching Sarah in her vehicle would have seen her smile begin to broaden. At least until she realized Tom wanted her to drop what she was doing and meet him and the Cornish brothers for dinner. She gripped the steering wheel. Her face paled with distress.

"Oh. No. I didn't realize that's why you were calling. I thought you were just calling to share the good news. . . . Tonight? I'm afraid that's impossible. Tom, I can't. . . . It's such short notice," she said. "What about tomorrow? Could we set it up for then?"

If only she could make him understand! If only he would let her out of this! But without really hearing her, her employer launched into a hearty accounting of the numbers. "It's asking a lot, Tom. I really don't see how I can do it. You see, I have plans with my family."

Success always involved trade-offs, Tom reminded her. She was one of the lucky few who still had a job in the financial district. If she wasn't delighted by her schedule, at least she and Joe had what they needed.

Sarah thought of the responsibility of the jumbo mortgage in East Lake Forest they had to think about, their faltering retirement account, and their gas bills in this unsteady economy, the upkeep on the Lincoln, the lease on the garage in Bucktown where Joe installed racing engines in Miatas. They were still paying off some of her college loans, and she was determined to pay off the balances on their five credit cards. She knew the extra income from an account of this stature would make a huge difference for them.

The pressure felt enormous. They were so much worse off now than they'd been a year ago. She really did not understand it, but it seemed the more money she made, the deeper in debt they became. The nanny was expensive, the cleaning lady she needed to keep up with the house was expensive, and the clothes she needed in order to be impressive were also expensive. At that moment Sarah felt as if she were being pulled apart. She didn't want to disappoint Joe and Mitchell, but she didn't want to disappoint Tom Roscoe either—and she definitely wanted to make more money and have more prestige on the job. She vaguely realized that not only did her head hurt really bad, but she felt a bit nauseated too.

For the first time that day, Sarah wasn't the woman with the power job and the personal digital device and the private nanny.

She was only the mother and the wife who wanted to get to the ballpark, the woman who felt like she was being pulled in a dozen different directions at once. "How much time do I have?" she asked, and he told her.

"Right now?" she asked. "Right now I'm stuck at the Lake Street Bridge.

"If I come back, could we compromise? Could it only take a few minutes to meet with them and let me be on my way?...Of course I understand. I know it's important, Tom. It's set, then?" she asked, keeping her voice even. "The Everest Room?"

The *Windy II*, only a third of the way through the passage, sounded its horn. The guy in the Beamer gave up and turned off his engine. Sarah unfastened the earpiece and stared at it like she wanted to deposit it in the depths of murky river.

She drummed out a short, apologetic text to her husband, entering the letters in much the same rhythm as the pounding in her head. She adjusted her rearview mirror and signaled, taking note of the curious onlookers in line behind her.

Indignant, she narrowed her brows and flared her nostrils at these complete strangers. *What do you think you're looking at?*

Sarah maneuvered the SUV into a slow, sad U-turn and headed back into the city.

∽❍ Chapter Three ❍∽

You think she's going to miss the game again?" Mitchell asked, and the little boy's eyes seemed suspiciously glittery in the stadium lighting. Beneath his little glasses, Mitchell looked perilously close to tears.

"Maybe she'll get here. She promised us this time, remember?"

"Yeah," Mitchell said, dubious. "But it might have been another one of *those days*." He turned around and scanned the walkway above them. "Maybe she can't find us."

"Oh, she'll find us. She's got her phone. She'll let us know when she gets here."

Joe would look back at this months later, at his halfhearted attempt to watch the game while he lost hope in Sarah, as the moment he might have realized their lives were falling apart and he was helpless to do something about it. But he felt no strong hint of that now, only a vague relief that something up in the sky had come along to distract Mitchell from the absence of his mother.

"Look at that guy! There's a man way up there, Dad."

Joe shaded his eyes and peered into a setting sun so fierce that it made his head hurt. The glare blinded him.

Chicagoans reveled in the lore of their ancient green scoreboard, how it had never been hit by a batted ball (although Bill "Swish" Nicholson and Roberto Clemente came close a half-century ago), how it stood where Babe Ruth had once called his '32 Series bleacher shot and slammed his longest homer ever, how every other team had succumbed to *progress* while the Cubs clung to tradition: their time-honored board with a man hiding inside, climbing from spot to spot on a labyrinth of catwalks and steps, posting numbers by hand.

"The scoreboard guy. He's up there, Dad. See him? Right there."

"Where?"

"There. Looking out through the hole in the eighth inning."

Joe hated to admit it, but he'd never really given these scoreboard stories much thought; he'd never really seriously considered he would see the guy. He took for granted that the score would go up correctly and instantaneously, the way it went up on the computerized displays at every other stadium he'd ever visited. Flags snapped overhead. Ropes clanged against the pole in the breeze. Joe squinted, trying to see.

"He's right there, Dad. See?"

"No," Joe said. "I don't."

At that exact moment, uncanny how it all worked, really, one of the flags curled aloft, caught by an updraft off the lake. It streamed across the sunset, briefly casting Joe's face in shadow. For one instant, Joe caught a view of the board.

"Mitchell, there's nothing there."

"There is. Right there."

"Better let me have a look through your glasses then. Maybe I need them."

Mitchell handed them to Joe, and Joe peered at a distance through the lenses.

"Nope. Nothing."

Mitchell's shoulders sagged with disappointment. And by the way he described the fellow, how he sat high overhead with his forearms crossed and his head inclined toward them, how his small amount of gray hair kept blowing across his scalp, Joe had to be impressed by the boy's imagination. He was being confronted with so much disappointment right now about his own life that he found himself feeling slightly jealous of Mitchell's childlike imagination. *Right now I would like to escape reality*, Joe thought.

"You think he lives up there?" Mitchell asked.

"Who?"

"That guy up there." Then, "Oops, he knows I caught him," he told his dad. "He went back inside."

Joe figured it out; he'd heard how kids used imaginary characters to deal with stress. Mitchell must have invented this crazy game because of his mother's absence. "I don't know, son." Best at this point to play along. "Of course he doesn't live up there. He only sits up there during the games and keeps track of the teams and watches. He keeps score."

"He keeps track of *all* the teams?"

"Yeah."

"So if I see him and you don't, maybe he's like an angel. Maybe he's helping God," Mitchell said. "Because he sits up high and keeps track of everything. Maybe that's why I'm the only one who can see him."

"Yeah." Joe had gotten somewhat distracted, looking for his wife in the crowd again. But he realized what he'd said and corrected himself. "No. Definitely *not* like an angel. Nothing to do with God. Because this is only a baseball game."

"You think he can see clear to the lake from up there?"

"Who?"

"That man up there. Does a guy stay in the scoreboard at every ballpark or just here? Does he make the clock run up there too?" (Which Joe might have answered, "No, Mitchell. The clock runs on its own. Each second takes care of itself. He doesn't do that part." But this barrage of questions overwhelmed him, and he didn't know where to start.)

"Does anybody ever see how he gets up there, Dad? Does he have a ladder? Does he have a trap door or something?"

"You want to stop asking so many questions?" Joe removed Mitchell's hat and punched it inside out to make it a rally cap; it seemed the Cubs always needed rally caps. "You're giving me a headache."

Scores were being posted for every team playing that day. On the scoreboard, Joe noticed that the sign for the Marlins came in two pieces, Flori and da. *Somebody ought to make you take a class when you get to be a parent.* He had no idea what he ought to say. "And it isn't heaven where he's sitting, Mitchell. It's just the scoreboard at Wrigley Field."

A passing vendor came by, clanging his cooler lid. "Water. There's *water* here!" which started people passing dollar bills along the row. The bottles dripped cold on Joe's knees as he passed them back. "You want water?" he asked Mitchell, but his son shook his head, looking unusually serious.

"You sure?"

"Yeah."

As soon as Joe settled into what was left of the game (he'd given up watching for Sarah any longer), Mitchell took off the paw. Joe looked down, surprised, when Mitchell grasped his hand.

"What is it, buddy? What's wrong?"

"If that guy's up there helping God," the little boy said, "maybe he could help Mom show up for things too."

Mitchell's words sent up an instant alarm. "I don't know, kiddo." Because to Joe, it seemed like nothing could ever change Sarah. Because he hadn't wanted Mitchell to sense how bad things had gotten between them. It exhausted Joe, having to pretend that all was well for Mitchell's sake.

He needed to talk to Sarah, to give her some ultimatum, to make her understand how hopeless and overwhelmed he was beginning to feel. And if there was anything that made Joe more nervous than Mitchell asking all these questions, it was Mitchell asking all these questions about God.

Joe didn't want to stand here with his son chitchatting about the spiritual well-being of the world. Joe had gotten dragged to church way too often back when he was a kid. He'd listened to all the same stories Mitchell listened to and, with that same simple logic, had believed them.

All that had changed now. Even though he and Sarah still attended services at their popular church in Lake Forest, Joe knew his adult convictions weren't much to brag about. He had a hard time taking all this "relationship with God" stuff to heart. You grew up. You got hurt and disappointed and couldn't figure things out. You forgot to ask for help or, when you did ask, you never got anything you asked for.

Somewhere along the way, you realized you were as lonely as one of those Great Lakes shipwrecks, rattling around inside yourself like old artifacts, rusting into oblivion.

Somewhere along the way, you figured out there weren't guardian angels waiting around every corner anymore. After all, how could a person believe God was managing everything in the world and angels were watching over us when everything felt so painful and out of order?

The chant began behind them, and soon the whole crowd had taken it up. "*Let's* go, *Cub*-bies! *Let's* go, *Cub*-bies!" The lady behind him whooped it up, stabbing him in the shoulder with her unwieldy sign: It Could Happen.

"Do you mind making that *not* happen?" Joe said to her.

The announcer introduced the seventh-inning stretch, the fans stood and cheered, and someone handed the performer a microphone. Just as the organ began to play, Joe's phone vibrated in his pocket and he had one last jolt of hope. A phone call! She'd come! Sarah had gotten to the ballpark and was trying to find them! But Joe flipped his Nokia open to find that it wasn't a phone call at all, only a text message.

One short sentence. One horrible word.

Sorry.

That was all she said. Seven innings into the game, with the Cubs behind by three runs and the organ sounding its scales, with the singer in the press box counting down "a one, a two, and a *three*," and her family finally knew that Sarah wasn't going to make it to Wrigley Field after all.

"Take me out to the ba-a-all game." Mitchell's little voice rang out above the others, senselessly beautiful. Joe halfheartedly sang too while he thought about the drive home tonight. He and Mitchell would have to go by the babysitter's and pick up Kate. The crowd continued to sing, "Buy me some peanuts and Cra-aacker Jack. I don't care if I never get back," while his thoughts trailed off into what he might say to Sarah later that night.

By the bottom of the eighth, the guy who'd wedged his way

into Sarah's seat stood and headed toward Waveland Avenue. "Excuse me," he said as he forced his way out, and they felt like they could breathe for the first time in hours. "Excuse me," as he blocked everyone's view and stumbled over women's purses and trodded on a fair number of toes.

"Hey, kid," Joe said, nicking Mitchell's chin with a crooked finger. "Don't look so disappointed. The Cubs will win the next one, don't you think?"

Silence.

And of course Joe knew this wasn't about the game.

"Hey. Chin up. We'll try this again with Mom some other time, okay?"

Mitchell climbed down and sat hard on his seat. He didn't say it would be okay. He chewed his bottom lip instead. Joe could see he'd been at it long enough to make it raw. Joe would have to get him a ChapStick. He felt resentment well up in him that Sarah could hurt Mitchell like this and not seem to even realize she was doing it.

Peanut Guy yawned. "If it's gonna happen," he commented to all those crazy, hopeful people who had carried the signs, "it's not gonna happen tonight."

Mitchell uttered a sigh that came clear up from his toes.

Joe asked, "You ready to go?"

Mitchell nodded.

"Don't forget your claw. That'll be good for another game."

Mitchell picked it up and, wordlessly, they trudged over empty nacho cartons and dented cups and crumpled hot-dog wrappers to get to the gate.

Wrigley Field had emptied fast. But even then, as the lights cast hard shadows along the empty seats and the batboys bagged the gear so they could drag it from the dugout to the locker room, as the janitors donned rubber gloves to pick up trash and someone started sweeping, even then, Joe couldn't shake the feeling that someone was watching them. He looked around, but no one seemed to be paying them any mind.

"Does that guy climb a ladder to get to the scoreboard?" Mitchell asked. "I looked, but I didn't see a ladder."

"Are you kidding me?" Joe asked, finally losing patience. "If you saw somebody up there at all, he isn't anything special. I don't see how he'd do God much good, Mitchell. He can't even help the Cubs."

But Mitchell wouldn't be dissuaded. He kept insisting there was a man in the scoreboard. Joe wondered if Mitchell kept talking to keep himself from thinking about how much his mother had disappointed him. And they had a long way home, first the trip on the "L" and then a stop to pick up Kate after they got the car out of the commuter parking lot. Still, Mitchell went on and on about the guy. Even after they'd joined the throngs of downcast Cubs fans on Addison. Even after they'd climbed the steps to the train.

⤳⚬ Chapter Four ⚬⤲

Sarah didn't usually cook breakfast on school mornings. She made do with a packet of microwave oatmeal for Mitchell, spoonfuls of Gerber peaches and maybe a teething biscuit for the baby, a cup of coffee for herself—all that just after six thirty—and sometimes a toasted bagel, which she shoveled down while she was driving. Joe fended for himself.

She'd set her alarm to ring at some horrific hour this morning so she'd have time to make pancakes. It was her way of trying to make up for disappointing Joe and Mitchell the night before. A fresh latticework of sun fell across the counter as Sarah measured flour into a bowl and cracked open the eggs one by one. Kate was sitting in her high chair fingering Cheerios and watching a *Baby Einstein* show on DVD. "*Chat*," the narrator repeated as a cat stepped across the screen. Baby Kate was learning to speak French.

Sarah heard the scraping of a chair behind her and turned to see that Mitchell had appeared at the table. His eyes were still full of sleep, his Cubs hat tilted sideways. His hair resembled a rather ruffled hedgehog. She froze with the electric mixer in hand, engulfed in guilt at the sight of her son. "Good morning," she said with false cheeriness. Mitchell scrubbed his eyes, trying to wake up.

She poured the batter onto the griddle, and in no time the hotcakes began sizzling. She'd made them in the shape of animals, a kitty for Kate and a giraffe for Mitchell. Sarah flipped them with her spatula, pleased to see they'd come out the way she'd intended. She slid the giraffe onto a plate and used chocolate chips to make eyes.

"Here you are." She set the plate in front of Mitchell to see what he'd say. Her heart fell as he stared at it without speaking.

"What's this?" she asked. "You don't like it?"

"Animals are for babies," he said.

"No they aren't," she said, surprised. "You've always liked animals."

"Well, I don't like them anymore."

"Really."

"No."

"Since when?"

"I just *don't*."

Sarah sighed. So *that* was it. She'd been hoping Mitchell wouldn't take her missing the game so hard. "Look," she said, "I'm sorry I didn't make it last night. My job got busy."

Mitchell turned his little face up toward hers. Beneath the brim of his cap, she could see tears. It wrenched her heart, but what could be done? "You and your dad both love the Cubs." She took his plate away, vowing that she wouldn't let an eight-year-old make her feel this conscience-stricken. "I'm sure you had a perfectly good time without me."

She worked at the stove, dripping a small quantity of batter in one direction and then pouring bits of it in another. When it was done, she tried again. "Okay. How about this one?" She made a big deal of getting it on the spatula. "Oops, his arm broke off. There. I've put it back on. What do you think about that?" She arranged chocolate chips without letting him see.

She slid the hotcake onto the plate in front of him, but Mitchell stared at that too with distaste.

"It's a baseball player," she prodded.

"I know that."

"It's Zambrano. He's pitching."

Mitchell worked his bottom lip with his teeth. He wouldn't be distracted so easily. "We saved a seat for you for a long time. Everybody kept trying to take it. Everybody got mad at us because we wouldn't let them sit there."

The baby was fussing. "I don't know what to tell you, honey. I had to go back to work. I'm really sorry." Sarah was just lifting Kate from the high chair and handing her a biscuit from the cabinet overhead when she heard Joe enter the room. She didn't turn toward him; even now she could feel his angry eyes boring into her spine. He'd been waiting up for her when she arrived home last night, and a big sponge claw he'd bought Mitchell had been lying on a chair. She'd picked it up and waved it at him, testing the waters between them.

"Nice of you to bother to show up here," he'd commented as he slapped his *Hemmings Motor News* shut, jabbed it inside the magazine basket, and made a getaway toward the bedroom.

"Don't you even want to know what happened?"

"No, I don't want to know. I'm going to sleep. I only wanted to make sure you weren't injured or hurt, that there wasn't some sort of an accident."

"Of course I'm not hurt. I was only—"

He held up his hand to stop her. "Because that's the only reason I could think of to make you miss time with your son again."

"Joe."

"I don't want to discuss it tonight, Sarah." Then, with a sarcasm she wasn't used to hearing from her husband: "You can give me all your excuses in the morning."

And so they'd each slept fortressed on their own separate sides of the mattress, each staring at the opposite wall, Sarah with her stony shoulders and her pillow punched up beneath her head, Joe's torso as set and stubborn as a concrete girder.

Now she heard him pouring coffee from the pot. She heard the clank of the sugar-bowl lid as he added sugar. Joe took one loud slurp, set the mug down hard on the counter, and waited.

Sarah shut the cabinet door with a little too much zeal. The hollow bang echoed down the hall.

Joe opened the silverware drawer with such force that every butter knife, teaspoon, and salad fork slid together with a resounding clang.

Sarah gave Kate the biscuit and balanced the baby on her hip. She opened the dishwasher and began to stack clean plates one on top of the other with deadly precision.

Thankfully, that very moment, Mitchell took pity on her and asked for more chocolate chips. "Ah," she said, breathing a sigh of relief and bringing the bag over. "Always after more chocolate, just like your mom."

"Nope," Mitchell told her, arranging the chips to his liking. "I want to make a *C* on his shirt. He's not Zambrano without a Cubs *C* on his shirt."

"And as soon as he's got that, you can bite his head off."

To Sarah's satisfaction, he finally dug in with his knife and fork, dismembering Zambrano headfirst.

To give Joe credit, he waited until she'd gotten Kate settled into the playpen in the other room and Mitchell had run out to get his backpack before he started in on her. "How come you made everyone breakfast?" he asked. "What is that? A guilt offering because you abandoned him again?"

Sarah's breath caught in her throat. If Sarah had been about to confess how guilty she felt, she wouldn't do it now. It was one thing to admit it, another to stand *accused*. She turned to face her husband. "I was almost to Wrigley when Roscoe phoned. He'd gotten a huge account, and he wanted me to handle it. The whole company's reputation at stake, that sort of thing. And after I'd lost the Nielsen deal last month, you know I couldn't turn him down."

"I wish you could have seen Mitchell's face, Sarah. I wish you could have seen your little boy searching for you the whole time, expecting to find you in the crowd."

"I saw his face this morning, Joe. Wasn't that enough?"

"You told him you'd come through this time, Sarah. You always promise him."

His anger had caught her off guard. Blood roared in her ears. She clenched her fists at her sides without knowing what to say.

"Sarah," he asked, "what's *wrong* with you?"

"What do you think? That I had another choice besides turning around? You think it was easy for me? I *told* you, Joe. I was halfway there." She thought, *There's nothing wrong with me. He is the one who has the problem. If I didn't have to be responsible for everything around here, maybe I wouldn't have to work so hard.*

Sarah wasn't even close to being ready to admit to herself that she did all the things she did because she wanted to. Her sense of worth and value was derived from her accomplishments. Actually, she needed her success much more than her family needed the money.

"And then there was the awful thing with the seat. I told all those people you were coming. I told people not to sit there."

"If you would buy tickets in the reserved section, you wouldn't have to turn all those people away."

"What good would that have done? What good would it have done to buy a reserved seat instead? Mitchell was so hurt, he started making up some fantastic story about the fellow in the scoreboard, some gray-headed guy keeping score for the Cubs, sent to earth to help straighten out his mother."

"And did you agree with him? That I needed straightening out?"

At that, Joe clamped his mouth shut. He could see that their conversation wasn't going in a good direction.

"A husband is supposed to support his wife, Joe. Is that what this is? Support? Because it certainly doesn't feel like it." Sarah was an expert at blame shifting when she felt cornered.

Joe was looking past her at the mustard-colored bus slowing at the curb outside the window. Its amber lights flashed in pulsing rhythm. "Mitchell!" he called. "Bus! Get a move on!"

Sarah didn't let the interruption distract her. "Joe? Are you going to answer my question?"

"I don't know what all of this is, Sarah, or what we're even doing anymore."

"I do. This is the way we've chosen to live our lives."

And it was true; they'd made most of these decisions together.

At least Joe agreed to what Sarah strongly felt was a good idea. Sarah was very strong willed, and Joe had a habit of going along with what she wanted just to keep the peace. That had been the reason for buying the house not only in Lake Forest, but in *Very East* Lake Forest, an acre of land for Mitchell and their rambunctious little schnauzer to run wild on, the grassy expanse covered in autumn leaves as large as stationery pages, as full of warm color as flame. Deer Path Elementary was close enough for Mitchell to have only a short bus ride. It was all supposed to be so wonderful, but here they were existing in the same house but growing further apart every day. Joe felt tired and defeated. He didn't like what was happening to them, but he wasn't at all sure how to stop it.

As Mitchell pounded downstairs, his knapsack seemed enormous, all buckles and straps bouncing on his back. Mitchell straightened the brim of his Cubs hat and galloped out the door. Sarah was glad to see he'd found his glasses somewhere; they seesawed precariously on his nose. "Hey," she called him back. "Don't forget your lunch." She dangled the brown paper bag in front of him. He grabbed it from her, slammed the screen door, and scampered across the yard. The driver had started to close the doors and pull ahead just as Mitchell appeared. Sarah and Joe watched as the bus held up, the doors opened again, Mitchell launched himself up the stairs and gave the driver a high five. He didn't glance again in their direction.

When Sarah turned to Joe, he was still staring down at her with sorrow. "I just don't know how much longer I can do it. I don't know how much longer I can stand by and watch you disappoint him."

It was too much. "Don't you think it upsets me too? But

someone has to take care of this family, don't you think? *Someone* in the family has to have a steady income."

She realized she'd just slammed him, telling him his job wasn't nearly as important as hers, but she didn't care. She saw him flinch as if he'd been hit.

"Joe. I don't know what else I can say." He knew how much it cost her to disappoint Mitchell. How could he use it against her? "It's an important, professional job. I keep this position for another few years, and we'll almost have the house paid off. We've made so much progress on the credit cards already. It's what we decided we would do, remember?" Then, "We can't all tinker around in a garage and wait for some car collector to stop by and buy something."

He began to bluster. "You said you didn't mind if I started this business."

"I didn't mind. I *don't*. Only when you use what I have to do to make up for it and turn it around and punish me with it. That's when I mind."

A loud clatter from the playpen interrupted them. Kate must have toppled something over on herself because by the time Sarah rushed in there, she found the Sit-to-Stand Giraffe sideways and Kate beneath it, howling. "Oh, there you are." Sarah gathered up the baby, bouncing her to calm her down. She showed Kate her face in the mirror. "Shhhh. What are those tears? Did that toy attack you?" Then, "You mustn't be sad. Mrs. Pavik is going to be here any minute to play."

Almost the instant she said it, the nanny van pulled into the driveway with its magnetic sign on the side: How's My Nanny Doing? Joe was still trying to talk to her, but she opened the door halfway and let Kate see the woman who was shuffling up the sidewalk. Having Mrs. Pavik arrive this way always made Sarah feel so satisfied. But, even so, when she turned toward Joe again, her eyes remained grim.

She brandished the baby against her chest as if she were brandishing a shield between them.

"There's nothing else I can do about this," she said to her husband, her voice rough with frustration. She saw something click shut in his face. "Will you make sure to be here when Mrs. Pavik has to leave this afternoon? And tell her I'll be checking on Kate via computer during the day."

Sarah could depend on www.nannyrating.com. The high-tech baby Web site was a conscience soother for her. If Sarah knew she wasn't spending enough time with the baby, well, she could turn on her laptop screen and know exactly what Mrs. Pavik was doing. And, after that, because she'd gotten the Cornish account and would be very busy today, Joe would have to take over.

"You're not going to come home again tonight? Even after this discussion?"

"This hasn't been a discussion," she said. "It's been you flinging accusations."

He stood there helpless and staring while Kate stuck out her tongue and blew, making noise and spit bubbles, daring either one of them to ignore her presence. The baby pitched forward and sinuously launched herself into her father's arms. He balanced her inside the crook of one elbow and straightened her tiny pink playsuit.

"We have to do this," Sarah said. "We have to work together and get through this. I promise things will change soon."

She read it in his eyes. *That's what you said last time, Sarah.*

Why can't you ever stop taking on new things and just for once put your family first?

"You can't back out on me now."

The baby nestled against her father's chest, her little blue eyes troubled, as if even a child this young could sense the stress between them.

"I've got meetings with my new clients tonight," Sarah said, her voice flat. "I don't have any idea when they'll let me come home."

⟊ Chapter Five ⟊

Tom Roscoe stepped from the downtown health-club shower and reached for the pristine towel hanging beside him. He dried his face with one swipe of his big hand and shook the loose water from his hair with a vigorous, satisfying shake. Droplets splattered on the mirror.

"Ah." Tom's exclamation of pleasure came from way down in his gut. Nothing like a strenuous lunchtime workout to clear the head for the rigors of the afternoon.

The dull thud of music sounded through the wall, the repetitive chorus that the trainer kept playing to motivate his clients to keep their pulses pounding and their feet moving. The beat of the music hammered the walls as Tom yanked up his trousers, unzipped his athletic bag, and rummaged through his shaving kit for his razor. He angled his chin toward the mirror and surveyed it on both the port and starboard sides, searching for renegade whiskers. Even though he didn't find any haphazard hairs, he pumped a giant dollop of lather into his palm, gave his jaw a bracing slap, and shaved anyway.

Tom, now smooth-skinned and smelling of Kiehl's Ultimate Man scrub bar, pictured his sweaty colleagues still laboring over barbells and bench presses on the other side of the wall. This gave him much pleasure as he fastened cuff links at his wrists and wrestled his feet into his loafers. He liked the feeling of everyone else running behind him. Never mind how disappointed he'd been when he'd found out his son Jonas wasn't interested in the internship he kept offering and that his other son had just dropped out of college for the third time.

He flung his suit coat over one elbow and hit the door, already late for his one o'clock. The street overflowed with people wearing computer backpacks or carrying briefcases, everyone scrambling back to their desks or frantically running errands or inhaling street-vendor pizza before they returned to the pits. Tom narrowly dodged a lady with a Nathan's hot dog that, should he have sidestepped two seconds later, would have ended up as ketchup, pickle relish, and onions plastered against his lapel.

Far ahead up the street he glimpsed a flash of red in the crowd. He thought he recognized the clothing. Tom hesitated for a moment, wanting to make sure. In only seconds, he was rewarded. She stepped off the curb to get around someone, and he caught the full view.

He could pick Sarah out anywhere.

Tom shouldered his way past a woman who'd stepped from her shop with a bucketful of bundled chrysanthemums. He shoved past a man who'd halted midstream to sort through his change and buy a *Tribune*. He wove his way between two cops arguing about the time left on a parking meter.

"Hey!" he shouted. "Sarah." And suddenly Tom wasn't quite sure what he'd say when he caught up with his employee. It was just that the past two nights had been extraordinary, both dinner at the Everest Room with their new clients and the strategy meeting at The Drake. In these days of financial insecurity, his firm had just roped in a large account. A moment of subtle appreciation surged through him. He couldn't have done it without Sarah Harper.

His one o'clock would have to wait.

Adrenaline surged through his veins; Tom still hadn't come down from his exercise high. He could see Sarah up ahead, the rear of her red jacket slightly rumpled, her skirt seams swaying to her steps. He quickened his pace to catch up with her, surprised to see her off the trading floor so early.

The sun glinted off Sarah's hair in squiggles of light. He'd long been thinking he'd like to get her alone and let her know how much he appreciated all she'd been doing for him. Tom didn't stop to consider, as he chased his associate along the street, that this pursuit might be of some concern to his wife. He and Maribeth had been far too busy lately, he with the pursuit of new clients and she with all her volunteer fund-raising at the club. Tom liked spending time with the people who shared his victories, and Maribeth hadn't been doing much of that.

He rehearsed the conversation in his mind as he followed her. *Tell me the truth. Have you ever had a meal like the other night? Quite the strategy Nathan Cornish was presenting last night at The Drake. What do you think, Sarah? Do you agree with his stance on metal futures?*

Just as he was about to call out to her again, she winced, grabbed onto a light post, lifted her foot, and ran her finger along the inside of her left heel. She never should have walked this far in those shoes. Why did women insist on wearing such ineffectual footwear? She could blame herself for getting a blister.

He saw her glance toward the shop window. Just as he expected her to start walking again, just as he was about to catch up with her and engage her in a conversation that would both exalt his company and remind her how much she owed him, he saw her lean from the waist and whisper something to a child. A boy. One with a shock of straw-colored hair.

From this distance, the kid could have been Jonas.

She spoke with a slight grin, her eyes probing the kid's face, the boy nodding and gesturing toward the sky. Tom realized then. For the entire length of the city block, the boy had been trotting at her side.

Tom stopped so fast that someone bumped him from behind. The lady apologized, and he answered without looking, "Oh yeah. Right. How about watching where you're going?"

Tom shouldered his athletic bag as people darted around and jostled to fill the empty space on the sidewalk. One man struck him with a computer case. Still, Tom didn't move. His feet might as well have been embedded in the concrete.

Seeing these two together left him feeling deeply angered and betrayed. What was Sarah doing with Mitchell in the middle of a workday? Didn't she know this was no time to be distracted from her work? The kid galloped ahead, with Sarah smiling after him as if she'd never before noticed a kid's legs pumping as he ran or a boy's way of hitching up the seat of his pants. He didn't want his employee thinking about her family during these dire times; he wanted her thinking about what she could do for his company. And Tom wasn't watching Sarah anymore; he was watching himself with his own two sons, Jonas first and then Richard, seeing the days he'd missed bringing them along to show them the city or the days he'd missed their baseball games or missed watching them leaping along the lakeshore ahead of him, back when they'd been delighted to be in his presence, back when they'd both wanted something to do with him.

In Tom's experience, boys never did anything except turn against you when it mattered.

"Why should you care what happens to me?" Jonas had snarled when Tom reminded him for the hundredth time how much he stood to gain by working for Tom's company. "You never want me around any other time, so why now?"

And Richard, listless and without direction, whose hangdog expression seemed to imply, *Yeah, you're right. I'm good for nothing.* Richard, with his head buried so deep in video games that he'd forgotten how to formulate a sentence. Richard, who had gotten picked up twice for shoplifting cigarettes and Pepsi. The shoplifting made no sense at all to Tom because he gave Richard money anytime he wanted it. Tom didn't realize that Richard's stealing was a rebellious act, a desperate attempt to get some kind of genuine attention from him.

Tom saw Sarah glance behind her as if she sensed she was being followed. He didn't want to talk to her anymore. Tom stared at a black spot of discarded chewing gum imbedded in the sidewalk. He held his breath, as if that would make him invisible to her.

She must not have noticed him. Otherwise, why had she kept going without even speaking to him?

What did Sarah Harper think this was? Take-Your-Kid-to-Work Day or something?

He detoured at the next corner, cut through an alley with its stench of garbage, and beat her to the office while his agitation gnawed on him like a dog gnaws on a particularly knotty bone.

Tom always got unreasonably upset when he didn't get exactly what he wanted. He had imagined an afternoon stroll with Sarah telling him how grateful she was for all he had done for her. Instead, she was so busy entertaining her son that she could not even find the time to speak to him!

She would have to answer to him for this, Tom decided. He wasn't paying her to bond with her kid on company time.

The line began beside the brilliantly lit case of croissants and cupcakes, stretched the length of the counter, and jutted past the shelves of mugs and CDs and fancy coffeemakers. Behind the counter, the girl released bursts of steam from spouts in a rhythm that, to Mitchell's ears, sounded like something in a hip-hop song. Mitchell pressed his nose to the glass and surveyed the many rows of baked goods, the lemon-knot cookies, the chocolate-covered granola bars, the pumpkin muffins made in the shape of tiny Bundt cakes.

"We don't have all day, Mitchell," said his mother. "I've got to get to the office. People behind us are waiting their turn."

The clerk stood with her finger over the cash register button, waiting for him to make a selection. Wouldn't you know? There wasn't anything with sprinkles and icing here. He glanced up at his mom and pointed toward the first thing on the tray. "I'll have that one."

"Macadamia nut, cranberry, or white chocolate?" the clerk asked.

He nodded without really caring. He'd had his heart set on Dunkin' Donuts instead, and then they'd gotten here and there hadn't been much to choose from. Add to that, his mom never gave him enough time to think. She was always in a hurry no matter what she was doing.

Beside him, she dug into her purse, paid the bill, and loaded their to-go cups in the cardboard carrier. She was already headed for the door when the lady at the counter reminded her she hadn't taken her bag.

"Aren't we going to eat here?" Mitchell adjusted the huge sleeves on the borrowed jacket he wore since he was going on the trading floor.

"I told you. I have to get to the office."

"We're eating cookies along the way?"

"Yes. That's what it looks like to me," Sarah snapped. The last thing she wanted to do was be impatient with Mitchell. After all, she had brought him to work with her to show how much she cared for him, but he would have to keep pace with her if he ever wanted to do it again.

He would have loved to sit at the table and nibble the cookie and watch everyone. He got tired of listening to people in his mom's office because they all talked about the same thing. But wearing the jacket made things somewhat better; this jacket might be the greatest thing ever. "It swallows you," his mom had said when he'd tried it on, which pleased him, the idea of something swallowing him. He liked the way it hung, wrinkly and large, green mesh with a smart white trim, and a plastic nametag on the collar. When he worried about borrowing it, his mom told him not to worry, that she had every intention of returning it to the closet after they'd finished. She said everyone had to wear a jacket like this when they visited the trading pit.

They'd almost made it outside when a lady carrying a computer case pointed at his borrowed nametag and said, "You're not Harry Tippin."

"I'm not," he said. "I'm Mitchell Harper. I'm visiting."

"But you're wearing Harry Tippin's jacket."

Mitchell shrugged, feeling as if this wasn't good, that somehow she'd caught him at something.

"Hello, Sarah. Heard you've been singled out for the Cornish account." The woman extended a hand to his mom. "Congratulations. I'm happy for you."

His mom didn't return the gesture. "I'll bet you are."

"Well," said computer lady, looking insulted. "No need to say it like that. I'm trying to be a good sport."

Once they'd gotten out on the sidewalk, his mom shook her head. "So now you've met Lauren Davis. You mustn't let her bother you. That woman would give up her own child if it meant she could get her hands on my accounts."

Mitchell wasn't sure what that meant. "Is she like Ryan Thompson in my class? He pushes me against the fence whenever I do better in Math Minute than he does."

"Ryan Thompson pushes you against the fence? You never told me that."

"He does."

"Have you talked to Mrs. Georges about it?"

"Of *course* not, Mom." What was she thinking? "If I did, they'd all know I *squealed*."

"I see your point. You're going to have to figure out a way to make him stop then. And, yes. It's the same thing."

His mom handed him his lemonade. Mitchell chewed his straw as they turned the corner. Suddenly he felt hemmed in by the giant buildings. The Chicago Board of Trade clock gawked down from the end of the street. As he watched, the clock's minute hand jerked from Roman numeral III to Roman numeral IV.

"Mom. Did you see that? Another minute just went by."

She'd been gulping her coffee in great mouthfuls, hardly stopping to swallow as they'd hurried along. Upon hearing his words, she picked up her pace.

"No, Mom," he said. "I didn't mean we were supposed to hurry up and catch it. I mean, we *missed* it." At school, Mrs. Georges had been teaching them about space-time continuums. It wasn't on the second-grade curriculum, she'd confessed as she drew some sort of chart that looked like a jumping spider on the blackboard, but her son was getting his doctorate in mathematical physics. She thought it only fair that she share with her class what she and her family often talked about around the dinner table.

"No, we didn't miss that minute. We were right here. We were talking."

"But I just saw it go by. And we didn't *do* anything with it."

"No, and we won't do anything with the next one either if you don't hurry up."

Mitchell stopped short. Some charity had placed a used-clothing bin in the middle of the sidewalk. Mitchell took his mom's hand as they made their way around it.

On the other side they almost ran into an old man who was digging inside a metal door marked Shoes Only! He clutched one scuffed wingtip oxford in his hand and apparently was searching to find its mate.

His mom didn't approve, he could tell. "Don't they realize they ought to put these in places where the homeless stay, not in the financial district?" She gave the man a wide berth. "No one wants these people to turn up here."

The man found his other shoe. He dropped to the ground and

positioned his backside on the edge of a windowsill to try them on. He rolled up frayed pants to reveal bare ankles. He wiggled his toes into the shoes and shoved them the rest of the way on. He yanked the shoelaces into neat loops and stood proudly to test them out, putting his weight first on one foot and then the other. The shoes were too big, but that didn't seem to matter. He glanced up at Mitchell, wanting some opinion. Their eyes met.

Mitchell could tell the old man had been sleeping under a bridge or something. He wore ancient clothes that were very dirty, his sleeves rubbed thin at the elbows, and his shirt didn't have much of a hem. He was missing a good number of teeth, and what teeth he *did* have protruded from his gums at slight angles. He walked with a slight stoop, and he smelled bad, and his scalp showed through a very small amount of gray, grease-caked hair. What hair he lacked on his head, he made up for in his bushy brows. Silver strands stuck straight out from the bony ridges over the man's eyes, stiffer than kittens' whiskers. Mitchell figured the man hadn't had a bath for days. He would like going without one himself sometime, but being clean and looking proper at all times was very important to his mom. Mitchell thought perhaps that was why his mom seemed so irritated at the man's presence. It probably just bothered her that he was dirty.

Something mysterious and familiar glowed in the man's eyes. Mitchell got the strangest feeling that maybe he'd seen this man before, only he couldn't figure out where. Mitchell couldn't help wondering if there was some special reason why they were meeting this man at this particular time.

The odd feeling ended, however, almost before it began. "Hey, lady." The owner of the oxfords held out a hand toward Mitchell's mom. "You need help finding your way around? Show you to the closest 'L' stop if you got spare change."

"I don't need you to show me anywhere," she said. "I'm not lost."

"Hey, Mom," Mitchell whispered. "I think he's just saying that . . . well, I think he's the one who needs help."

His mom shouldered her large purse. "You mustn't help people like this. They have to learn to help themselves."

"What if he needs money because he's hungry?"

"He isn't hungry. He'll only get as much as he can and then he'll get drunk on it. You have no idea how much these people drink, living on the street like this. I work for my money, and I am not going to give it to somebody who doesn't want to work."

But Mitchell hung back. "Are you hungry?" he asked.

"You bet I'm hungry." The interesting stranger shot him a broad, plaque-infested grin.

Mitchell's mom gave him that look that said, *Mitchell Harper, if you don't cut it out right now, there will be big consequences, young man.* He was just about to give up and follow her when he remembered the cookie he'd been carrying. He held out an arm with the sack caught between two fingers. "You want this?"

"Sure I want it," the man said. He peered inside the bag and withdrew the cookie. "God bless you for this. I say, God bless you." From the careful, reverent way he peeled off the paper and bit into the gift, you'd have thought he was biting into some fancy French pastry. "I say." He pulled the small sweet out of his mouth and examined it after his first bite. "This is the *best* cookie I've ever eaten." Then Mitchell heard for the third time, "God bless you."

"Those are some nice shoes too," Mitchell said, nodding toward the man's feet. "I like those. You're lucky."

"Don't got nothing to do with luck, I tell you." The stranger stared down at his feet like he'd almost forgotten they belonged to him. "They sure are nice, aren't they, though? They'll clean up nice, don't you think?"

"Yeah."

Mitchell figured he was in deep trouble for not obeying his mom. "If you do not come with me *this minute,* young man," she said, covering her mouthpiece with her hand because she'd answered her phone again, "you will be grounded from Cubs games for as long as I'm alive."

He was just turning to follow her when the man in the wingtip shoes called, "Hey, kid." He pointed to the collection bin. "You want me to dig you something out of here?"

Mitchell shrugged and called back, "Don't need anything much." But then he brightened. "I'd take it if you found a Cubs shirt."

"Plenty of Cubs shirts in here," he said. "You stop back by, I'll have you one. Folks throw those out all the time. Now take White Sox shirts. Those are a whole lot harder to come by. Folks hang on to those."

Mitchell did a double take as he got a closer look. Behind his glass lenses, his eyes went round as hickory nuts. "I saw you from the bleachers, didn't I?"

It all started to make sense. The way the man leaned on the open bin and propped his arms into a wide D against the door. The way what was left of his hair sprang from his ears like the feathers of a half-plucked turkey.

Mitchell felt the awesome thrum of his pulse. His heart felt like it might thump clear out of his chest. "You were at the game, weren't you? In the scoreboard?"

In spite of his disheveled appearance, the gentleman snapped to attention with military precision. "You recognize me, don't you? Yes, I was there." His gaze popped right, to his left, to his right again, hoping no one would overhear. "But maybe now's not the best time to tell everybody about it."

"Mom!" Mitchell called. "This man is our friend. I saw him at the Cubs game. He was keeping score. He was watching me and Dad!" Sarah kept getting phone calls and taking them; otherwise, they would have been long gone. She certainly wasn't paying any attention to what he was saying right now; she just looked frustrated that she had a plan, and for some reason it kept being thwarted.

The fellow raised his bristly eyebrows and clamped his mouth shut tighter than a varmint trap.

Mitchell was unsettled now, but for completely different reasons than his mom. He fished inside his pocket. He had almost a dollar in there if you counted all the dimes he'd made carrying groceries for Mrs. Fogelman down the street. "If I had time and I was lost, you could show me the 'L' stop. Here's all the money I got."

"That's not why I'm here, Mitchell."

The little boy held out a sweaty palm with every coin to his name in it. "Here. Take it."

"*Mitchell*," his mom said, interrupting her latest cell-phone call and anticipating his move. "You may *not* do that."

"How come you know my name?" Mitchell whispered, marveling and somewhat confused. "Until now, my mom never said it in front of you."

His mom took his hand and pulled him after her. "Come away from him now. *Please.*"

"But, Mom."

"I said *now!*"

For the entire length of the block, Mitchell couldn't stop craning his neck, peering behind him.

-⊂◦ Chapter Six ◦⊃-

Tom Roscoe had just crumpled a cup and pitched it inside the wastebasket when Lauren Davis appeared beside him. "Tom," she said. "We have to talk."

He noted the dark concern in her eyes. "What about?"

"I've made a decision, and I need to speak with you right away."

Tom led her to his office and closed the door. He braided his fingers atop his desk and waited. Lauren seemed nervous. She wasn't saying anything yet. Finally he could stand the silence no longer. He blurted, "I didn't think you needed reminding. It's your duty to present strong numbers for us. That's why I hired you." Tom was a bit nervous himself. He figured Lauren was getting squeamish about the proposal he wanted her to offer Nielsen. Tom was willing to do anything in an attempt to punish his old clients for their defection.

"Which I will do." Lauren leaned forward in the massive leather armchair, matching Roscoe's predatory body language limb for limb. "I'll put together the strongest portfolio possible and present it to a prospective client," she said in her measured voice. "But I won't help you manipulate those prices. It's revenge."

"What?"

"I'll only do my job by honorable means."

"Honorable means?" Roscoe asked. "Will you let the Nielsens decide what's honorable or not? They're the ones who broke the contract. They're the ones who pulled out first."

She said, "I'm afraid I have to turn it down. I'm sorry."

"What?"

"Don't look so stricken, Mr. Roscoe. I'm sure you can find someone else who will do this for you. It doesn't have to be me."

Tom wasn't one to mince words. He had one goal and one alone—to keep this company going. He wanted to continue to live his life in the manner to which he was accustomed. He wanted to leave an inheritance for his sons that would allow them to do the same.

He wanted them to have dugout seats in the club section at Wrigley Field. He wanted them to be able to live in Lincoln Park and play golf at the country club and send their children to the finest schools. He wanted to give them everything he'd struggled through the years to build. He wanted them never to have to live as he had, with a father who was an alcoholic and who had left his mother to feed a family of six on money she made doing other people's ironing. Like Sarah, Tom failed to realize that money and things were not what his children needed. It was *him* they wanted.

"Look," he said. "All I asked you to do was have a look at the list."

"Which I did. I looked at the list."

"And?"

"It was quite the lineup." Then she reiterated her position, her words controlled. "Tom, I'll put together the best managed-futures fund I can for the Nielsen family. I'd be happy to rely on my own intuition and expertise to bring them back into the fold. But I won't resort to manipulating prices under the table as you've suggested. I won't resort to paybacks."

Tom hadn't built this company by being indecisive or under-handed, and he convinced himself that he wasn't being dishon-est now. He was simply taking advantage of the same creative options that other successful commodities traders knew to employ. If he was willing to be somewhat more inventive than others, well, just chalk that up to his experience and his com-mitment to his sons and to his single-minded focus on leaving a legacy for them.

Lauren Davis had made one mistake and one mistake alone. She had confronted Tom Roscoe. That was something nobody did and stayed around to talk about.

"If you won't do everything under your power to pursue your career here, Lauren," he told the woman sitting across the desk while her eyes blazed at him, "I'll have to hire someone else who will."

Sarah punched the button on the elevator in the Roscoe Build-ing. The brass door slid shut and, above it, the numbers started to climb.

She leaned against the wall and stared at the ceiling, discour-agement a leaden weight in her chest.

Sarah had planned a special day for Mitchell to make up for

missing the Cubs game. To her disappointment, it hadn't worked that way at all.

Where she'd hoped Mitchell would be interested in the ticker numbers streaming across the boards, he'd spent his time spinning round and round in the pit, getting tangled up in about a thousand Ethernet cables instead.

When she'd wanted to introduce him to the ninth-floor guys who called her "Andretti," Mitchell had conveniently gone missing in a sea of legs.

When she'd tried to teach him how to buy and sell with hand signals, Mitchell had turned so timid and scared that he'd cried, "Mom, this isn't for kids," at which she'd lost her patience with a horrible snap. "What's the difference? If you can get excited for Zambrano and Edmonds at the ball game, then at least try to do it for me!"

She berated herself. *What is it with you, Sarah? Can't you do anything right for them anymore?* Her job might be strenuous, and maybe she struggled putting in long hours down in The Loop, but Mitchell and Kate meant everything to her. Why was she always losing her temper with the kids?

Sarah loved them both so much she couldn't catch her breath when she thought of it. If anything ever happened to one of them...she couldn't imagine how she would keep going. Imagine someone who could talk a cookie right out of the hands of a little boy! Imagine someone who could convince a child in one minute, *one minute*, that he could be a trusted friend! The very thought filled her with terror when she remembered how fast Mitchell opened up to a complete stranger. And a street bum at that!

I saw him at the Cubs game. Mitchell had seen more than forty thousand people at the Cubs game. *He was watching me and Dad.* Those words sent chills up her spine.

She'd scolded Mitchell soundly about it the minute she'd gotten him away. "Didn't I tell you not to talk to strangers?" she'd asked, gripping his shoulders. "Didn't I tell you to ask an adult before talking to anyone like that? Didn't I tell you to always check with me first?"

He'd scuffed the curb with his toe and hadn't raised his eyes.

"Don't you remember talking about stranger danger?"

He'd nodded so hard, his bangs flopped and his glasses slid sideways.

"Have you really seen this man before? Do you think he could be following you?"

Mitchell shrugged, apparently deciding it best to be vague.

"Have you?" she pressed.

"I'm not sure," he said, on the verge of tears.

"You don't talk to adults who ask for help from children. That's not the way it works."

Mitchell jammed his hands so deep inside his pockets that he might have been reaching for China. But she couldn't let up on him, not about something as crucial as this. "Mitchell, it's one of the most important rules you'll ever learn. There's danger everywhere."

They stood all alone in the elevator with Mitchell gripping her hand, and just thinking about it made Sarah want to reprimand him again. But before she had the chance to start up, the brass doors slid open to reveal the Roscoe lobby.

Together they stepped out. Sarah knew immediately that something was wrong.

A hushed gloom had fallen over the office. No one smiled in

the foyer. Discussions, usually punctuated with laughter, were being carried on in low, serious voices.

What happened? she mouthed to Leo over Mitchell's head. *What's going on?*

He shook his head. *Don't ask.*

She raised her brows, questioning him.

"Ah, nice trading jacket," Leo diverted, pumping Mitchell's hand with vigor. "Very cool.

"How was the game the other night? Was it the best?"

"Yeah."

"I was so jealous, thinking of you guys. Man, Mitch, I would have given anything to be there."

Sarah interrupted. She certainly didn't want the conversation to go in *this* direction. "Leo?" She held out a hand. "Messages?"

But for the moment, Leo ignored her. He focused on Mitchell. "So, what else is going on in your life, kid?"

Mitchell brightened under Leo's attention. "After we're done here, I'm showing Mom how I can throw down one-wheelers at the skate park."

Sarah had made this promise on the trading floor, a last-ditch effort to put a smile on his face. "We can?" he'd asked. "Yes." "You sure?" "You have your board with you, don't you?" "It's in the car." "Then we'll do it." Even then, she'd hated how his brow furrowed with skepticism. "I *promise*," she'd told him.

"That rocks," Leo said now. "Very cool."

"And I'm in a Math Counts competition tomorrow. There's kids coming from different schools, and Mrs. Georges, my teacher, picked me. Mom's getting me Cubs pencils for good luck."

Oh my word. Sarah was horrified. She'd totally forgotten about the Cubs pencils. She'd intended to pick them up from a souvenir booth at the game. "Mitchell. I've—"

But Leo didn't let her finish. "That is so great, Mitchell. You must be brilliant in math. A real genius."

"Mitchell," Sarah was trying to tell him. "I don't have the—"

But Leo shot her a look. "Hey, what can you find to do in your mother's office?" he asked Mitchell. "Set up a Facebook page? Copy your nose on the printer? You know how to do that? I need to assist your mother for a minute."

Mitchell's glasses magnified his rounded eyes. "Really? You don't mind if I make faces on the copier?"

"Just don't look at the light. Don't blind yourself. Your mother will blame me."

Leo pointed to the leather swivel chair, herded him inside, and closed the door behind him. Sarah cupped her hand over her mouth and sucked in a huge gasp of air through her fingers. "What am I going to do? I don't have those pencils."

Leo slid his drawer open and, with a flourish, handed her a good half dozen of them. "Now you do."

She stared at the pencils in her hand. They were white with blue Cs, and CUBS written in red.

"These are yours? You just keep these around?"

"Of course I do. You don't think Mitchell's the only Cubs fan on the North Side, do you?"

"You just... keep Cubs pencils in your desk?"

He grinned.

Sarah closed her fingers over them. "Do you know how many times you've saved my life?"

"No. But I think I'll start counting. And when it comes time for me to apply to this firm for a *real* job—"

"You'll have my glowing letter of recommendation," she finished for him. "Just say the word."

To get them past this pleasing yet awkward subject, Leo sorted through the message slips again. "Your nanny called to say it was applesauce, not peanut butter."

"Tell her to text me. I want that in writing."

"Rothman wants to know what you think about the price direction on silver."

"You can tell Rothman I think he needs to do his own research."

"You'll get back to him with an answer. This afternoon." Leo made another note. "Oh, and your stepfather called. Something about a missed appointment. He sent you a text, but you never showed up."

She'd totally forgotten. "When? Yesterday?" She couldn't even remember when she'd been scheduled to meet him. "Oh, Leo. Can you get back to him for me?"

Ever since she could remember, Harold had been like a true father to her. She felt like a traitor for having forgotten him. Her life was reeling out of control, and she felt powerless to make it stop. Forgetting appointments and not even being able to remember making them, snapping at Mitchell, hurrying all the time, trying to please everyone and not even being able to please her own husband. Her head was hurting again, and she was so tired. Sarah felt trapped. She didn't know how she could go on like this. Yet at the same time, she didn't know how to stop.

"Maybe I could give him some sort of estimate? When you'll call him back? He sounded kind of forlorn."

But she couldn't answer that. "Tell him I'll call him when my schedule isn't nuts. When things get better. When I haven't made promises to Mitchell. You know what to say." It was just too much. Every time another person demanded something of her,

Sarah felt even more depleted. She didn't have anything to give anyone else. She was just plain worn out. And yet everyone kept asking for more. It was endless. It took all the self-control she could manage not to scream.

Leo didn't dial right away. "Guess who's been asking for you ever since the floor closed."

"Oh no. Really?" She pointed to the stack of files on Leo's desk. "Are those Tom's *notes*?"

"Afraid so. I'll let him know you'll be right up."

"Thanks."

But Leo kept looking at her like he wanted to warn her of something. "Tread lightly."

"Why?"

"Lauren Davis just got canned."

Sarah's hand froze on the file folder. "What?"

"Not kidding you."

She felt the color drain from her face. She just stood there in shock. So this was the reason everyone kept tiptoeing around like they might step on a land mine, meeting each other's eyes with grim, knowing glances.

"Why?"

He shook his head, at a loss. "He told her to clean out her office. She left with everything packed in a cardboard box."

Sarah couldn't explain the jolt of terror she felt, the sudden, improbable grief she felt for Lauren, who, just this morning, had been comfortably sipping coffee and making comments about Mitchell's trading jacket and hadn't any idea that, like a plunging stock price, she would be worth nothing by the end of the day.

"Rumor has it that Lauren wouldn't deal with an account because she didn't want to do it his way."

"Oh." Sarah forgot everyone around her. She forgot Leo, who had asked if he could leave on time tonight because he had something planned with his sister. She forgot Joe, who didn't approve of her anymore, who'd said, *"I don't know how much longer I can stand by and watch you disappoint him,"* and who didn't see how hard she was trying. She forgot Mitchell, whom she'd just scolded for being friendly with a good-for-nothing stranger in the street and for whom she'd planned a day that she'd hoped would rival a major-league all-star game.

All she could think of was the pounding panic in her heart and the possibility that with one slip of her tongue, one wrong word or one misplaced idea, the same thing could happen to her.

She could get fired too. And then where would she be?

Ashamed.

Afraid.

Worth nothing.

I don't care how hard I have to work—Tom Roscoe will never have a reason to fire me.

I don't care how tired and confused I feel—I'm going to do whatever I have to do to protect my position.

One by one, Leo began crumpling the pink message slips and making arcing free-throw shots into the trash can, returning Sarah's attention to the matter at hand. "Leo?"

"Yes?"

Sarah glimpsed a reflection of herself across the way in the mirror on the wall, and the woman she saw was someone she didn't recognize. Yes, even though she was one of the lucky few to keep her job in the financial market, she looked older than her years—and frantic. The more stressful the choices she had to make on the trading floor, the more she worked to prove her worth to people around her, the more it seemed these people expected more and more. Everyone was in control but her, she thought. Yet it was more than just the job or her relationship with her husband or the things Mitchell and Kate needed from her. Sarah felt this deep dissatisfaction but couldn't quite put her finger on the cause.

She felt alone even though she was surrounded by people all the time.

"Keep Mitchell entertained as long as you have to, would you?"

Sarah's weariness went way beyond the hours of work and the challenge of managing a family and of being a good wife. It went way beyond the guilt she felt for missing Mitchell's classroom parties even though she always sent snacks, way beyond worrying about getting the schnauzer to the dog park or managing a drive schedule so Mitchell got to the field house for his Scout meeting, way beyond the nuisance of people trying to ply her for trading tips whenever they wanted.

Even now, her life seemed to be dangling on a thin string, and she feared it could break at any moment. Sarah didn't know how to make herself or the people around her happy anymore. And wasn't that what being alive was all about, about being *happy*?

She opened her office door a crack and called to Mitchell.

"I'm headed upstairs, kiddo. I'll be back any minute."

Then, to Leo, "Text Tom again for me, would you? Let him know I'm on my way?"

Leo raised his chin as if to say, *Go ahead. I got you.* Then he nodded broadly. "You don't even have to ask."

∽ Chapter Seven ∾

The red convertible stood angled in the middle of Joe's repair shop with its hood yawning open. From beneath the hood came a series of thuds and grunts. After a bit, a wrench fell to the ground with a resounding clatter.

"Hey. Anybody in here?" Joe's best friend, Pete, knocked on the doorjamb with the same solid strokes he would use to pound a post into the ground. "You working hard or hardly working?"

Joe muttered something unintelligible, untangled his excessive height from under the hinged cover, and swabbed his forehead with the greasy chamois from his rear pocket. "A little of both."

Which was all the invitation Pete needed. He joined his friend beside the front fender and examined the workings of the car.

"Need help with that?" Pete surveyed the gleaming pistons and the polished valve covers with reverent awe. "How could a blockhead like you make a performance engine fit into this heap?"

With a satisfied humph, Joe slid beneath the car's chassis, fished for the wrench he'd lost, and located it beside the front tire. "Just wait until you hear this thing start up. Then you call me a blockhead." He handed Pete the wrench, making it clear that his best buddy could definitely make himself useful.

"How long'll it take to get her going?"

Joe shrugged. "We'll find out, I guess." He ducked inside the open maw of the sports car again, found the bolt he'd been tightening, and extended his palm so Pete could hand him the wrench.

"Actually"—Pete placed the tool in Joe's hand—"I stopped by to invite you and Sarah over for Gail's birthday."

Joe wiped the wrench against his thigh, then went after the bolt with Herculean effort. If it occurred to him that he'd surely pay for this later, that somewhere along the way he'd certainly have to remove these bolts and mounts and clamps again, he didn't care.

"You want to think about it?"

Joe shook his head. "You may have to count us out."

"You kidding me?"

Joe whaled into another bolt, then another, not wanting to discuss his wife. "You know. Sarah's got this awful schedule."

"Isn't there time to rearrange it? Gail's birthday's still a couple of days away."

Joe set the wrench in Pete's outstretched hand and felt around for the pliers. He knew better than to be honest. *She never puts anything but work on her schedule.*

You just get disappointed if you depend on her to be someplace she says she'll be.

Something will come up, and I'm not making excuses for her anymore.

"Well, don't you even want to talk to her about it?"

"No."

Pete shifted his weight from one boot to the other. "Well, that puts me in a tough place. You're the only folks Gail wanted for the big day."

"Sorry."

"What'll I tell her? You know how a woman gets when her feelings are hurt."

With one rotation of his knuckles, Joe crushed the metal clamp and smashed the hose into place. "Guess I do." He hefted the new air-intake duct, grabbed the gasket, and jammed it into place, as if everything he did to this car might clear his mind of his wife. "I could invite you two over to our place that night, Pete, but I couldn't promise Sarah would be there either."

Joe ducked out from under the innards of the old car and smeared what he could of the grease from his hands. He couldn't rid himself of the feeling that the cold shoulder Sarah gave him was somehow his fault, that he'd made some mistake, that he'd done something to make her pull away. She had a way of making him feel guilty even when he knew darn well he hadn't done anything wrong.

"Is everything all right between you two?" Pete shot him a troubled frown.

Joe swigged from his giant water bottle and backhanded his mouth dry. "Sure," he lied.

Pete stood with his hands shoved in his pockets, rocking from his heels to his toes and back again, studying the spotless crankshaft.

Joe shoved back his dusty cap, scratched his forehead, and studied the new bazooka tailpipe from five different angles.

Pete started to whistle.

Joe offered Pete a stick of Juicy Fruit. He unwrapped his own piece, shoved it inside his jaw, and absently folded the empty foil into smaller and smaller squares. "Tell me something," he said with false nonchalance. "Does Gail fight straight when she's mad? Does she cry and slam doors and carry on, things like that?"

Pete looked at his friend like he'd just asked if the sun came up at his house every morning.

"Does she bang the cabinets and stalk around the house with bird-stiff legs and tell you you're not being fair?"

"Sarah's doing that?"

"No. Sarah's *not* doing that. Sarah *used* to do that. Now I can hardly get her to look at me."

Pete chewed his gum slower and slower.

"Or when she does look at me, she stands there like she'd just as soon be having a conversation with the Chicago Water Tower."

"Well, Gail doesn't throw any left hooks or anything like that, if that's what you mean."

"Of course she doesn't. She's a woman."

"Don't know what to tell you. You asking me to understand a woman?"

"Nope. Just asking you to try to explain one."

"Well, isn't that the same thing?"

Joe couldn't decide which reaction of Sarah's alarmed him the most, her hotheaded accusations when he tried to make her see what she was doing to Mitchell and Kate or her cold detachment when he tried to get her to tell him what was wrong. Just last night he'd found her sequestered at the computer desk after supper, her bedraggled curls captured in the vise grip of a hair claw, her neck about as stiff and out of joint as a worn-out axle shaft.

"Sarah. I've thought about it a little bit. Well, actually, I've thought about it a lot." He was trying to get her to talk, and he hated himself for struggling with the words. Foolishly he toyed with one of her curls, winding it around a finger. Then his knuckle brushed the hollow of her scalp, and she jerked away from him. He felt her go as prickly as a pincushion.

"Stop, Joe."

"What? You don't want me to touch you?"

An alarm sounded on the phone by her elbow. She dropped everything to read the text message.

"No," Joe said as she flipped open the Nokia. "Will you stop and look at me? Do you see that I'm in the room? Can't you show me a little respect?"

He waved his hands between her face and the computer screen. "I'm here, not online. I'm here, not on an instant message or a text or a cell phone." He waved his arms in the air. "I'm right in front of you."

Her dark emotionless eyes reflected the rows of data on the screen. Her cell phone vibrated again. She reached, but he beat her to it. He stuffed it inside his shirt pocket.

"Maybe we could go away together. Leave the kids with your mom and Harold. Or maybe Mrs. Pavik would stay overnight."

He waited a long time for an answer that didn't come.

"Couldn't you make time for that?"

"I'm making time for Mitchell. That's what you wanted, isn't it? I'm taking him to the city."

"Won't you just *stop*?"

"You're changing the rules on me," she said blandly. "Every

time I start to do something right, you raise the bar a little farther."

"No I'm not. I'm not raising anything. I'm not changing anything."

When she pivoted toward him in the chair, her eyes accused him. Other than that, they were as void of emotion as two stones.

"I don't understand where you're coming from anymore, Sarah. I thought the fast pace would eventually end. I thought we'd work hard together, pushing forward together for a while, and then we'd both be able to slow down and enjoy life together. I didn't know you wouldn't be able to do that."

"You told me you wanted me to make time for the kids," she persisted, her voice thick with injury. "I get so tired of you blaming me. Don't you see how hard I'm trying?"

"I'm not blaming you for anything," he said. "It's you blaming yourself. It's like you're trying to earn membership in the human race or something."

She glared at him.

"Why do you feel you have to push yourself so hard? What are you afraid of?"

To which she didn't respond. She returned to the computer as if they'd never spoken.

After a horrible length of silence he said, "Guess I'm going to bed now."

Her fingers were on the keys, the only things moving in the room. He didn't think she'd heard him.

"Sarah?" he pressed the point. "When are you coming to bed?"

Tap. Tap. Tap. Tap tap tap. Her fingers never left the keyboard.

"I'm not coming to bed," she said at last. Sarah knew she and Joe had serious problems, but for right now it just seemed easier to blame them on him rather than try to understand their inability to get along. She already had one of her headaches.

And Joe couldn't have felt more like a loser if a Wrigley Field umpire had been counting strikes against him and then signaled with a hammered fist in front of thousands of people, "You're *out*." He could never remember feeling more defeated than he did right at that moment.

Pete practically stood on his head at the repair shop to peruse the car's racing header. He must've forgotten all about their discussion of the feminine mystique.

"What do you think?"

"Hmmmm. About what? About women? Or about this baby that's going to blow the roof off when you hit the ignition?"

"About this." And Joe laid a hand over the fender and patted it in a gentle motion that he never would have dared risk with Sarah lately.

Pete said, "I think she's something."

"I think so too."

"I think she's going to go so fast, she'll leave her paint behind."

Joe had to smile at that one. "I think so too." He figured he might as well talk about the car because talking about Sarah didn't help anything, and Pete didn't seem to understand anyway.

The two men stepped back and stood shoulder-to-shoulder. They crossed their arms over their broad chests, surveying this great feat of Joe's.

"You're going to hang around here, aren't you, until you can see what she'll do?"

Even though Pete shrugged nonchalantly, his eyes had gone bright with anticipation. "Guess I wouldn't want to miss the big moment."

"Guess you wouldn't, at that."

Opening the gigantic shop bay and checking the carburetor one last time should have been such a celebration. Hearing the engine spring to life after all those days of trial and error and tinkering should have brought Joe so much satisfaction.

But Joe's happiness was dampened by his unfulfilled desire for things to be different with Sarah.

Joe climbed into the front seat, shot his friend a dull A-OK signal, and flicked the key in the ignition.

The chassis shook. The engine gave a low growl. Pistons thundered to life.

"Yes!" Pete shouted. "Oh my word. Just listen to it!"

"You think she sounds good?"

Horsepower roared under the hood. But in the driver's seat, Joe didn't sense the excitement he thought he would. His feet didn't tingle to the vibration as usual. His fingers didn't rest on the steering wheel in reverent wonder. He was just too preoccupied with thoughts of Sarah, the kids, and where their life was headed.

"Do I think she sounds good? Are you kidding me?" For several beats, Pete just listened to the car in awestruck stupor. "Whoa." The man finally whistled. "Oh, *man*."

There'd been a time when Joe would have felt over-the-top pride at his friend's reaction. Pete's words would've made him feel he'd made the greatest accomplishment since Chennault created the Flying Tigers.

But Joe already knew he'd be heading home tonight to a house that felt more empty than an abandoned tenement. He and Sarah would exchange meaningless words when the kids were in the room, pretending everything was all right. Sarah wouldn't spend time with him or talk to him when they were alone. She would manage to stay busy all night on office work.

He'd be heading home to a life that had become unbearable. He should be celebrating and looking forward to telling Sarah about his accomplishment today. Sadness filled him because he knew it wouldn't happen.

Joe didn't know where to start to make things better between them. He didn't believe anything would ever change. He needed to come up with a plan.

When Leo found Mitchell Harper still waiting in his mother's office, he couldn't believe a kid could stay patient so long. The kid, who sat dwarfed inside the big swivel chair, must have used up a whole tree's worth of paper on the copy machine. Surreal black-and-white copies of faces and hands, or at least pieces of those things, a smashed nose, a knobby wrist, fingers in a V, an eye, lay spread across the entire width of the huge executive desk. The pictures stretched from one end to the other. Another good stack of them rested beneath Mitchell's elbow. "What?" Leo asked, trying to make this unexpected schedule change seem like it was all in good fun. "Looks like you ran the machine out of paper."

"I did."

"I'm sure we could get you another ream. That's a good five hundred more pages. You could use those up too."

"Nah," Mitchell said. "It's okay."

The entertainment had obviously gone downhill since then. After all the excitement, Mitchell had been reduced to making a chain of paper clips and dangling the chain over a magnetic cup.

"What, then? No computer games?"

"All Mom has is solitaire."

Which didn't need comment from either of them. "I'm sure your mom just can't get away up there. She never knows when she'll get called up to Roscoe's office."

Mitchell shrugged noncommittally. "Doesn't matter to me."

But it did. Leo could tell the kid was disappointed and hurt. "I'm sure she'll be back any minute. Your mom's got quite the reputation," he said. "She's very determined, always busy. She never stops."

"My mom's really important here, isn't she?"

"Yes. She is."

"She must be because that's what she always tells my dad." Mitchell's voice stayed level. "That she can't always walk away from things here when we need her."

"She tries really hard. I know she made a big deal out of getting to the ball game on time," Leo said, not knowing any better. "I know how excited she was about that."

Mitchell diverted his eyes. He twisted another paper clip open and added to the string.

"She *did* make it to the game the other night, didn't she?"

Mitchell finally put the paper clips down and met Leo's eyes. "Leo? Do you believe there's such a thing as angels?"

"Well, I..." What had brought this question on? He couldn't imagine. "No. Guess not. But, you know, I haven't thought about it much."

"The other night I thought I saw one. Inside the scoreboard at Wrigley." Mitchell stood tall. "At first I thought it was a man, but now I think it might have been an angel."

"Oh really?"

"What do you think, Leo?"

"Hmmmm." Leo didn't know exactly what to say. Angels were outside his area of expertise these days. He just wanted to change the subject.

He hoped Mitchell hadn't noticed how many times he'd checked his watch. He didn't know how long his boss intended to leave him responsible for her son, but he hoped it would not be much longer.

"Hey, Mitchell, are you going to take those paper clips apart again? It's always a bummer when you go to pick up one of them and get the whole string."

Leo left Mitchell plying paper clips apart and going around in circles in the executive chair. And when Leo made the call he dreaded, "You're still there?" the girl on the other end of the line asked, dumbfounded. "That woman walks all over you, did you know that?"

"She's my boss. She's given me the opportunity of a lifetime, working here. What I want doesn't matter."

"Oh, come on, Leo. She lectured you about taking an extra ten minutes off at lunch to get a haircut last week."

"So? I should have scheduled the haircut on my own time."

"She lectured you about having to get stitches in the emergency room. What were you supposed to do? Stop your bleeding on your own time too?"

"You don't know what it's like." Leo shook his head with profound blind loyalty. "She's the ticket to my career. I owe her a lot."

Tom Roscoe gave Sarah a big buy order he wanted her to execute for a client. He explained that he wanted her to buy the same list of commodities for him first, even though the order might drive the price up for the customer. Sarah knew what would happen. When the order went in for the client, it would further raise the price. Then Roscoe would sell his own contract at a profit.

Sarah said, "I thought you wanted me working solely on the other account. I don't—"

He stopped her. "I know I promised exclusivity. But sometimes there isn't any choice but to be flexible." His eyes burned with purpose. "We both know I need someone with a head like yours, especially in a market that's this unpredictable."

"I'm flattered, Tom. I am."

"I'm asking you to take on more than your fair share. I'm aware of that. But we both know what you're capable of doing."

"Isn't front-running illegal?" Sarah asked.

But even if he'd answered yes, Sarah wouldn't have argued. She felt a sting of conscience but pushed it away. Ever since she'd found out about Lauren losing her post, Sarah couldn't shake the feeling of impending doom. Even if Tom's suggestion was legal, Sarah knew it wasn't ethical. Would she also get fired if she didn't do exactly as he wanted?

Her heart raced. Her headache pounded. She had to remind herself to breathe.

Tom made it simple. "It's just another weapon in the arsenal. Everyone does it. And just because I know that Buck Nielsen happened to short sell a large amount of wheat futures and this will make the price go up, well, *c'est la vie*."

Tom lavished admiration on Sarah. He told her that Lauren had complained about Sarah's appointment to the Cornish account and that's the reason he'd let her go. "No one threatens this team," he said, "and we all know you're the best I've got. I like the way you think on your feet, Sarah. There aren't many women like you. You're an elite breed. You're a go-getter."

With each word Tom spoke, Sarah's heartbeat ran a little slower. Her shoulders relaxed. She wanted to do good and not hurt people, but she needed this. She *needed* this. Her drive to succeed outweighed everything else. Each of Tom's words felt like a hit of a drug. They soothed and rescued her. *Why can't Joe make me feel this way?* she thought vaguely.

Outside his door, she leaned against the wall, held her hand over her rib cage, and was finally able to take a breath. It was a breath that, for the first time in three hours, finally went clear down to the depths of her lungs.

Sarah found Mitchell slumped over his arms at her huge desk, sound asleep.

"He waited a long time for you," Leo whispered on his way out.

Sarah peered down at Mitchell. His eyeglasses were seriously askew. She removed them, shook his shoulders, smoothed his hair off his forehead. "Hey, kiddo," she whispered. "You still with me? Time to head home."

He lifted his head, and his brow furrowed. There was a red imprint of his sleeve on his cheek. He was still fuzzy from sleep.

"Mom?" Mitchell asked. She followed his gaze out the window. The sunset bloomed over the outline of the city, watercolor streaks of apricot and lavender and magenta shining softly through the soiled gauze of Chicago smog. "We're not going to the skate park anymore, are we?"

She shook her head. "We're not, buddy," she said. "It's too late."

He was almost too big to carry, but not quite. With her head down and her body hunched, Sarah shouldered him and her enormous purse and toted them down the elevator.

As she strode past the enormous marble security desk, as she burst out through the revolving door the same way a springboard diver bursts through the surface after being under water too long, as she carried her son out to the car in the Smart Park Tower, she was right, it was already too late.

It was too late for a great many things.

Chapter Eight

Sarah hadn't told Joe, or anyone else for that matter, that she'd made the appointment at Dr. Faber's office. Something like this wasn't important enough to bother her friends with. And Joe had been so busy playing the entrepreneur, starting his car business from scratch, that she hadn't wanted to distract him with anything else.

When she'd walked in the door yesterday, Sarah had noticed the slight flash of joyful expectation on Joe's face (he must have been expecting Mitchell) before he'd realized who she was and shut down again. *Someone has to make a living around here,* she'd told Joe. She hadn't meant to hurt him; she could kick herself for letting those words escape. *Why couldn't I have kept my mouth shut?* But she knew the answer: Joe had a way of always making her feel so *angry.* When he backed her into the corner like that, she couldn't keep herself from going on the attack. She imagined he knew exactly what buttons to push to get her to explode and delighted in doing so.

As Dr. Faber recounted the results of her tests, Sarah felt doubly glad she hadn't told anyone about this meeting. For a great while, every time she'd considered phoning for an appointment, she'd managed to talk herself out of it. Why spend the money if she didn't need to? Why worry everyone if there wasn't going to be anything wrong anyway?

She didn't really believe she was sick. Still, she couldn't help wondering why nothing seemed to make her happy. Nothing gave her the sense of contentment she wanted. Could something be physically wrong with her? After all, she did have a lot of headaches. They were becoming more frequent and intense. She was tired most of the time.

As the physician explained her blood counts to her, he assured her that everything looked perfectly normal. He couldn't find any medical reason after the laboratory tests for why she hadn't been feeling herself lately. "Physically, you're doing very well," he told her. "Could be stress," he said, and even though she laughed at that, she felt irritated that he would even suggest such a thing.

"I have always lived a fast-paced life, and I've always felt great about it," she told him. "Actually, my work is what keeps me going. What I accomplish in life means a lot to me."

Her doctor flipped through her file as if searching for more clues.

"I didn't come for you to tell me to slow down. I need something that's going to fix me," she told him. "I have to build up my energy level so I can keep up the pace." But she didn't say the rest of it, that work took first place over everything else. That it had begun to cut into her time with her family. That she'd missed going to the game with her son this week even though she promised him she would go. That she couldn't stop punishing Joe for the guilt she felt.

The doctor suggested she try a low dosage of antianxiety medication. She assured him she wasn't anxious and that she was able to handle life without anxiety medicine. She had left his office without making the follow-up appointment he suggested.

Now, as Sarah drove home from her disastrous day with her son, Mitchell fiddled with the radio buttons until he found the Cubs game. On the air, the announcer said, "Two men on, nobody out. Runners go." The bat cracked against the ball. The crowd roared to its feet. "That's a base hit to center field! Soriano scores. The ball off the glove of Cabrera, and Sheffield, with a burst of speed, takes an extra base..."

Sarah glanced across the front seat, trying to read Mitchell's expression. "Sounds like a good game, huh?"

"Yeah." Mitchell's voice was flat. His face was lost in the flicker of shadows from passing cars. He sat with his skateboard upside down in his lap, absently fingering one wheel. His glasses concealed his eyes.

"You okay?"

"Yeah."

"You sure?"

No answer.

"Mitchell?"

He spun the skateboard wheel again. "It took you a long time."

"I know."

"I made about a hundred pictures of myself on the copy machine. You always say you'll be back any minute. But then you aren't."

As they clipped along the expressway, their headlights loomed on the exit sign for the Village of Buffalo Grove. "I do," she said. "I *do* come back." And in a fit of total frustration at the way she felt so trapped all the time, trying to please everyone and seemingly never doing it, Sarah swerved to the right, barely sandwiching the Lincoln between a white pickup and a motorcycle that sped around her, its driver glaring. She took the exit with a hard right veer.

Mitchell glanced out the window for the first time. "Mom?"

"Just a slight detour."

"Where are we going?"

"To Nona and Harold's house."

He sat taller. "We are?"

"Into the right-field corner. Good to score at least a run," the radio announcer shouted. "Ramirez is plated. Lee to third, and Ryan Theriot has come through here in the fifth."

"We're going to Nona's house *now*?"

"How about we surprise them?" Sarah couldn't face going home just yet.

They drove past a stretch that had once been broad, open field dotted with apple orchards, now built up and marked by curving cul-de-sacs and executive houses. They passed Dollar DAYZ and the White Hen Pantry and a massive car lot where light fell in spotlight pools upon the latest automobiles and flags flapped their greetings in the evening breeze.

They rounded the corner, past the American Legion Post, past the pink and green awning bedecking the shop that sold Rizzi's Spumoni, and found themselves in territory that transported Sarah to her girlhood days. They passed the building that had once been the courthouse and the senior-spirit painted windows at Woolworth's where Sarah's mother had bought her notebooks and pencils for school. They passed the huge Lathrop Steel Casings Company where Jane had taken dictation and answered phones and been a senior stenographer for forty-one years running. They passed trees in the park with their leaves scything to the ground, the revamped city pool that had seen its last visitor on Labor Day and wouldn't open again until next summer.

Sarah gripped the steering wheel, her knuckles pressed into sturdy, white ridges. Whatever had possessed her to leave the expressway and turn down here anyway? She should never have been so spontaneous. She should have thought this through.

Around the next corner, there stood the remodeled church, looking every bit like the long-ago architectural rendering Sarah's grandmother had been over the moon about, a beautiful contemporary building with the floodlights upon its cross and its unmarred, white steeple. "Oh just look at it, Sarah," she remembered her grandmother exclaiming the first time the framed drawing had gone on display in the foyer. "Imagine worship in a beautiful place like that! You see the steeple, Sarah? They've designed it from the old pictures. That's the way it used to be." Sarah had not thought about church in a long, long time.

Tonight the triangular building crouched atop land the way a vast ship might crouch atop water's horizon, beckoning the way a ship might beckon, "Come journey! Come be carried to a different world." Sidewalks framed the manicured crest of lawn. Some farsighted landscaper had seen fit to save a few of Buffalo Grove's old apple trees. The churchyard's ridges and rises remained studded with them, their dark trunks reaching toward the sky with the same ancient courage as an arthritic hand.

Try as she might, Sarah couldn't erase her grandmother's voice from her head. "Just imagine something this fine in the center of Buffalo Grove. People will come from all over just to attend church here. Don't you think?"

"Yeah," a little-girl Sarah had answered. Sarah remembered clenching a hand just as gnarled and timeworn as the tree trunks along the hill. "I do think." And she remembered gazing into the eyes of the only woman who she ever felt really loved her, eyes that, in spite of age, had remained a clear, sharp blue. She remembered Annie's face that heightened into pink whenever she was happy; Annie's silver hair, so thin you could see the flush of her scalp beneath it, iridescent and finely spun on the top of her head into the shape of a Q-tip.

Sarah had never called her grandmother anything except Annie.

At first her mother had interfered, saying it wasn't respectable for a two-year-old to call a grandma by her first name. Annie had tsk-tsked Jane's objections almost before they'd started. "It's the only thing she can say; she can't even *say* 'grandmother' yet. I'll live by any name with which my granddaughter christens me. And if it happens to be my given name, well, then so much the better."

Now, passing the church, Sarah remembered the smell of the wood-paneled rooms and the homemade play dough, the wax candles dripping on the altar, Annie's lilac perfume. She remembered the cool shade splashing over her face when, later in the day, they sat with their cheeks together beneath one of the trees, Annie's breath smelling faintly of root-beer mints, reading aloud the stories in the Sunday-school paper. Now, passing the church, Sarah missed her grandmother with an ache that resembled hunger.

She braked. "I can't do it, Mitchell. I don't want to go to Nona and Harold's after all."

"But Mom, we're almost there."

How quickly one little boy's face could shift from joy to a troubled frown.

"I want to see them, Mama. I want to talk to Harold. I want to see if I can find apples in the tree."

The car had drawn almost to a stop in the center of the street. She clenched her teeth and drew in air. She ran a hand through her hair, draped it behind her neck, and kneaded the tense muscles there. She didn't want to see Mitchell disappointed, not again today. Not again. Not ever.

She went through the same emotional upheaval every time she came to the house. She dreaded it and yet she hoped that perhaps this would be the time her mother would be glad to see her. But the same disappointment met her every time she walked in the door, every time she saw Jane and saw how nothing had changed. She shouldn't have done this; she felt too tired and weary to put herself through it again right now. But it was too late.

"You never want to come to Nona's house anymore. Mom, please?"

Her shoulders rose and fell with her sigh.

"Please?"

"Okay. I promise," she said, her voice resolute. "We won't turn back now."

She hadn't even stopped at the curb before Mitchell unhitched his seat belt and flung open the door and galloped to the front porch. Sarah opened her window. Even this late she could smell the apples.

Most of the fruit was snagged from the limbs just as soon as it ripened. But a few pieces fell and fermented in the grass with a sticky sweet smell that attracted wasps and reminded old-timers of long-ago orchards. Annie had always told her the whole town smelled like McIntosh apples at harvest time.

Harold's silhouette appeared against the light from the living room. "Harold!" Mitchell shouted, bouncing on his toes. "It's us! We came to see you."

"Woo ha-he-*goodness*," the man's voice bellowed. "We've got company, Jane. Who's this in the dark jumping around like a chimpanzee? It's Mitchell." Sarah could see her stepfather surveying the yard, checking to see who else might be out there. "And I'll bet Mitchell didn't drive over here all by himself, did he?"

"Of course I didn't drive," Mitchell said as he pushed his way past Harold's leg and went inside to find his grandma. "I'm only eight years old."

"You're eight? And nobody's taught you how to drive yet? Well, if I had my keys and a phone book for you to sit on, I'd get on that job right now."

"I don't think so," Sarah said, giving her stepfather a squeeze. "But when he gets to be fifteen, I might take you up on it."

Harold hugged her back, and it felt so good that she wished he'd never let go.

She stepped back and searched his expression. "Are we bad, coming so late?"

"Of course you're not. You know we'll take you anytime we can get you."

"I'm sorry for missing our coffee date, Harold. I wouldn't have done that to you. I totally spaced it out."

He gave a little humph, gripped her shoulders, and searched her expression. "Sarah? Are you okay?"

"Yes." Then, "No." Then, "Of course I am. Why would you ask? I'm fine."

"I do need to talk to you."

She raised her eyebrows in a question.

"Not now. It'll have to be for another coffee date."

Her teeth clenched in embarrassment. "Did you wait a long time?"

"Ate three whole pieces of pie."

"I'm so sorry."

"Maybe next time you can punch it into your computer and have the thing give you an electric shock in the pants or something," he suggested.

"Harold. I'm *so* sorry."

I'll get over it, his brief smile said. He held open the screen to allow her entrance.

The minute she stepped into the house, she knew she shouldn't have come. The wooden floors complained beneath each of her steps: *You don't have any right to be here.* The old boiler rumbled to life, knocking and hissing like it disapproved of her presence.

"Mama?"

"Good heavens, Sarah. Don't you know better than to pop in to see people in the middle of the night like this?"

The ancient, upright piano huddled like a watchman in the corner. It was missing several select ivory keys the same way an ancient boxer missed teeth. Beyond the piano, the tiny woman must have leaped from her chair, distraught at first sight of her grandson. Her reading glasses rested upside down in a pool of ice cubes on the floor. With a stained tea towel, she flogged and thrashed at her bathrobe as if she were trying to punish the soda she'd spilled in her lap.

"Hello, Mama."

"How could you have not made a phone call? For Pete's sake,

you're one of those with the phone implanted surgically to your ear. Most of the time you're so busy making calls that you don't even talk to the people in the room."

"Nice to see you, Mama—".

"Mitchell came romping in here, and I didn't have a stitch of clothes on other than these bedclothes. And you know we watch the nine o'clock news. If you had called, we would have told you not to make us miss the news. Why didn't we get a phone call?"

"You watch the nine o'clock news? I forgot about the nine o'clock news."

"And did you forget my workday begins at Lathrop before seven o'clock in the morning?"

My *workday begins early as well,* Sarah wanted to say.

"There wasn't time to call," Sarah explained instead. "We were on the expressway. We were only five blocks away."

"I thought you had better manners than to just show up without calling."

Sarah heard Mitchell's shouts from outside. Every so often, a flashlight beam would slash across the curtains. Mitchell and Harold must be rifling through leaves, searching for the remaining McIntosh apples. As she listened to her son's happy chatter, Harold's low-pitched, patient suggestions, it occurred to Sarah that, of all the things she'd tried, she'd finally found the one pursuit to win herself back into Mitchell's good graces.

"Did you forget the importance of my job, Sarah? I don't even have a high school diploma and look what I've done after forty-one years. No degree and I'm making more money than Harold."

Sarah felt even more drained than when she first walked in. *I should have known better than this*, she thought.

Trying to remember something positive, she thought about how many times she had hugged Harold good night when she was little. How many times he had asked her to tell him about the things that made her afraid. Often when she'd been scared, he'd tucked her in with that flashlight. Oh, how she enjoyed seeing that flashlight of his!

"Would you just listen to those two out there?" Jane had given up on her sodden robe and was now using her hands to scoop ice from the carpet. Sarah bent to help. Each cube ringed the glass with a condemning *clink*. "Just look what you're asking of Harold. He's not even the child's grandfather, and you've got him out there climbing trees."

Sarah's hand froze. Yes, she'd expected her mother's bitterness. But she was surprised by its force. "What did you say?"

"In the middle of the night. Taking care of your child. Don't you think that's asking a great deal of him, Sarah?"

"I know, Mama." *Oh, don't say it. Don't let her bait you into this.* But she couldn't stop herself. "Wasn't it asking Harold a whole lot to ask him to raise me too?"

Jane's face shot up. The censuring twist of her mouth couldn't have cut Sarah any deeper if it had been administered with a scalpel. *Clink* went the ice in the glass. *Clink. Clink.*

In her mother's embittered eyes, Sarah read the accusation again, the same resentful indictment that had been pouring into Sarah's heart as long as she could remember. *Well, you'd sure better amount to something in your life because you certainly made a mess out of mine.*

The door slammed open and the two boys, one big and one small, tottered inside with their arms laden with apples. "Well now." Harold helped Mitchell balance his stash as they headed toward the kitchen. "I guess we found a few more out there."

Sarah shot up off the floor. "I guess you did." The items swam atop the piano as she tried to focus.

The FDR campaign button on its wire stand, passed down since 1944.

The glass jar that made Sarah cringe because Harold once used it to store her tonsils for the neighbors to see. Stored in alcohol, mind you! As if having her tonsils out had been the proudest thing she'd ever accomplished.

The three-generation portrait of the Cattalo women with its black-and-white likeness of Annie, Jane, and Sarah: grandmother, mother and child, the same as always, even then.

Annie smiling.

Sarah hiding behind her mother's skirt.

Jane madder than a hornet at the world, not caring one whit if the cameraman knew.

Sarah went in search of the boys. "Mitchell. I'm sorry, honey. We have to go."

"But we just got here."

"I know. But it's late."

Harold took several apples and, with great care, placed them inside a bag so the skins wouldn't bruise. "Get these wrapped up so you can take them to your dad. Show him how good you did."

Above Mitchell's head, Harold mouthed to Sarah, *Don't get upset. You know how she is.*

It about broke Sarah's heart to see Mitchell start to lift his arms to his grandma, but then step back because he was afraid.

"Good night, Mother," Sarah said carefully. "We'll see you again."

"Why don't you call before you come next time? You shouldn't visit anyone this late," Jane said with the same enthusiasm as a porcelain bedpan.

Chapter Nine

The crème brûlée Lincoln MKX tore into its space at the Smart Park Tower a full fifteen minutes earlier than usual. Once again, Sarah had left Joe to get Mitchell on the school bus and Kate settled with the nanny. "Here so early?" asked the doorman as he turned the key in the lock at the Roscoe offices and let Sarah inside the lobby.

The janitor dipped his mop into the suds, trailed it in paisley patterns across the marble floor, and remarked, "You're here at the crack of dawn."

The uniformed postman wheeled his cart into the elevator and pressed the button to go to the basement. "Mrs. Harper," he said, "when do you sleep?"

Sarah ignored each comment, footnote, and wry observation. She wasn't in any mood to respond. Instead she trotted the width of the lobby at a fine clip, her personal-data-assistant alarm sounding to remind her of three different meetings, her cell phone erupting, her footsteps snapping everyone to attention as her shoes clicked the length of the hall.

If Sarah had never worked hard before, she worked like a mad-woman today. She sent Leo for office supplies and to research the daily commodity analysis and to the Cornishes' international headquarters to snag second-quarter earnings numbers. She sent him for coffee, she sent him to pick up legal documents at Daley Plaza, she had him join her to take notes during three client meetings, and when he ran out of other things to do, she sat him down with stacks of file folders to transpose onto the computer.

That done, she asked him to spend several hours cutting down her e-mail list.

Sarah read her news feeds while she was in a meeting with Roscoe. She checked the www.nannyrating.com Web site three times to spy on Mrs. Pavik, and if people wanted to criticize her about it, well, let someone just try! She typed a blog entry while she was embroiled in a conference call. She made snide comments via text to Leo across the boardroom table (DO YOU BELIEVE THIS? DO YOU THINK THIS GUY BELIEVES A WORD HE'S SAY-ING?), her thumbs flying across the words.

She'd shouldered her way into the trading pit, attached herself to the tangled mass of cables and headphones and screens, only to find that Leo's market-analysis notes had been way off the mark. Where Sarah looked to sell, a string of red told her to hang on. Where she intended to buy, the numbers had already soared. She found no bargain pricing. She found no solid profit taking. She stalked the entire length of LaSalle Street after the market closed, and when she returned she stood in the middle of Roscoe's offices and took her frustration out on everyone within earshot.

"What happened out there?" she stood in the middle of the hallway and yelled. "Didn't anyone have any idea? Didn't anyone have anything to tell me?"

People hid from Sarah in the break room. The lobby

receptionist collapsed in her chair, rested a wrist against her forehead, and said, "If this gets any worse, I'm giving my notice." The Andretti guy from ninth said, "Don't let her on the streets; she'll kill somebody." A friend from human resources asked, "Is this worse than any other day?" One of the senior partners asked, "Does she think we control the commodities trading market?"

Just after five that afternoon, with timid hesitation, Leo cracked open Sarah's door. "There's someone to see you," he announced, expecting to get his head bitten off. "It's Joe."

"Joe?"

In a careful undertone, Leo said, "He's got *Mitchell*. And *tickets*."

Her face went white. "Tickets?"

There couldn't have been a worse night for Joe to finally catch up to her with Cubs tickets. All she wanted to do was prove that she held mastery of her job so she didn't feel this awful shame. All she wanted was to do more, to be more, than she'd been before visiting her mother's house yesterday. She didn't know why it was so important to her, but she was determined to prove to her mother that she was worth something.

Leo shot her an apologetic glance, then scampered away before she could do him bodily harm. That's all the notice she had before Mitchell bounded in wearing a big foam Cub claw and his best shirt with buttons and a collar, his face taut and new-nickel shiny from soap.

"Joe," she said. "You should have warned me."

"You've had plenty of warning before, and it never worked." He sat in her chair, which made her livid, and braced his fist under his chin. "I thought this time I'd surprise you."

I'm not always up for surprises, she wanted to say. Her mouth opened, but she forced it shut again. It opened again and, this time, she clamped it tight. She didn't want to act the same way her mother had acted the night before, when she had been surprised.

"I got Kate to the sitter myself," Joe said with pride. "I've been working on this plan." And for the next five minutes, as he recounted the list of the baby's belongings (diaper bag, stuffed elephant, pink blanket already starting to unravel), they both knew he'd gathered up Kate's things before. He was really only hedging for time so Sarah could get used to the idea.

"Reserved seats?" he said, looking a little pale, holding the tickets out so she could inspect them.

"Not the bleachers?"

"Dugout. Right beside home plate."

The last thing Sarah wanted to do was go to a baseball game with her husband. She wanted to go home, put her feet up on the couch, and try to forget about her horrible day. Her mouth looked like it had been pulled tight with a drawstring. She shot Joe a look strong enough to sour milk.

Joe stood waiting for her, holding the tickets fanned in his hand.

Sarah had no other choice. Everyone in the office was watching. Leo looked about ready to jump out of his skin, he wanted to go to a game so bad.

She lifted her purse and flung it over her shoulder. *We might as well get this over with,* her sullen expression said.

Sarah and Joe drove the few miles to Wrigley Field in stony silence. Only Mitchell chattered, carrying on a one-sided conversation about the batting lineup and wondering if Zambrano could throw the sinker. No matter how many questions he asked, no one answered him. By the time they turned into a lot a good five blocks from the corner of Clark and Addison, by the time Joe paid an exorbitant fee so they could park the car, Mitchell wasn't talking anymore. With a worried frown, he climbed from the car. He walked between his mom and his dad, glancing from one of them to the other, all the way to the ballpark.

For all the gaiety an outing like this one should have entailed, it held all the rowdy joy of a property-tax meeting. To be sure, Mitchell watched self-absorbed as the players took their warm-up swings right in front of him. With one of his Cubs pencils, he jotted down the game stats, biting his tongue in concentration. He pointed and waved when Theriot glanced his direction. He stared and shouted when Soto ripped one down the third baseline.

But somewhere during the fifth inning, the novelty of the fancy seats began to wear off and Mitchell began to gaze with longing toward the bleacher section.

"What is it, son?" Joe asked. "What's wrong?"

Mitchell screwed up his mouth and scratched his elbow. He rubbed his cheek. He studied the peanut hulls that he'd crunched flat with his left sneaker. "Dad, I like these fancy seats, I really do. But I wish we could be in the bleachers where my friend looks down on us from the scoreboard."

"What? Are you kidding? We're right here with the players. If Lou Piniella blows a gasket, we'll be right here with the dirt flying. You want to miss that?"

And while Mitchell and Joe jabbered on about full counts and windups and checked swings, Sarah sat in the seat beside them with her mouth pursed and her cheeks burning, trying not to overhear. She was livid. Joe had ambushed her, plain and simple. She'd looked forward to coming to Wrigley, and she'd exhausted every effort to join them that night—she *hadn't* taken it lightly—and now Joe was getting her back by putting her in a position where she had no choice. Sarah did not like being backed into a corner. She did not like being tricked and manipulated as if that was the only way she would spend time with her family.

While Mitchell tried to carry on a lively discussion with Sarah about the swing-away sign versus the bunt signal from the opposing third-base coach, Joe whistled a tune with false bravado and peered off toward the rooftop party seats on Waveland Avenue. He jiggled his knee, feeling nervous. If Sarah was mad, well, he guessed he'd let her vent her anger and just take it, but Joe couldn't help himself—he felt strangely gratified getting any response from her whatsoever.

Sarah sat in the very expensive dugout seat with her hands crossed over her *Game Day* program, peering through the net that kept foul balls from smashing into the crowd, with her gaze trained toward the red brick and green paint and woven ivy.

Joe sprang from his seat in a frenzy every time bat connected with ball. "If you're going to jump up and down like that, mister," complained the man behind him, "next time why don't you sit in the bleachers?"

Other than smiling at Mitchell occasionally, Sarah didn't glance to her right.

Other than talking to Mitchell, Joe wouldn't look to his left.

After a five-game losing streak, a surprising thing happened and the Cubs won. And although the game went into extra innings, neither husband nor wife spoke to the other for the entire length of the game.

The drive home was punctuated by distant bursts of lightning over the water. A storm gathered to the north and lit the clouds intermittently with flashes of electric discharge. They came closer, and a jagged fork of light scissored toward the ground.

Their trek had been excruciating ever since they'd left Wrigley Field. The animosity they'd managed to conceal in a ballpark filled with thousands of spectators now hung in the car like a glacial rock ready to drop.

"That was sure some run by Lee! Did you see Mike Fontenot's throw? The way he backhanded it?" Mitchell chattered, still overcome with enthusiasm. When no one answered, his little words faded into empty silence.

A strong wind blew by the time they neared the sitter's. It almost ripped the car door from Joe's hands as he stepped out. The leaves around the porch rattled and shuttered and hissed as he knocked.

Kate was already asleep when the sitter went to fetch her. Kate's little rump was warm and smelling of Johnson & Johnson's as Joe bundled the baby beneath his chin. "You two should forget about that fancy nanny you hired," the babysitter said just before Joe departed. "You know I'm perfectly willing and able to take care of this baby." The sitter had asked for the job, but Sarah wanted someone more professional. She enjoyed the control the nanny Web site offered her. Anytime she felt guilty about working so much, she comforted herself with the thought that at least she knew what was going on at all times.

Thankfully the drive home was short because the silence seemed to be getting louder.

It took forever to get Mitchell calmed down and ready for bed. Joe watched, feeling powerless, as Sarah situated Kate in the crib and checked on Mitchell in the tub, picking up the clothes their little boy had jettisoned.

Mitchell could scarcely brush his teeth for talking about Aramis Ramirez's game-winning hit. Joe glimpsed Sarah and Mitchell with their heads together, Mitchell talking a mile a minute and Sarah pretending to be interested while she towel dried his hair. Joe watched Sarah steer their son to bed with her hand on his head.

And then, finally, the moment he'd dreaded. From Mitchell's room, the bedtime story ended and he heard Sarah say, "Good night. Sleep tight."

"What is it?" She stood in front of him with her hands extended from her sides, her entire body pleading the question. "What is it you want from me?"

There had been a point tonight when Joe would have said simply, "I thought it was a good idea." But the words gummed up his throat like sludge gums up a carburetor.

"You show up at my office and put me in a position where I have no choice but to do what you want! I don't like it, Joe. I don't like it one bit."

"Was it so bad? Was it so horrible that I came up with good tickets and brought your son to the office and made a show of kidnapping you?" Then he risked it. "I thought it was kind of cute myself."

He waited for her comment.

She gave him a disgusted look.

"Sarah," he said, too astonished and hurt to cover his reaction. *What happened to her? When did she become so brittle and hard?*

"You trapped me. You made it so I couldn't say no or I'd look bad to Mitchell. You're always trying to make me look bad in front of him."

"Would you have said no? If I wasn't standing there in front of you with tickets?"

"Yes."

"No?"

"Tonight I would have said no."

His arms stayed riveted at his sides. "That beats all."

"You have no idea what sort of day this was. It was horrible. It was"—she searched for the word—"monstrous. My day was monstrous."

"Sarah. You make them all that way."

"Joe. Don't do this again."

"You say you are doing all of this for us, but somehow every day ends up being all about you. How hard you work. How tired you are. How nobody understands you. Did it ever occur to you that I have rough days too? Do you know how long it's been since you've asked me how my day went?"

She reached for her desk and turned on the computer, and his insides wrenched tight. The monitor's indicator light began to swell from faint to bright as if the machine had begun breathing. The screen took on the same backlit gray as predawn.

A burst of lightning flashed through the curtains, and thunder rattled the glass not five seconds later. As rain began to beat against the window, the Apple logo appeared. The cursor raced around the dial as the system booted up. Some program must have needed updating because at that moment the computer spoke aloud in its robot voice. "Excuse me. Your computer needs your attention."

Joe extended a hand toward Sarah, palm up. "Excuse me. Your husband needs your attention."

"Don't be ridiculous," she said, staring him down. "I've got to check my e-mail. I've got to check my news feeds. I've got to post to the commodities trading blog. In case you hadn't noticed, Joe, I never run out of things I need to do."

He couldn't have felt more vulnerable if he'd been standing at the end of a pirate's gangplank, ready to be shoved off. "Sarah, not now. *Please.* Not another discourse on how hard you work and how nobody appreciates you."

For the first time in a long, long time his heart formed a clear, stark prayer. *Oh, Father. Put words in my mouth to help me break through to my wife.* Joe hadn't been in church in so long he couldn't remember the last time, but he felt desperate. Maybe God could help because he sure didn't know what to do.

With the hand she wouldn't touch, he took her chin and made her turn toward him. And as quick as that, he knew. "This is what I want to say to you."

"What?" she asked. "Haven't you already said enough?"

"This is not about your job, it isn't about the bills or the kids or any of those things you usually talk about." Not until he uttered those words did he know how true they were. "This is about you and me." At that moment Joe realized how deeply he had let Sarah hurt him. He was sadly aware that she had belittled him so much that he didn't feel like much of a man anymore.

He saw her throat contract. He saw the challenge in her eyes.

Joe dropped his grip and didn't mince words any longer.

"If I depended on how you treat me to determine my value, Sarah, I wouldn't think very highly of myself."

This clearly caught her off guard, this talking about his feelings, this honesty about how he saw himself.

"If things don't change, I'm not sure what I will do. I want this to work, but I can't take much more of how you behave."

She had too much pride to give in. Sarah's face had gone white, but she still acted like she didn't know what he was talking about. "How I behave? You can't take it?" Angrily she called his bluff. "You don't like my *behavior*? Well, perhaps you haven't heard, but there is help for people who aren't happy in their marriage. It's called divorce."

"No, Sarah. That isn't what I want. Not yet. But you have to get a grip on the reality of our relationship and realize how unhappy I am."

"What about me?" she asked. "What about me being happy?"

He only shook his head. As usual, the conversation turned back to her and what she needed and wanted.

～◇ Chapter Ten ◇～

After Joe went to bed that night, Sarah worked until the numbers on the screen began to run together. She worked until she couldn't remember whether she'd been looking at bullish numbers or bearish ones. She worked until she felt like someone was grinding sand into her eyes.

And then she worked some more.

No matter how she tried to concentrate on the computer screen, she couldn't forget Joe's words. Each tap of her fingers on the keyboard restated the cutting words and constricted her chest.

This isn't about your job. This isn't about the kids. It's about you and me.

I want this to work, but I can't take much more.

You have to know how unhappy I am.

"Oh, Joe," she wanted to say as she raked her hand through her hair and her shoulders rose and fell with an exhausted sigh. "Don't the two of us have everything we've ever wanted? Why isn't it enough for you?"

The answer came from deep in her heart, unbidden.

Because he's your husband. He wants you to give him yourself, and that's something you don't know how to do.

Sarah left the desk and went into the family room. Why couldn't she give herself? Why did she keep hurting Joe even though she really didn't want to? The storm outside sounded like one of those Midwestern deluges that would settle in for days: the distant roll of thunder, the steady drumming of rain against the house, the water's refrain as it streamed down the gutters. Lightning still played in the distance, flickering through the curtains, transforming the furniture into eerie, imposing shapes.

When Sarah flipped on the lamp in the corner, the room filled with a soft glow, warm and bright. Without any answers, she stood in the center of the Oriental rug, her eyes dry, her heart a muddle of pain and confusion. Their little schnauzer had awakened and padded in to find out why Sarah wasn't in bed. He stood at her feet, his nose black as licorice, his sober, fluid eyes asking, "Why aren't you in bed?" Sarah picked up the dog and buried her face in his wiry fur. She smelled his familiar dog scent, and somewhere between deciding the dog needed a shampoo and knowing she couldn't keep her eyes open much longer, her answer came.

Because I am afraid if I give myself I will be rejected. Because I hurt so bad that I want Joe to hurt too.

In the wee hours of the morning, she finally slipped in beside her husband. His light snoring stopped, and she winced. She hadn't meant to awaken him.

She curled into the fetal position to keep from touching him. In spite of her anger, Sarah suddenly ached for her husband to hold her. She'd never been this cold. She might as well be sleeping on a slab of Antarctic ice.

She moved over into his territory, drawn by his warmth, shame rolling through her. But when she found the spot where he'd lain, he wasn't in it. He'd moved away. She waited there, rejected, furious, unable to cry, until a sliver of sunrise crept over the windowsill. No one had ever told her it would be like this. No one had ever told her she could feel this empty.

Sarah never knew how much she slept that night; she only knew that it was still raining and dreary when she heard the baby stirring. With her head still pounding and her eyes feeling like they had cinders in them, she shoved her feet inside her slippers and trudged to get Kate. She found the baby already sitting up, wide-eyed and gnawing a fist. Sarah balanced the baby's backside on one hip and wiped drool from Kate's hand.

Kate reached for her mother's nose with her tiny wet fingers. In a burst of tenderness, Sarah closed her eyes at the brush of the baby's tiny thumb, the slight prick of her little fingernails. On this morning of all mornings, Sarah buried her face in Kate's feathery hair and remembered how good a baby could smell, like baby powder and a touch of last night's milk, sweeter than almost anything.

That's when her morning began. Sarah's cell phone vibrated. It almost toppled off the edge of the coffee table before she could get it. With Kate's plump little legs dangling, Sarah bent to catch the early-morning text message. Tom Roscoe had a breakfast meeting with Nathan Cornish. Could she join them?

Of course she could.

Into the high chair went Kate. Out came the Cheerios. Sarah lobbed waffles into the toaster and set the handle. She poured Mitchell's milk and set it alongside his chair with the fortitude of an army general making a combat decision. The butter saucer slid across the table. She heard Joe's footfalls in the hall, and he came stalking in, stuffing in his shirttail, just as the toaster sprang. Sarah flung the waffles onto a plate and shouted for Mitchell to get a move on as if today were any other day.

Joe stood in the middle of the room, his eyes fixed to a spot just above the faucet hot-water handle, while bitterness once again clamped Sarah's chest tight. In her thoughts she aimed all the hurt she'd carried through the night straight at the man in the middle of the room. What could Joe be thinking, risking their marriage? He was the one to blame for this! What could he be trying to accomplish, saying such hurtful things to her?

How dare he dump this on her?

She made a wide berth around him with her son's breakfast in hand. "It's raining cats and dogs out there, Mitchell. Where are your galoshes?"

"I'm eight years old," Mitchell argued. "Nobody wears galoshes when they're eight, Mom. Those are for babies."

"Put on your rain boots," she said in a tone that left no doubt whatsoever. She seized them from the closet and deposited them on the floor beside his chair with a resounding clump. "Do you understand me?"

Mitchell nodded, wild-eyed.

The little boy departed in the bus that hissed its way up the wet road. Sarah, with only minutes to spare, had yet to get out of her bathrobe. She turned toward Joe, filled with rage, ready to take him to task over this, raring to continue the fight.

Joe turned toward Sarah, his face decisive as stone. He wasn't budging, and she knew it. If she'd expected him to backpedal or apologize, she'd been sorely wrong.

While the flame beneath the kettle sputtered and popped, the kitchen sizzled with tension between husband and wife.

"I have to go." Sarah diverted her eyes to read another text. "I told Tom I'd be early." Her voice so falsely nonchalant she might have been speaking to the schnauzer.

"Sarah, I bared my soul to you. Doesn't that mean anything at all? After everything I said last night? You're just"—he gestured toward the front of the house—"out the door?"

The kettle's lid clattered as she moved it on the stove. "That's right."

"So that's it then."

"Yes."

Sarah didn't look back when she left. As she sped out onto the street, the bruised, foreboding sky suited her mood. Heavy brushstrokes of storm slanted across the Chicago skyline, almost obscuring the high-rises. She drove on with her throat aching, clogged with tears that she didn't dare cry.

Wasn't she always busy trying to do what was expected of her? Maybe Joe wasn't happy all the time, maybe neither was she, but they were surviving. They were busy trying to build a life. Wasn't she doing what she was supposed to do?

As quick as that, the bottom of the sky dropped out and the storm dissolved into a violent downpour. Guilt besieged her as water pelted the car in fat, wet drops. The windshield wipers couldn't keep up.

What's wrong with you, Sarah? You've never been able to do anything right, have you?

No wonder you can't give yourself to anybody. You're not worth anything.

Water gushed in muddy streams along the curb. For perilous seconds, she couldn't see the road. The wipers beat back and forth with what seemed like frantic speed, unable to scrape the glass clear before the deluge filled it again, every beat of the wipers punctuating her grief-stricken heart.

Here you are, always messing up other people's lives. You messed up your mother's life and now you're messing up Joe's, Mitchell's, and Kate's too.

She leaned forward, as if that would help her peer out the windshield. She braked. The tires sent up thick walls of spray.

What were you thinking? How far did you think you could push Joe and expect him to put up with it?

When the phone vibrated on the seat beside her, she wanted to chuck it out the window into oncoming traffic. But this phone was her lifeline to her employer, who waited for her at a five-star eating establishment with a demanding client at his side and eggs Benedict on order. He waited while steam rose from the spout of a silver coffeepot and the *maître d'* laid out place settings for three. Mr. Tom Roscoe, whom she hadn't disappointed, who liked the way she thought on her feet, who'd said she was part of an elite breed, who'd told her he thought she was capable of anything.

His text sounded more harsh than usual.

You coming or what?

I can't do this, she cried in desperation to the God her grandmother had once taught her about. *You've got to fix me. I don't know what's wrong, but I can't go on like this anymore. Nothing's working for anybody. I've tried my best, but I just can't make it happen.*

Gridlock besieged the city. Inbound traffic, the Kennedy, the Ike, the knotted interchange everyone called the Hillside Strangler, all slowed to a crawl because of the rain. Sarah took the first exit ramp she could, flipped on her blinker, steered left around a corner and headed toward the bridge. That's when she spotted the boat drifting along the river, taunting her with its purposeful glide upstream. Her breath hitched tight in her throat.

Oh no you don't! Only idiots would set sail in this weather. *If you think I am going to get caught with the bridge up while you glide by, you are wrong!*

With eyebrows knit and teeth bared at her rearview mirror, she located an unnervingly small space and, without signaling, shoehorned her way into it. The driver behind her laid on his horn. She passed to the right and swerved directly to the middle lane, cutting off a second driver, practically knocking off his bumper because he had the audacity to slow her down.

Red lights would start flashing along the bridge any minute. Barricade arms would begin their slow, excruciating descent to stop all travel in both directions. The bridge would jolt apart and rise as slowly as syrup, gigantic gears screeching in complaint. And so help her, she wouldn't be brought to a standstill behind that web of rising girders and the trussed arches parting and the road gaping open. Not today.

Her temples began to throb. With one hand she sifted through the contents of her purse in search of aspirin. The CTA bus hissed to a halt directly in front of her. Even one-handed, Sarah was ready. She dodged left, barely missing a bicycle. The cyclist shot her a look halfway between outrage and terror. Behind her he jumped the curb, dismounted on the sidewalk, and apparently chose to walk the rest of the way.

Ahead, the boat struggled to make headway, low in the water, her heavy cargo lashed in place with chains. Water churned in the wake of mammoth propellers. Smoke plumed from one smut-tarnished stack.

If the ninth-floor guys got a kick out of her NASCAR driving, they would've been awestruck if they could see Sarah Harper now. Every racetrack-inspired maneuver numbed the icy emptiness of the night before. Every Mario Andretti move kept her from replaying Joe's plainspoken, painful words. Each Indy 500 tactic gave her license to conceal the hurt behind other long-ago scabs and scars.

Each time Sarah finagled her way into another lane, she was in her very own speed contest, running from the truth.

By the time Sarah gunned her engine and pulled around a delivery truck, the warning lights on the bridge burst to life. The bells started ringing as the barricades began their torturous, slow descent. Brake lights flickered ahead. She leaned forward, as if her body language could inspire the three drivers in front of her to keep moving. "Not yet. Go go go go *go*."

For one maddening moment, she thought she couldn't proceed. Everything ahead seemed to be drawing to a standstill. In slow motion, one compact car passed from the opposite direction. It doused the side of the Lincoln with one fateful burst of spray. Then, nothing in the oncoming lane, only open road.

Sarah saw her way clear. She downshifted and slammed the accelerator to the floor. Her tires squealed on the asphalt, shimmied where they hit rain. The stiff-armed barriers were folded midpoint like a drill-team captain halfway through a routine. Sarah swept past the idling vehicles blocking her way. She swept past clanging lights and concrete abutments. She slalomed through the barricade, skidding left, veering right, without slowing down.

Somewhere in the back of her mind, Sarah smelled burning rubber. Just let someone try to come after her! By the time they could stop her, she'd be placing a linen napkin on her lap, sipping coffee from a china cup, and discussing commodity-futures prices. In surprise, she saw the gaping mouth of the bridge already yawning open. She saw the huge jaws of its mouth parting to reveal a taunting grin of steel teeth.

She remembered her motto: *Life is there for the taking.*

Sarah felt the bridge's iron gearwheels rumbling beneath her feet. She hadn't realized she was driving steadily uphill. In one swift second, she considered whether to put the pedal to the metal or throw on the brakes. She cataloged the danger and shoved it aside. She could make this.

The speedometer needle nudged eighty. The sky passed in a blur of balustrades and steel. Sarah felt wheels leave the ground and suddenly, horrifyingly, knew she'd been wrong.

Already she heard sirens in the distance. In her wake a bridge-authority operator had thrown an emergency switch. She heard tons of metal shudder to a stop. Below her the ship's throttle had gone into full reverse, whipping up water. But it was too late. The road ahead had already opened. She had nowhere to go but down.

The bridge's underpinnings hung in her path. She crooked an arm over her face and braced for impact. The car missed the bridge by inches. For long seconds she hung in an awful void, suspended between all that was behind her and all that was yet to come.

And then she plummeted.

The Lincoln's nose struck cold water at full velocity. Metal sheered off. She tasted blood. Adrenaline shot through her, numbed her with needlelike precision. *I'm in trouble.* Her heart pounded faster than it had ever pounded before. When she tried to scream for help, nothing came. Fear clamped her throat, leaving her no voice. The constricted sound that escaped was something between a gasp and a reedy cry.

Somewhere in the distance, the talk-radio host ranted on about some foreign policy. Water sloshed around her elbows as she struggled with the seat belt. How many times had she clasped and unclasped this buckle with ease, never stopping to give it a second thought?

She jabbed the button with her thumb. She yanked the straps, trying to make them release. With water to her neck, she remembered the tiny pocketknife in the glove compartment. She had found it in the parking garage and pitched it in there a few months ago. As her face sank underwater, she took one last, frantic breath and reached for the dashboard.

Sarah's personal data assistant wafted in front of her hand. No more memos or alarms or schedules. Its screen had gone dead.

She couldn't reach the glove compartment no matter how hard she stretched or how long she tried.

She tried to kick herself free. Somewhere in the past moment, the XM channel had dissipated into silence.

One last time she tried to unfasten the seat belt on her own, holding her breath, bubbles escaping her mouth. The bubbles moved away from her face at an odd angle; she was losing her bearings fast.

I'm in trouble. Her last thought. *I'm in trouble.*

The icy river closed overhead, leaving no trace of where she'd been.

⤙ Chapter Eleven ⤚

Mitchell Harper could tell you how a kid could find ways to get in trouble in class, especially a restless kid like him. The day had barely started and, for some reason, he couldn't stop squirming in his seat. Ever since the bell had rung and Mrs. Georges had announced they wouldn't have math as scheduled today but would jump directly into their assigned oral presentations, he'd been feeling anxious. He couldn't have felt more fidgety if he had centipedes in his pants.

First of all, he hadn't exactly *finished* his oral presentation. He'd planned to work on it last night, copying down interesting facts from the Internet about the rainforest jaguar. But he'd forgotten his homework the moment his dad showed up with those Cubs tickets. If Mrs. Georges asked him to stand and give his presentation now, the only things he could tell the class about jaguars were that they had four legs and maybe spots. (Did all jaguars have spots or just some?) He could also tell the class that jaguars weren't afraid of anything.

The first time Mrs. Georges singled him out for disrupting the class that day, he hadn't meant to be spinning his Cubs pencil. He'd been admiring it secretly behind the ledge of his desk, thinking he'd never seen an eraser this color before, examining the tiny wrap of red tin, thinking how it looked nice with those red *C*s and the blue shiny paint. Sometimes when Mitchell worked math problems, especially a particularly complicated column of subtraction, he chewed his erasers. He hoped he wouldn't get nervous and chew this one because Mrs. Georges didn't like it when he did.

Mrs. Georges interrupted his thought. "Mitchell Harper. Would you step to the front of the class please and share that item with us? The one you insist on playing with? Is it a toy?"

His face went hot. He felt the tips of his ears burning. "No, ma'am. It's a pencil."

He felt everyone watching as he traipsed up the three rows of seats toward the chalkboard. Mrs. Georges made him deposit the pencil in her palm, closed her fingers around it, and informed him she would return it at the final bell if he would make an effort to remind her at the end of the day.

The second time Mrs. Georges singled him out, he hadn't meant to be squeaking his shoes against the floor. His teacher asked, "Mitchell Harper, are you making that frightful sound?"

Until that second he hadn't noticed the squeaking. But when he froze in embarrassment, the sound stopped.

"Is it you?"

Who knew rubber soles could screech and squish like that when they got wet? His sneakers had gotten soaked clear through when he'd made the mad dash out the door to the school bus. His mom was going to have a fit when she found his rain boots shoved under the table, right where she'd dropped them.

He nodded.

It horrified him to imagine that Mrs. Georges would make

him walk forward to give up his shoes the same way she'd made him give up his pencil. Thankfully, she didn't. She eyed his feet with distaste, her mouth pursed as tight as if she'd been eating lemons.

"Absolutely no more squishing your soles, young man. Do you hear me?" she said. "Mitchell, I certainly don't know what's gotten into you today!"

He slouched in his seat, stared at gum stuck to the floor, and tried his best to be invisible.

Now Mitchell couldn't help being torn about whether he wanted Kyle Grimes, who stood giving his presentation in front of the blackboard, to speed up or slow down. Mrs. Georges had announced her intention to call on them in alphabetical order, and Mitchell had the roll book memorized. He knew he was next in line.

At Mitchell's right elbow stood a fish aquarium, a twist of limp ivy, and a bookshelf filled with tattered-spine chapter books and easy readers. At his left elbow sat Lydia Smith, who gnawed on the ends of her hair and threw spit wads at him when no one was looking and put out Elmer's glue to dry in little globs, only to peel them off and stick them to her fingers and brag she had fake nails.

Kyle Grimes finally finished his address on poison-dart frogs and sat down. Mitchell pulled off his glasses and wiped his forehead with his sleeve. He swallowed hard. When his left sneaker squeaked again, he wanted to smack himself on the forehead for being klutzy.

Just as Mrs. Georges ran her finger along the list to see who was next, a knock came at the door. She glanced up, surprised. She scowled at her students and shrugged.

"Bear with me, class." She boosted herself from her chair. "This shouldn't take a minute."

As seven- and eight-year-olds will do, they strained forward in their seats to eavesdrop. Their teacher lowered her forehead, giving the distinct impression that whoever waited outside had better have an excellent excuse for causing this untimely interruption. Even after she stepped into the hallway, her hand curled around the doorknob, holding it open so she could keep track of her pupils.

But Mrs. Georges exited completely after a moment of murmured conversation, letting the door swing shut behind her. When she returned something had changed. With her wrist she swiped at the underside of her nose, which seemed a little drippy.

"Mitchell," she spoke almost under her breath. "Would you come here, please?"

Was she calling on him to start his presentation? He didn't know what to think. She didn't say *Mitchell* in that sharp way that meant, as she always reminded him, he was "getting on her last nerve."

"Mitchell. Oh, honey. Mr. Nagler would like to speak with you in the hall."

Mitchell stumbled from his chair and, with wet shoes squishing and his chin hanging and his heart uncertain, headed in the direction Mrs. Georges pointed him. With each step he took, his feet felt heavier.

"Uh-oh, the *principal* wants to see you," Lydia singsonged. "Now you're *really* in trouble."

The last thing he heard was Mrs. Georges informing Lydia she would not tolerate that sort of reproachful behavior in her classroom. Which might have been the biggest surprise of all. Lydia Smith never got in trouble for anything.

Mr. Nagler, the Deer Path Elementary principal, had let them throw pies at him during the spring carnival. He'd promised he'd shave bald if the Cubs made it to the World Series. At the last school assembly, he'd carried a trash can around the gym, coaching the student body to yell when he yanked off the lid and go silent when he slammed the lid in place.

But Mr. Nagler wasn't smiling now. Mitchell stood tall, clasped his hands behind his belt, and confessed the guilt that kept gnawing at him. "I know I'm in trouble because I didn't finish my report."

Mr. Nagler laid large hands on Mitchell's shoulders. "Oh, Mitchell. I'm sure Mrs. Georges will understand."

"I was going to do my homework last night, but I forgot."

"That's okay, son. I don't think there'll be any problem working that out."

"There won't?" Mitchell touched his glasses, stunned by the sudden generosity. "Why not?"

The principal pinched the bridge of his nose and didn't offer any explanation. After Mitchell joined him in his office, Mr. Nagler told him that his grandparents were coming to pick him up, that they were already on their way.

"Nona and Harold?"

The principal nodded.

"But Nona and Harold would never come to school," Mitchell argued, his heart sinking, finally understanding something had to be bad, bad wrong. "Nona says too many kids in one place gives her angina."

Mitchell was relieved when the principal walked him outside

and waited with him until his family arrived. Mitchell recognized the car as it pulled in at the curb. He told Mr. Nagler goodbye and skipped forward the minute Harold came tramping up the front walk.

"Where's Nona?"

"Nona's in the car waiting for us." Harold held out a hand. "You're coming to our house for a little while, okay?"

Mitchell wouldn't take Harold's hand. He felt much too skeptical and left out. Why wouldn't anybody tell him what was going on?

"What's wrong, Harold? What is it? Why wouldn't Mr. Nagler tell me?"

When they got to the car, Nona waited in the front seat while Harold gripped the boy in an anguished embrace. "It's your mother." Harold choked on the words. "She got in an accident, buddy. A real bad one."

"But she's okay, right?" Mitchell heard his own voice, thin as a grass whistle. "She'll be okay, won't she? She's in the hospital, right? When she comes home, me and Kate and Dad can take care of her. She'll get better, right?"

But the look on Harold's face told Mitchell the answer was no. Harold said that nobody knew for sure yet, that his father had phoned and had wanted to be the one to tell him, but everyone needed him to answer questions and sign things and make decisions.

Mitchell felt his face flatten. He thought, *I should have worn my galoshes. Mom wanted me to wear my galoshes.*

"Sometimes things happen, Mitchell," Harold said, swiping tears from his own face with his thumb. "Any minute, life can change."

Mitchell stared at him.

"We think we know how life will turn out, but it doesn't always work that way," Harold said, trying to prepare Mitchell without coming right out and telling him that the police had said there wasn't much hope after his mom being in the water that long. At least, that was what Joe had said between sobs when he called.

"No," Mitchell repeated. "No. *No*," he said, pummeling Harold with his small angry fists, shoving away both the man and the devastating news.

An armada of rescue vehicles lined the riversides, lights spinning and flashing and shimmering, reflecting red, gold, and blue confetti on the water. Boats patrolled the river too, slipping in and out beneath the bridge in silent vigils. Divers in wet suits sleek as seals surfaced and headed down again. Their cohorts hoisted them onto a platform only long enough for them to report they'd found nothing, only long enough for them to change to fresh air tanks before they leaped off and disappeared.

Flares burned, reflecting long, pink flames on the wet street. Gapers had slowed traffic to a near standstill. Joe Harper stood numbly on the bank, alone, watching. Everywhere he turned, people babbled on two-way radios. An EMT team waited at the ready. The ambulance stood poised nearby.

When Joe had first arrived at the scene, he'd yelled in desperate anger, stripping off his shirt, popping off buttons in his haste to leap in and swim. He didn't have any idea who finally managed to stop him. He hadn't gotten a good look at the fireman in the blinding coat, the reflective yellow stripes, who'd restrained him and kept him from going in.

"You have kids, don't you?" asked a gruff voice, the owner of which kept his hands in handcuff grips and buckled his elbows around Joe's arms while he thrashed. "You're not thinking straight. What good would it do those kids if you jump in and don't come back either?"

"I've got to get to my wife."

"What good would it do if you jumped in?" the voice asked in his ear. "What good would it do if you got lost in the river too? Think about it."

But Joe couldn't think straight. This was the hardest thing he'd ever done, waiting here with nothing to do, feeling this helpless. It was the worst thing he could have done, driving here by himself, but he hadn't had any choice.

His stomach had already retched itself inside out until there wasn't anything else left to come up. Joe struggled to break loose, fighting the man's grip even though it was futile. He twisted one arm free and flailed. "Please. My wife—"

"We have dozens of professional rescue workers looking for your wife. We're not going to leave her down there, sir."

Everything was a blur as Joe wheeled. "But she might still be alive," he shouted.

"We'll bring her up, sir. I promise."

But after too much longer, Joe knew they'd eventually switch from rescuing a live person and start efforts to remove a body.

One after another, squalls passed over the waterway, raking it with driving rain. The accusations Joe had flung at Sarah the night before resonated in his head, as immense as claps of thunder in a Midwestern storm. *I want this to work, Sarah, but I can't take much more.*

Maybe she'd gotten trapped with some air and could still

breathe. Maybe she swam to safety. Maybe she was lost and dis-oriented somewhere. Joe couldn't let go of even the most remote possibilities. *God, how could you let those be the last words I ever say to my wife?*

Just like that Joe's grief ignited into rage. Rage at crews that took so long to find her. Rage at the hands on his watch that kept ticking forward as if this were any other hour, any other minute, any other day.

"It's a beige Lincoln MKX," he repeated to an officer for the umpteenth time. "Crème brûlée is the color. Why can't you fig-ure out where she went down?"

Joe didn't see the police captain glance at members of his squadron. "We got sludge. We got water about as clear as Shaw-nee Hills swamp. Sunshine would help, but, as you can see"—one of Chicago's Finest peered overhead, not wanting to tell this guy about shipwrecks and aircraft that had never been found—"that's in short supply."

A diver emerged, sending widening circles riffling across the surface. Every team member straightened to attention. They each waited for the whistle, the shout, anything that might sig-nal success. And when the signal didn't come, when the diver swam with regular strokes past the diving bell, when they lifted him onto the platform and, even from this distance, saw him shake his head, dozens of shoulders drooped in disappointment. Dozens of steps became more dogged.

"I've got to do *something*." Joe sprang toward the water and was up to his knees before a paramedic restrained him. It took pre-cious minutes trying to wrestle everyone off. When they finally overcame him, he couldn't stop the violent trembles. His teeth chattered. The harder he tried to clench them to make them stop, the worse they got. He waved off the offer of a blanket. "Tell me what I can do," he begged them. "Please let me do something."

"You have to keep safe for your kids. That's what you have to do."

"This is our chaplain." A police officer whose name badge read Patterson doffed his cap and stepped into Joe's line of vision. "Would you like the chaplain to say a few words? Would you like him to stay with you?"

"No." Hopelessness seeped into Joe's bones, obscuring the sharp outlines of everything he cared about, absorbing everything in its ominous, soggy gray. "No, I don't think so. Please go." Joe could have said, *I know a pastor. I can notify him if I need anything spiritual.* But he'd been desperate enough to pray a few days ago and look where it had gotten him. He had said words to his wife they'd never be able to work through. Words he'd never be able to retract, even if he wanted to. It had been so long since he'd even thought of reaching out to God for help that now he felt betrayed because he finally had and Sarah was dead. He turned away from the chaplain and said, "No. Nothing. There is nothing you can do now."

"You're sure? It isn't good for you to wait by yourself. You need someone with you. For support."

"I have a friend coming."

Ever since they'd notified him at the shop, Joe had been on the cell with Pete and Gail. Harold had agreed to pick up Mitchell. Mrs. Pavik had said Kate was fine; she'd do anything she could to help.

Pete kept calling to check on Joe and report their progress. They inched along at an excruciating pace. Because of the rain and morning rush hour, the highway was clogged for miles.

"How you doing, man?" Pete asked again, desperate to keep Joe on the line.

"We fought last night," he said. "Did you know that? You should hear some of the things I said." Soon Joe might list every word in a litany of grief. But for now, the shock numbed him. His emotions had shut down.

"Don't think about that now. You'll go crazy. You have to think of happier times."

"She drove off the bridge, Pete," Joe said. Now that his anger had dissipated, his voice had gone flat. "Isn't that nuts? She drove off the bridge." The police had told him they'd talked to people who had witnessed it. "I don't know how I can face this."

"We're on the way," Pete kept repeating. "We're creeping along, but we're making some progress.

"Joe. Joe? Say something. Are you there? Listen to me, Joe. Sarah was probably just in a hurry like always."

But Joe couldn't speak. He dropped his forehead onto his arms.

"You hang in there, Joe. You hang in there. We'll be along as soon as we can."

⌘ Chapter Twelve ⌘

Bright light! A light so bright Sarah couldn't even look at it at first, but then it seemed to be drawing her. The light was warm, and the closer she got the better it made her feel. She felt safe for the first time in as long as she could remember. She felt totally safe, and it was wonderful.

Suddenly the bright light started turning a beautiful honey gold color. Everything glowed. Sarah looked at her hands, and even they glowed. Everything was sunshine gold. Apple jelly gold. If she was in heaven, it smelled like apple jelly—wasn't that funny? Gold fell over Sarah's arm, warm as the sun.

This was the most beautiful place Sarah had ever seen. She couldn't imagine anything more perfect. Water splashed from a waterfall and ran into a beautiful stream that seemed to be singing as it flowed along its path. Peace and joy filled the air—and singing. The hills and valleys seemed to be singing. The mountains were singing. Singing from every direction. Singing in every tone and tongue, yet no note discordant. Singing about a God who loved more than Sarah could even begin to imagine.

Then suddenly she was inside Annie's house, the one Annie had when Sarah was a child, but everything looked absolutely perfect. There were jars of gold liquid so rich and clear in the window, and she thought she heard her grandmother singing like she used to. "We shall tread the streets of go-*o-oold*."

Sarah felt a longing inside. She wanted the peace and joy that surrounded her to be in her heart. She ached for the innocent wonder she'd lost, for the little girl who'd yearned for an embrace, a smile, anything from her mother, the little girl who'd found approval only in her grandmother's arms. She didn't want to be afraid anymore. She wanted to rest.

Sarah had heard plenty about how to get into heaven. She remembered hearing about how Jesus knocks on the door of your heart and if you open the door he will come in. She had heard the Christmas and Easter stories—how Jesus was born in a manger, to a virgin girl. How he died for her sins on a cross and was raised from the dead. Was this what she'd believed when she was a little girl?

Was she dreaming? Sarah wondered. Because if this was heaven, she didn't think she had any right to be here.

But maybe it wasn't heaven. Even as she took in the room, she realized that she was lying in a bed with a quilt draped over her and a soft pillow beneath her head. Someone had taken great pains to make her comfortable. Besides, she hadn't prayed or asked for God's forgiveness for anything since she'd been eleven years old.

She had believed then. Annie believed in Jesus, and Sarah wanted to also. She let Annie pray a prayer with her inviting Jesus to live in her heart, and she remembered believing that he was in there after that. She even talked to him, asking for his help. How was it that her simple childhood faith dissolved so quickly as she grew older?

Suddenly Sarah remembered. She'd left Tom Roscoe waiting

for her! He'd be in his office by now and Nathan Cornish would be well on his way and Tom would be gnashing his teeth that she'd disregarded the request of a client. Panic rushed through her like an electric current. Her clattering heart banged in her ears, more dissonant than plates in a downtown diner.

Tom Roscoe would have her cleaning out her desk before the end of the day.

I don't have time to be here, wherever "here" is.

She felt she was being pulled in two different directions by two different worlds: the one she was experiencing for the first time—the bright, golden, warm, loving, peaceful, happy one; and the one she was accustomed to—the one with constant frustration, pain, disappointment, and never-ending pressure to perform.

I've got to use my cell and find Leo and have him get Roscoe on the line. But she couldn't find her cell phone. She wanted to order someone to do something. Now *that* would make her feel better. *Have him make some crazy excuse for me; I don't care what he says. Just tell him to get me out of this.* But when she tried to speak, nothing came.

The golden glow seemed to be taking over again. Sarah's panic was being swallowed up in peace. What she felt right now was infinitely better than the anxiety she felt when she thought of Tom Roscoe, her cell phone, being late for the meeting, and the possibility of getting fired.

She heard someone tramping up the steps to the porch and fiddling with the doorknob. "Please. You've got to find my cell and—" The door swung open. When a man entered, Sarah's words lodged in her throat.

"*Bryl*-creem," the stranger sang as he pushed his way inside.

Only he wasn't a stranger anymore, not really, because Sarah had met him once before. "A little dab'll do you. Use more only if you dare! But watch *out*, the gals will all pursue you. They'll love to put their fingers through your hair." Which seemed an absolutely ridiculous song for him to be singing since the sparse hanks of hair springing from his head looked more like a badly weeded thistle patch than anything a girl might want to run her fingers through.

"You!" Sarah felt every muscle and nerve in her body come to attention when she recognized him. "What are you doing? Get out! You... you don't have any right to be here!"

"Seems to me," he noted, "you'd better figure out where *you* are before you start telling me if I have a right to be here or not."

"You're following my family! I know you are!" Sarah lost the pillow on the floor and grappled for the quilt to shield her chest. "You're stalking us."

The man broke into a whistle and shouldered the sugar bag.

"He's our friend," Mitchell had said the last time she'd laid eyes on this man. *"I saw him at the Cubs game."*

Sarah clenched the quilt. "Who are you? Why are you here? What's so important that you've got to follow me—" She glanced around the room. *Where?*

He took one step forward and, shooting bullets with her eyes, she bunched the quilt tight as a barrel around her. Still, she couldn't shake the odd feeling. In one way she felt afraid of the man but at the same time, she sensed his kindness.

Apparently her reaction didn't ruffle him much. He barely even glanced her way before he plopped the heavy sugar bag on the sideboard with a resounding *thwack*.

"Guess you'll figure it out directly."

He started whistling. Sarah noticed a slight grin on his face before he was suddenly gone.

For the first time Sarah surveyed her surroundings. The house did look just like her grandmother's house. With its narrow linoleum-covered counter and its sink as big around as Cook County and its single pipe buttressed beneath it in the shape of a bent knee. Somehow these old household belongings looked brand-new even though the style of them was old. A gleaming Zenith radio perched on a table beside an upholstered chair with crocheted doilies draped over each arm. The gas range squatted in the corner like an overdressed guest, its legs Betty Grable curvy, its black knobs winking like buttons on a bodice.

The stove's brushed-nickel plaque announced its maker with simple new-minted pride: Kalamazoo. Sarah didn't understand what was going on, but she kept thinking how totally beautiful everything was. It had a beauty that was beyond anything she had ever seen or read about or imagined.

A steady flame licked the bases of two shiny new aluminum pots. Tongs rested sideways on the counter. Sunlight spilled over rows of empty canning jars. Skeins of vapor rose from the pots, scalloping the windowpanes. Everywhere, the smell of home-grown McIntosh apples. Mouth-pucker tart, yet sweet as honey and crispy as spice—the way her grandmother had always described them "back in the day."

The cell phone beeped beside her, and Sarah practically fell out of bed trying to get to it. She knocked over a lamp in the process, but managed to grab it before it toppled to the floor. What was she doing here in a bed like some sick person, anyway? She kicked her legs out of the tangled quilt and performed a level-four gymnastics move so she wouldn't end up on the ground.

Maybe Leo was trying to find her. Or maybe a nervous client needed reassurance about oil prices. It could be one of the firm's senior partners, seeking her input on the precious-metals fund. Sarah flipped the phone open, intent on taking the call. With anticipation hammering in her ears, she surveyed the screen, expecting a number she recognized.

SEARCHING FOR SIGNAL.

It took precious seconds for the words to register and her hopes to plummet. "What do you mean, *searching for signal*? I always have signal!"

Only then did she realize the beeps sounded at regular intervals. LOW BATTERY. In desperation, she pried open the battery panel, yanked out the battery, and slammed it back in its place. Once again, she checked the screen. Nothing had changed. The red indicator flashed its warning. The narrow bar stood empty.

Someone had dressed her in a nightgown. The clothes she had donned in haste this morning flapped in the breeze on the clothesline outdoors. Sarah frowned. The sight of her blouse flapping its arms at her, the skirt kicking up its narrow pleat, made her freeze in her tracks. A chill raced the length of her spine. Suddenly she remembered this morning. She remembered the bridge and the water. She remembered Joe. She remembered what happened before she'd gotten here.

With her hopes dashed and fear tugging her insides, Sarah glared at the phone. As if in defiance, the final three-note alarm rang and the thing shut itself off in her palm.

"You really think that phone's going to do you any good in this place?"

Sarah lifted her eyes toward the owner of the voice. If it had been any other time, if she'd been eleven years old again, if Annie

Cattalo had been seventy, Sarah would have shouted, "Oh my goodness! Oh my word!" and launched herself laughing into the woman's arms. But not this moment when the woman standing before her was beautiful and young, a pinup girl instead of an old woman, as vigorous and sparkling as all the other articles in the house. Not this moment when her grandmother seemed more like a youthful actress out of a World War II movie than anyone Sarah had known before. Not this moment with the grave memory of squealing tires, descending barricades, and pounding water leaving Sarah's stomach to pitch with nausea and regret.

"Annie." No more than a breathless whisper. A beloved name. "Did I die? Did I drown? Am I in heaven, or am I dreaming?"

Her grandmother propped her hands on the hips of her red polka-dotted dress and pressed her calves together like a model in the Buy More War Bonds poster. "We'll have a conversation about that."

Now Sarah knew who'd dressed her in the nightgown—it suddenly made perfect sense. Annie had been the one to take care of her, even before her mother had finally married Harold. When Sarah was little, whenever this woman had come to visit, Annie had been the one to lift her from the sofa when Sarah was left watching television and had fallen asleep alone. This woman had been the one to whisper, "Sarah, sweetie, will you wake up a little bit? Let's get you into bed," as she tugged the shirt over Sarah's head. "Can you get your arm in here for me?" as she helped work an elbow through small pajama sleeves.

Still, Sarah wasn't one to get sidetracked by sappy memories. "Wherever we are, I don't have time to be here. I have to get back."

Gone was the fine silver hair Sarah remembered so well. In its place, lacquered yellow curls jutted forward like a finch's nest ready to topple from a tree. She was a lot younger, but it was Annie all right. Sarah would have known Annie at any age.

The woman narrowed her eyes and shook her head with the same spunk that would continue to serve her kindly over the decades. "Oh, you've got everything all scheduled for yourself? You have the plan figured out, do you?" Annie stood before Sarah with her knee cocked and her mouth in a dubious pucker. "All I've got to say to you is this, young lady." She brandished a paring knife and attacked another apple. "You'd better be careful what you pray for. Otherwise you might just get it."

"I haven't prayed for anything in thirty years," Sarah said.

"Actually you have," Annie reminded her. "You told God you couldn't go on anymore the way you were. And anything you say to God is a prayer."

Well, Sarah hadn't thought of that.

Apple skin peeled off in one perfect, red spiral. Annie met her granddaughter's eyes with such intensity, Sarah worried Annie might slice her thumb. "I have prayed," Annie said. "And so has Joe. And that's the reason I'm here now."

"Joe prayed?" Sarah asked. "You're here because of *Joe*?"

"No." Annie retrieved another shiny McIntosh, polished it against her apron, and turned it in her fingers. "I'm here because of Jesus. Because he loves you and has a plan for your life. One that you have been totally missing."

Sarah's grandmother scrabbled through a drawer and came up with an extra blade. "I was beginning to think you might sleep until sunset. How about some help paring these apples?"

But Sarah wasn't one to be diverted. "If we're in heaven, we don't have to go through all this, do we?" she asked. "Couldn't we just get it over with? You could take me by the hand and walk me right up and you could introduce me to Jesus, couldn't you?"

On the shelf above Annie's head stood a small ancient clock, "Enfield" written in script on its face, with its crystal missing. When Annie saw that its hands weren't moving, she eyed it disagreeably and gave it one good *whump*. Still, its hands didn't move.

"Don't you see? That's what I did every day of your life from the day you were born until you turned eleven and I got taken on to Glory—I tried to introduce you to Jesus, but maybe this time I get to introduce you to yourself as well."

Annie felt amiable enough to banter back and forth with the fellow who kept appearing at the window, but Sarah felt anything *but*. She felt afraid every time he came around. The knife shuddered every time she sliced an apple. She shot countless furtive glances in his direction, trying to figure him out.

There had been bushel baskets of apples to peel, core, and pare. Each of Annie's peels came off in one perfect, single whorl. Sarah's came off in a pile of stubby, short slices because her nerves made her clumsy. Sarah nicked herself again and, with a sharp cry of pain, sucked her thumb.

"Are you going to tell me who that man is and what he's doing here?" Sarah asked, letting the knife clatter to the counter. With the knuckle of her injured hand, she swiped at her hair-plastered forehead. "Is he a friend of yours or something?"

"Who? Wingtip? A friend of mine?" Annie pressed her hand against her apron sash and gave a hearty laugh, which didn't make Sarah breathe any easier. "Of course he's my friend. In this place, we're all friends."

Sarah commented, "His name really is Wingtip," her voice dry.

As if mention of his name had caused him to spring forth, Wingtip appeared in the open window again and crossed his arms on the sill. "Sure it is." He shot Sarah the same broad grin she remembered from the clothing bin in Chicago. He lifted a foot so she could see the wingtip. "Guess the Heavenly Father thought it'd be cute to name an angel after his shoes."

So *that's* why Annie had teased him about living in eternity.

Some other person might have accepted this angel information with awed reverence. But not Sarah. She searched her mind, rifling through the details from that day on LaSalle Street. She accosted him with the same vigor as an attorney defending her rights. "Why were you following us that day? Are you what they call a guardian angel? Why would you think I'm someone who needs looking after?"

"In God's kingdom, we don't get to order up our own duties. The way it works, we all do what we are asked and we do it with great joy."

Well. Maybe she hadn't expected *that* answer. Sarah gave every ounce of her attention to the McIntosh in her hand. She set it down hard on the counter and, with one flash of the knife, sliced it in half. "I don't believe you." The apple fell in two, revealing a core and seeds.

"That's your problem, Sarah," he responded. "You don't believe in anything except what you can see and touch and accomplish by your own effort." He paused before continuing on. "I tell you, that kid you got, Sarah, he's something special. You ever notice his rally cap punched inside out? The way he pumps his fist at those come-from-behind runs? Now, how cute is that? Your kid knows how to enjoy life, that's for certain."

"Well, of course I've seen all of that. He's my son."

"Kid bites his tongue every time he keeps track on his score-card. You noticed that?"

"I have," she lied.

"As a matter of fact, you don't see most things that are really worth noticing and remembering. When he gets stats wrong on that card, he pushes his glasses up his nose and erases so hard he leaves a hole in the paper. Have you seen that?"

"Just stop it. Please."

"When he swallows his gum, he—"

Resentment and pain sliced through her. "Please. I'll picture it every minute of eternity that I'm gone from them. Please stop asking me what I've seen and not seen." Now that Sarah had lost so much, she realized she'd never taken the time to be grateful for even the most basic things. She'd never even thought to be grateful for being alive. "I am very aware that I failed at being a good wife and mother."

Anyone could see at that moment that Sarah cared about her boy.

"That kid of yours sort of gets me right here." Wingtip thumped his chest right above his heart. "Come to think of it, he's a little version of his mama. Quite the little math whiz." He shook his head as if he'd just realized something. "Guess that means I've taken a liking to you too."

Sarah Harper would go after a good argument any day. Here she stood, bursting with angry pain, raring to go at it. Just let him say she didn't measure up as a mom. Just let him say she did everything wrong. She'd take him on about all of it!

But Wingtip's gentle humor gave her pause. The care in his eyes disarmed her. As fast as the fight had flown into her, it seeped out again. "Can you see my family from where we are?" she asked with hope in her eyes.

Wingtip nodded. Yes.

"Are they okay?"

"They're being looked after, just like you always were."

Sarah pictured Mitchell with his cowlick sticking straight up after he showered and practically gnawing the end of his pencil as he worked a thorny math problem and plopping in her lap at the city swimming pool. Mitchell, who, Sarah realized, had told her Wingtip was a friend, only she'd been too terrified to listen.

In that one moment, Sarah missed her children so much that it seemed more than she could bear. Both of their precious faces were branded on her heart. The pain of losing them felt like a fist wringing out her heart. Why hadn't she looked Mitchell in the eyes that day? Why hadn't she heard what he had to tell her?

She said, "I don't get the part about you spending time at the ballpark. For an angel, you sure know a lot about the Chicago Cubs."

He stood mute for a beat too long.

"No. Don't say it. You're not the angel for the Cubs."

Wingtip lowered his gaze at her and waited for her to make her own deduction.

"No. You're telling me the Cubs have had an angel up in that old scoreboard all this time? And counting."

"You told me not to say it."

"You're *not*," she argued.

"Well, don't you think they could use one?"

"If you're an angel, then why were you pretending to be a bum on LaSalle Street?" She gawked at him, speechless, before she started shaking her head, fending off the idea.

"Would it be so bad," he asked, "if the Cubs had an angel and that angel was picked by God to watch over you a little bit and show you around?"

You need help finding your way around? A vagabond's question from LaSalle Street. And her answer, *I don't need you to show me anywhere. I'm not lost.*

"You knew this was going to happen," she said.

"Who knew?" he asked. "Who knew what choice you would make?"

"Annie?" Sarah drew a deep breath, turned toward her grandmother. "Where does my family think I am?"

Her grandmother had been in the process of carefully peeling off her silk stockings and gently kneading her vermillion-painted toes. But Annie's fingers paused. Slow-motion like, her foot returned to the floor.

"They think you're at the bottom of the river. So does everyone else." She said it as matter-of-factly as if she'd said, "The soup is on the third shelf, the second row, at Boldt's Grocery and Meat Market." Which sobered the mood between the three of them considerably.

Sarah stared into the pot as if trying to see through the surface of the cold, tea-colored water that had closed over her head, the rippled surface she couldn't quite get to, its shimmering dancing light. What was Joe doing right now? What was he thinking? Feeling? Was he frantically looking for her?

I didn't mean to leave like this, she wanted to cry out to Joe.

And then the horrifying realization of where things had been left between them. *Suppose he thinks I did this on purpose.*

Suppose he thinks I was trying to punish him. Or that I was trying to escape.

Sarah felt again the breathless loss, the hollow cramp of sorrow that had come unexpectedly as she watched him sleeping beside her, heard those light snores he made, that sharp mind-boggling emptiness she felt when she tried to imagine living without Joe. How she wished she had told Joe how much he meant to her. She wished with all of her heart she had told him how wonderful he was, how talented and creative, but all she'd done was find fault with him. Now it was too late.

She gripped the sideboard, her vision swimming, her head pounding. The noise behind her ears was deafening. Why had it seemed so important to beat those barricades this morning? What had she thought so important that she'd made such a reckless dash to the other side?

Annie's voice came then, gentle and full of sorrow. "Sarah, I know how hard your life has been for you. Being resentful and feeling sorry for yourself hasn't done any good. All you've been thinking about is trying to make yourself happy, and God wants you to understand that's why nothing in your life is working. It is impossible to be both selfish and happy, Sarah."

"Oh, Annie," she whispered, and she might have been a little girl again, hearing the mournful way she sounded. She gripped her grandmother's hand. "If I could just go back and do it all over again, I would do things differently."

Annie shook her head solemnly, her voice measured. "Don't you know most people think the same thing? Why would you be any different?"

Sarah sighed, feeling sufficiently chastised.

"Everybody wants second chances. And no one realizes that taking a really honest look at changing things isn't easy. But if you genuinely want to change, God will help you. You cannot do anything about the way you got started in life, but you can determine how you will finish."

"Annie, I'm scared. Are you saying I can have another chance? That I'm not dead after all?" Sarah whispered.

"God loves you, and he wants you to feel better about yourself. He wants you to live the life he intended for you to live. You don't have to be scared about that."

The timepiece above Annie's head stared at the two of them. It wasn't ticking, but it was pointing at 7:35. Sarah wondered if the clock was right. She had no concept of just how long she'd been gone. The clock stood silent as a stone.

"The Father holds every second in the palm of his hand, Sarah," Annie said. "His timing is always just right, and everything that happens to you is intended for your good. Even the disappointments you had as a child hold a treasure if you will ask God to work something good out of them."

In one way Sarah hated the thought of leaving this place. She loved the light, the golden glow, the feeling that nothing could ever be wrong here. But maybe she had a chance to see Joe and the children again. Maybe she had a chance to tell them how sorry she was for the way she had been treating them. She wanted to promise to go to a ball game with Mitchell and not disappoint him and be really happy about being there. Sarah wanted a chance to learn what was really important in life and how to live for someone other than herself.

❧ Chapter Thirteen ❧

What does a person do at a time like this, Joe thought, *when you really don't know how to pray?*

Joe crouched beside the riverbank and stared into the murky water. The police captain had been right. Even where the river lapped onto shore, he could barely see an inch beneath it. He glanced over his shoulder to see if his friend Pete was watching. Then Joe slipped his hand into the water and watched his skin instantly tint a sickly shade of green. Another four inches deeper and he couldn't see his fingers at all anymore.

As surely as he felt his hand attached to his arm beneath the water, Joe felt his wife somewhere down there too, crying out to him, floating away from him. And even though an army of professional rescuers searched for Sarah, Joe couldn't shake the feeling that he was the one who was supposed to find her. Maybe if he just kept hoping she was alive, that would draw her to him. All he knew was that he couldn't give up . . . not yet, anyway.

He should have let the chaplain stay. That would have been better than phoning the pastor at the church they'd attended a few times. It would have been easier and better and *guilt free.* How did you say, "You don't know me, but I need you"?

Maybe pastors got calls like that all the time. Joe wondered.

The day Joe had met Sarah, everyone at the Chicago bank had told him he couldn't cash his paycheck. Here they'd been, a group of college guys who couldn't have looked more bedraggled if they'd been hiking cross-country, making a scene in the lobby and refusing to leave.

The teller had examined the draft he'd slid across the ledge toward her. "It's out of state." She'd laid both hands flat, one on either side of the check, and said, "There's nothing I can do. I'm sorry."

The teller had been kind of cute and he'd had an audience—four of the guys he hung out with stood nearby. Joe leaned forward on crumpled sleeves that hadn't seen the inside of a washer for a good month. He veed his fingers alongside a jaw that hadn't seen a razor for days. "What's wrong?" He shot her a come-hither glance that he knew worked magic with women. "Don't I look like someone you can trust?"

"I'll get my manager," she said with distaste.

"Yes. You do that."

Joe winked across the lobby at his buddies, one possessive arm still crooked across the counter, making sure the guys noticed he had pull in this place. He expected an old battle-ax to emerge through the swinging door, someone he could charm with his quick wit, his ready smile, and his round, dark eyes. Especially his round, dark eyes. He put a lot of faith in those. Generally he could get anything he wanted when he flashed them.

He should have known what he was up against the moment Sarah Cattalo strong-armed the door the way a running back would strong-arm a tackle. With the door still wagging behind her, she surveyed him with crossed arms. "What can I help you with, sir?"

If she didn't have her mouth screwed up tight as a persimmon, he thought, *she'd be pretty good-looking.* "This is a bank, right? This is where I go to get money, right? Well, that's what I need." He thumped the check to draw her attention to it.

She didn't even glance in its direction. "If you want to open an account here, you're welcome to make a deposit. After the deposit clears, you'll have access to the money. Does that sound like something you're interested in doing?"

He sent her the message with his eyes. *I could be interested in you.* And this time, he really meant it. The more he looked at her, the more he thought she was about the prettiest thing he had ever seen.

For a moment he almost considered opening an account, just to talk to her longer. He had an apartment here in town, but when he left to take the temporary job in St. Louis for a few months, he closed his bank account. He didn't see any point in paying monthly fees to keep it open if he wasn't going to have anything in it.

Now he and a bunch of guys had decided on the fly to take their final paychecks and head back to Chicago where they could all invade his apartment. Reality had hit, and they realized their paychecks were no good unless they could cash them. Joe was determined to flirt until his charm won the boss lady over to his side.

They had been driving five hours, devouring Pringles and telling man jokes and listening to punk rock in the CD player. At twenty-four, he hadn't been one to think ahead. His friends had agreed to fill up the car with gas. He'd made the pilgrimage without so much as a dollar to his name.

"If I open an account, how long will it take to get my money?"

He'd expected her to say something like thirty minutes. "Four days at least."

"Well, that answers that question."

"Don't you have an ATM card? We have a machine right out front. If you have funds in your account at home, you ought to be able to access those."

He had the card from his old account that was now closed, which did Joe no good whatsoever. With all those guys watching, the last thing Joe wanted to do was walk away empty-handed. He selected a lime lollipop from the jar, slowly unwrapped it, and tried to figure out how she could be a bank manager and so young. Either she was a fast climber or she must have started working when she was like ten. "So. You got a boyfriend or something? Is there someone who's going to come slash my tires or beat me up if I ask you out?"

She drew herself to her tallest height. After twelve years of marriage he still teased her about her answer that day. "You don't have a prayer."

Joe could never determine for sure which motivated him more, the ribbing he got from his pals that night or the flicker of self-doubt he'd noticed before something clicked shut in her face. He did open an account, which gave him a good excuse to keep returning to the bank until finally he'd convinced a reluctant Sarah Cattalo to join him for dinner at a dive on Lawrence Avenue, just around the corner from Hoyne Savings Bank.

When Sarah said, *"You don't have a prayer,"* it made Joe that much more determined to win her over, and later she told him she secretly admired his determination and confidence.

Sometimes now, with the two of them struggling, it was easy to forget the times he'd savored being married to her. Sharing the bathroom, shifting his body so she could reach past him to the sink, the way their eyes locked in the mirror, the way he liked to kiss inside the crook of her arm. The times he'd cupped the back of her head in his hand and felt her hair falling through his fingers. The times they'd lain in bed and he'd been fascinated by the ebb and flow of her breathing, the fiddle-curve of her spine.

On the day she'd given birth to Kate, he'd found her with a foot propped on the coffee table, trying to paint her toenails. Only problem was, she couldn't bend over and reach them.

"What are you doing? Isn't it about time for the hospital?" he'd asked.

She'd groaned, bending over herself with the bottle of Maybelline's Saucy Brown. "Things were too crazy at Roscoe. I didn't have time to get a pedicure downtown. Nobody wants to go through childbirth without painted toenails. Your feet are up high and waving around and everyone in the hospital sees." The way things looked was very important to Sarah, probably way too important.

"Oh, so that's what they're looking at," he'd said, laughing at her. "Here. Let me do that."

"I don't want any smudges. You have to be careful."

"Just give me the bottle, Sarah."

Mitchell had already been picked up to spend the day with a friend from school. And there they'd been, Joe touching the tiny brush to her toenails with the same attention to detail he employed repairing dings in his auto shop. She'd gripped his shoulder and breathed through another mild contraction, inhaling through her nostrils with her eyes closed, counting to ten as she exhaled through the *O* of her mouth. She knew she still had time; her contractions were too far apart to be concerned yet.

"So do you have your hair ribbons packed too?" He screwed the cap on the nail polish and grinned at her. "Pink ones? And all the little pink clothes?" They'd had an ultrasound and knew it would be a girl.

"Don't tease me about it anymore." Sarah's eyes smoldered with something he didn't understand, her words fervent. "It's important. I want everything right for her when she comes, Joe."

"Why would you worry so much about that?"

"She is going to be perfect and I want to look perfect for her and I want her to look perfect when I bring her home."

"She's not going to know any difference."

"Yes she will. She'll know later. She'll see the pictures. I want her to know how much I want her."

The Windy City had been living up to its nickname that day, complete with lake-effect snow, when Joe toted Sarah and her bare feet to the car. Her coat was open as she clung to him, her arms locked around his neck. When she laid her head against him, he could see her pulse rising in the hollow of her neck. Even carrying her weight this way, even with their pulses tangled, Joe knew there was still a part of her that he had never been able to penetrate, an area closed off in her soul that she wouldn't let anyone into.

He remembered how, about a week before their wedding, with gift money in their hands and a couch in their sights on the showroom floor at Colemans, she'd grabbed a throw pillow from its display, hugged it against her chest like it was something she wanted to hide behind, and asked, "Joe? Are you sure you want to do this?"

"What?" he'd asked wearily. He wanted her to have whichever color she liked best. "Pick the brown tweed over the plaid? I think so. Yes."

"No. Not the couch. I'm not talking about the couch."

"What, then?"

"Are you sure you want to marry me?"

He'd taken the pillow away, held her face in his hands. "Why would you ask a question like that? Of course I am."

"Because maybe you haven't known me long enough to *really* know me. Maybe you won't like me when you get to know me better."

He could see her, he'd told her. He could see everything about her. He *loved* everything about her. But now, as surely as water obscured his hand just below the surface, as surely as her words had been a mystery to him, he thought maybe she'd been right. Even then he'd sensed that he didn't really know her like he thought he did.

I wanted to make things right for you, Sarah. I just didn't know how to do it.

Joe had never been much for words when it came to asking for help. His simple, blunt request to God had come from desperation to save his family, not from any trust in prayer. Even though he believed in the existence of God, Joe's life creed had always been: "Do the best you can, stand up for yourself, take life as it comes."

God, I asked you for help, not more problems than I already had.

How could he trust a God who didn't fix their lives the way Joe wanted them fixed?

What am I supposed to do? Who am I supposed to rely on now?

Things had changed in a moment....Just like that, everything was different. He stood at a precipice, with two children who needed him, not knowing what to do and having nowhere to run.

He soberly realized that now he would never be able to reconcile with Sarah or have the life with her that he longed to have.

Mitchell sat wedged between Nona and Harold in the front seat, his wet feet straddling the hump and the Kleenex box, air blowing in his eyes from the vents, which made him squint. The inside of Harold's car smelled funny, like dust and decaying foam rubber. When he tried to get comfortable, the seat scrunched beneath him like hay.

When Harold had hauled Mitchell into his arms at school, Mitchell couldn't remember ever being held that tightly.

There were too many things to think about. Mitchell missed his mom. He wanted her right now, for her to cup his face in her hands and tell him everything would be okay. He didn't want to think about what Harold had told him, that she had somehow gotten lost in the river and the firemen were trying to find her but they might not. It felt scary to be let out of school with all his friends still in Mrs. Georges's class.

"Will Mrs. Georges tell them why I didn't come back to class?"

Beside him, Nona had been blowing her nose. She rested a frayed tissue in her lap, inside the curl of her hand. Harold drove with both hands, his fingers clenched so hard around the steering wheel that his hand looked like a skeleton. Which made Mitchell shiver.

"She'll tell them," Harold said. "That's what teachers are supposed to do."

"Are we going to get Dad?" Mitchell asked.

"Your dad's busy. We're taking you to our house."

In spite of the horrible events, Mitchell felt a sharp thrill at this idea. His friends had told him about spending weekends with their grandparents and being encouraged to do all sorts of interesting things. Lydia bragged about how her grandma let her try every flavor of syrup at IHOP. Ryan Thompson drew jagged-teeth pictures of stalactites and stalagmites and told everyone in class that his grandfather had taken him to explore a cave. Kyle Grimes went with his grandparents on a houseboat at the Lake of the Ozarks.

Mitchell couldn't remember ever being alone with Harold and Nona. He never got invited to visit them without his mother coming along too. Mitchell couldn't quite decide whether it was because Nona felt uncertain and awkward around him or because his mother wanted to protect him from something he didn't understand.

"You want me to make something to eat?" Harold asked when they got to the house. "How about popcorn?"

"I'm not hungry."

"Something to drink? We've got Pepsi."

"I'm not supposed to have soda. It rots my teeth."

"Oh. Sorry."

"But you're the oldest grown-up I know. So if you said it was okay, it probably would be."

They perched at the kitchen table and, with the stealth of criminals, popped open a couple of cans. Harold guzzled his down. Mitchell traced the condensation on the can with a finger, trying to be brave. "Mama knows how to swim, you know."

"Does she? She's a good swimmer?"

"She used to be a lifeguard one time. She wanted to take Kate to Aqua-Tots this year, only she didn't have time so Mrs. Pavik had to do it."

"Mitchell. I—" Harold stopped. Pain snagged in his throat. A grown man trying to comfort a child, at a loss for words.

"When can I talk to Dad?"

"Anytime you'd like. Do you want to call him and tell him we got you here safe?"

Mitchell nodded, his bottom lip starting to quaver.

"Come on. I'll dial his number for you. I'll bet he wants to talk to you too." Harold hoisted himself from the chair and headed for the landline. He dialed Joe's number and handed the receiver to Mitchell.

"Dad?" Mitchell heard three rings and then the click. "Dad?" But no one answered, only voice mail. *I can't come to the phone right now. If you're trying to reach Harper's Mazda Car-Care Clinic, please dial . . .*

Mitchell wiped his runny nose with a shirtsleeve and waited for the beep. "I'm at Nona's, and we got here fine. Will you call us, Dad? I want to talk to you."

Harold produced a hankie from his pocket after he'd taken the phone from Mitchell. After that he invited Mitchell to come with him to the greenhouse. "You could dig around in the dirt out there. I have tomatoes that could sure use transplanting."

Nona had told Mitchell plenty of times that she didn't like him to get his hands dirty. So Mitchell shook his head even though Harold's suggestion sounded like fun. Instead he went in search of his grandmother. He found her in her brocade chair, gripping a tissue in both fists directly below her chin. She'd worked the Kleenex with her thumbs until there wasn't anything left of it, just a wad of shreds.

"Nona?"

It seemed a necessary thing: that a grandmother in a chair would reach toward a child who needed to be embraced. But Nona didn't. She sat there, looking stricken, her limbs crimped tight against her, a cocooned butterfly unable to unfurl its wings. Mitchell's throat tightened. He hated to admit it, but his grandmother frightened him.

"Do you like Mike and Ikes?" he asked timidly. He would try anything.

"What? What are you talking about?"

"Those candies. They're different colors and they're shaped like pills and they get stuck in your teeth when you chew them."

Her name had been Jane. His mother had once told him this. Mitchell thought about that sometimes, how your name could change when you got older and somebody gave you a nickname and it just stuck.

"There's lime and lemon and cherry and orange and strawberry. Do you know what your favorite color would be?" he asked. "I like green the best. But if you thought you'd like those best, I could save the green ones for you."

She didn't answer. She sat in the chair with her shoulders hunched forward to make herself smaller, as if she didn't think it appropriate to take up so much room in her own chair.

"Or I could save another color for you if you'd like."

When she pretended not to hear, pain squeezed his ribs. He inched closer, not knowing what else to do. He saw the picture frame of a young girl in her lap. "Who's that, Nona?" Mitchell pressed closely against the chair. "Is that a picture of my mother?"

"Yes." A whisper, faint as a breeze winnowing its way through the grass. "That's her."

Even though he wasn't invited, Mitchell climbed into the chair with Nona, and for once she didn't have the strength to push him away. "Can I see?"

Nona didn't raise her head, but she handed the frame to him. Mitchell held it between two hands (his mom would be so proud of him because he hadn't gotten his hands dirty today) and looked at the little girl's face.

When he glanced up at Nona, she was staring at the girl's face too. It surprised him that Nona didn't look angry anymore; she just looked sad. Mitchell realized that Nona was feeling bad about his mom too. And even though she'd always acted bristly to him, even though he'd always been afraid of her, at that moment, Mitchell didn't care. He laid his head against her bony shoulder.

The afghan in her lap folded to the floor unheeded, like ripples of cake batter, as he threaded his fingers into Nona's hand.

Chapter Fourteen

It could be a fearful thing traveling with an angel, Sarah thought, even an angel whose forehead was covered by sparse hanks of hair (which occasionally lifted like a hinged lid on a teapot when he got caught by the Chicago breeze), who'd acquired his best pair of wingtip shoes from the clothing bin on LaSalle Street, whom God had relegated as the long-standing guardian of the Cubs.

They made an unlikely trio as they set off: Annie, the Christian grandma who had never stopped praying for the little granddaughter she'd adored. Wingtip, the angel who'd been inexplicably drawn to one small boy rooting for the Cubs in the bleacher section. And here she was too, given the gift of traveling with them, unable to turn back, not knowing what it meant to go forward. Not knowing why her heart felt so empty inside even when she'd had everything she ever thought she wanted.

It wasn't like being lifted up and flying exactly. It was more like a hot-air balloon ride—at least that's how Annie described it. A whoosh of warm air overhead (or maybe a whoosh of wings, she couldn't be sure) while below them the bustling village of Buffalo Grove gently, silently, fell away. It was like watching

Google Earth on the computer—the view widening as they rose, the rooftops growing smaller, the street layouts resembling the pattern on an Oriental rug, before Wingtip took their hands, waited for them to say they were ready and, together, they dipped toward the tilting world again.

It was night when they returned. Stars pinpricked a navy sky, so sharp they seemed like they were prickling Sarah's skin. A gathering of teenagers caroused on a wooded rise overlooking town. Against the dark sky, tree limbs stood outstretched like a catcher's glove, reaching to snag the ball of a moon.

Moonlight glanced off a row of car fenders. Somewhere down the line, a radio played. Johnny Rivers was singing "The Tracks of My Tears."

Sarah gasped. "This is the night it happened, isn't it?"

Why would anyone bring me here? Sarah rounded on them, her fists knotted at her sides. "I thought God wanted me to look at *my* life, not my mother's!"

Wingtip asked pointedly, "Isn't this the night your life began?"

Resentment burst forth in Sarah the way an ember bursts into flame. "This part certainly isn't important."

"Isn't it?" Annie asked. "She let it affect her entire life, and you have been doing the same thing."

"But it wasn't my decision, and I don't understand why I have had to pay for it. *I* didn't have anything to do with it." The bitterness shone in Sarah's eyes.

Then Sarah saw them. None of the other kids paid much mind to the couple necking beneath the tree. Intent on a kiss, the young woman braced her hand at the small of her back against the tree trunk, even while the young man angled her spine against the rough bark. They were only silhouettes, these two who had slunk beyond the far shadows so no one would see. His head lowered, her gaze lifted, and who knew if the whispers came from the rustling leaves or the promises he made as he told her he would always love her. Who knew?

A flash of white collar and the thin bow at her neck where she'd folded and refolded it to look perfect with his letter sweater. A glimmer of leather where her finger hooked his belt loop, something to hang on to.

The radio played in the distance. The song changed, and somebody whistled along to the words of Frankie Valli's "Can't Take My Eyes Off You." Sarah stood with her fists clenched, indignant, wondering what God intended to do, watching her mother let herself be coaxed out of sight over the ridge, Jane's wrist clasped in his hand. She didn't try to wrest it away, her black-and-white saddle shoes taking unsteady tiptoe steps in the grass.

Even in her anger, Sarah stumbled forward, trying to follow them. "Mama," she shouted. "Don't!" But Jane didn't hear. Sarah gripped her grandmother's arm. "Annie, you've got to make her stop it. We don't have to let her do this."

"Oh yes. We do. We do have to let her do this. She made the choice long ago."

"Annie, *please*." Because this cut through her bitterness, it was all she could figure out. "Don't you think that's why God sent us here? To change things for her?"

"God didn't send you here to change things, child. He sent you here so you'd ask him to help change things that you can't. The things that happened can't be changed, but you can change, and so could Jane if she wanted to."

Tears welled in Sarah's eyes.

"One mistake does not have to rule a person's entire life. Jane is stuck in a moment of time, and she has let it ruin her life, but you don't have to make the same mistake."

"Please." She spun around, gripped the cuffs of Annie's short sleeves. "*Please.*"

"Think about it." Her grandmother brushed hair from her eyes, then gravely rubbed one of Sarah's dark ringlets between her fingers, twisting it like an old telephone cord. "Child, God always works good things out of our mistakes if we let him. If your mother wouldn't have gotten pregnant, then *you* wouldn't be here."

Sarah balled her hands into angry fists. "What difference would that make, Annie? Wouldn't Mama have been better off? She hinted all the time at how different her life would have been if I'd never been born."

And Annie said, "Your mother didn't have to spend her life mad, but she chose to do it. She made a wrong choice in a moment of passion, and she spent her life blaming others for the results."

Hearing it in her grandmother's words, Sarah finally began to understand it wasn't her fault.

"Even now she is still trying to get someone to pay her back for the bad things that happened in her life, but only God can do that."

Jane Cattalo wasn't the most popular girl in school or even much of a looker in her adolescent and teenage years. She was just a nondescript bobby-soxer who played the French horn in the high-school band, without a glittering personality, everyone agreed, and with a nose a little too wide for the rest of her face. "She might have been sort of cute," one of the parents noted from the third row in the meeting hall that night, "if she ever stopped being so sour."

Still, thanks to her persistence and being a senior, she was elected drum majorette that year. Everyone knew she'd been working on a miniskirt and matching hooded cape—a Butterick pattern, double-breasted with those big brass-plated buttons and yards of facing—for her 4-H clothing-construction project. This was the arena where she would earn her distinction; everybody knew it. The detailing on the cape alone would earn grand-prize rosettes at the fair.

Everyone knew Ronny Lee Perkins had given Jane his letter jacket for a while that summer. And after a couple of months, after football season had started, he'd taken it back, which surprised no one. First, everyone knew Ronny Lee had to go to college so he wouldn't get drafted. Second, for a boy like Ronny Lee Perkins, something more interesting would always be coming along.

Jane's Latin teacher, Mr. Gregg, was first to call everyone's attention to the problem. During the "public discussion" portion of the School District 11 Board of Education meeting (so full that Sarah and Annie found it difficult to peer through the crowd when Wingtip led them in; even angels can end up in the rear when it's standing room only), the teacher rose from his chair, walked toward the microphone when called upon, and asked, "Mr. Chairman. I wonder if we could discuss the situation I mentioned to Principal Steed in his office last week?"

Around the table, the board members frowned. They didn't know the situation to which he referred. The chairman of the board asked, "You spoke with Dr. Steed about a matter? Can you tell us what this is?"

When Mr. Gregg announced the young lady's name, it rang out like it had been broadcast over a bullhorn. "Jane Cattalo, sir."

At the mention of Jane's name, a woman in the fourth row sat a little straighter. Sarah felt Annie tense up next to her.

"Is that you?" Sarah asked. "Were you present at this meeting?"

"Yes," her grandmother answered. "I'm sorry to say I was. That's me sitting right there."

They were still talking in the boardroom. The chairman asked, "And you've already spoken to Dr. Steed about it?", bringing them back to the matter at hand.

"Graham Steed seems to want to ignore the situation."

"I do not!" The high-school principal leaped from his seat as if a lightning bolt had struck him. "It is a sensitive issue, Gregg, and you know it. We should have discussed this privately, but now you have *trounced* on my authority by introducing it in front of the entire town."

The board chairman jutted a chin toward the Latin teacher. "And how do you know that much about Miss Cattalo?"

"She's in my fourth-period class, sir."

Jane Cattalo was one of those stay-at-home girls who you didn't think about much. She'd gotten brave enough to try out for the senior play, *South Pacific*, and although she wasn't the type to play Nellie, her reasonable singing voice had gotten her a part in the chorus. She certainly wouldn't be one to sample illicit drugs or to be drawn in by The Beatles or to say something objectionable about the boys in Vietnam. Which is why you could have heard a gnat come in for a landing right before the teacher remarked, "She has flaunted it in front of us, sir, and until now, we haven't noticed."

"Excuse me, but where is this girl? What is she flaunting?"

At the back of the room, Annie touched her granddaughter's arm.

"It's me, isn't it?" Sarah whispered. "She's trying to hide that I'm on the way."

Annie hugged Sarah. "I'm afraid so."

The horrible man hemmed and hawed, apparently trying to figure out how to state such delicate facts in mixed company. "Jane Cattalo's barely seventeen years of age and..."

A few people just stared at him.

"She's, well you know, she's...I don't know how to say it in front of the women, sir."

But the women were starting to get the idea. The room erupted in gasps of disbelief and indignant humphs and murmured conversations.

"Well, perhaps you shouldn't have brought it up at *all*."

The woman in the fourth row, Annie when she was the mother of a high-school-aged daughter, rose from her chair. "Whatever you have to say about my daughter, you had better stop hinting at rumors and innuendos. If you have something to say, come right out and say it!"

"All right, I will. Are you her mother? You ought to take blame for this too." At last the man found the words he'd been searching for. "How could you even show your face in town with a daughter who's in the family way?"

A great deal of time passed before the hoopla died down and either the school-board chairman or the superintendent of schools could get a word in edgewise. Everyone in the hall seemed to have an opinion needing to be expressed. Finally, when he could be heard, the superintendent tried to take charge of his own meeting.

Mr. Graham Steed, who had not even discussed this subject with his wife, who had not even decided how he would present the idea in front of a small group of male colleagues, let alone a roomful of people, felt the tips of his ears go pink as a turnip.

What regrettable luck that any of them should find themselves in this position, having to report this delicate matter.

But no reliable public educator could let a girl in Jane's condition go unnoticed. How might something like this affect the well-being of other young ladies in the classroom? After all, a thing like this was almost unheard of and quite shocking.

And the entire time Mr. Gregg was talking about the young woman and the situation at hand, Sarah Harper, formerly Sarah Cattalo, stood with her fingers resting lightly on the stackable chair in front of her, her stomach twisting in anguish, all the resentment she felt toward Jane coupling with the helpless realization that she hadn't been the only person censuring her mother. Sarah felt sympathy for her mother for the first time as she realized how embarrassing this must have been for her.

The whole lot of them criticized Jane as if no one else in the meeting hall had ever gone astray or done anything wrong. How easy it can be to forget your own mistakes when you're busy pointing a finger at someone else. Sarah stood by, powerless, as she watched her mother accused, tried, found guilty, and rejected before the entire town.

"How do I know this information for sure, Mr. Gregg?" the chairman asked.

The instructor gave a righteous chuckle. "If you take a close look, it is becoming quite evident and more so as each day goes by."

Mr. Gregg's voice grew shrill as he recounted the story. The girl had risen from her seat, he said, and he couldn't help but wonder at her bulging silhouette as she'd worked the pencil sharpener. Just as he'd managed to convince himself this was no business of his—he must be imagining things, she'd dropped her pencil. As she stooped to retrieve it, her blouse hiked above the waistband of her skirt. Before she could tug it down again, Mr. Gregg had seen the safety pin holding her skirt closed. The skirt had a button—he'd noted that too—so it wasn't a case of laziness with needle and thread. The garment couldn't stretch much farther. Its seams were ready to pop. The waistband alone was a good inch-and-a-half, two inches too small. Jane Cattalo was pregnant as all get out, and doing a masterful job of hiding it. And only three months before graduation to boot!

At the back of the room, Sarah gripped Annie's hand. Sarah whispered, "Did you know the truth about Mama before this announcement?"

"I'd been wondering," Annie said. "You know how it is when you have children. A mother sometimes just senses things. I think I suspected, but I didn't want to admit it to myself."

"I can't believe they just...attacked her this way, Annie."

"I was as shocked as everyone else to have it brought to light in such a public way."

"It must have been awful. For both of you."

"I didn't want to think she would hide something so important from me."

Sarah asked, "Even then, she was cutting people out of her life, wasn't she?"

"I did everything to let her know that I'd be there to help, that even though she'd made a mistake, it didn't change the way I felt about her," Annie admitted. "But Jane's disappointment, shame, and bitterness prevented her from being comforted in any way."

"Oh, Annie."

In the boardroom, the tension had grown thick. "Well, I believe we have some decisions to make, then, don't we?" asked the chairman. Board members leaned across each other's elbows and exchanged opinions. One by one they came up nodding, and the consensus was taken.

If Sarah had heard the story once from her mother, she'd heard it dozens of times. Stripped of her title as drum majorette. No longer allowed to enter the 4-H competition with her handiwork. No longer able to stand onstage and sing in *South Pacific* because "What sort of message would *that* convey?" No matter how hard she'd tried, Jane couldn't hide a baby coming. When her belly began to swell, they'd made her drop out of everything.

Who was the father of the baby? Neither the school superintendent nor the rows of concerned parents nor the teachers thought it important to name him. Who had done this to her? No one thought to ask.

Although, of course, some names would get tossed about. There would be speculation. Rumors. The students would talk. But eventually some new tidbit, some other scandal would come along, some other girl's reputation to defame, and the gossip would fade away. And Jane Cattalo would never tell.

⟶ Chapter Fifteen ⟵

Plenty of youngsters visited the friendly confines of Wrigley Field, scrambling over tiers of bench seats, shoving and climbing to find the best view of the ballpark, and Wingtip didn't pay much attention to any of them. But this one blond kid with the claw, who kept jerking his dad's sleeve and peering in every direction, who kept his little hand flat against the metal bench in spite of guys five times his size trying to convince him otherwise, well, Wingtip could spot a courageous young soul when he saw one.

Wingtip honored God. He'd served in the ranks and would be serving for all of eternity. The Heavenly Father had different assignments for each of his servants, and when Wingtip knew his he didn't hesitate. He marched forward like a revolutionary soldier ready to go anywhere, anytime, and do anything the Father asked of him.

The Father had given him the address in a brisk, no-nonsense matter: 1060 West Addison Street, Chicago, Illinois. "The corner of Clark and Addison," he'd added.

"Will I know it when I see it?"

"Oh," God had assured him. "You will."

And when Wingtip found himself at the entrance to Wrigley, he couldn't believe what God had done! Here again was proof that the Father took a deep desire and, with it laid before him as an offering, used it to fulfill his good plan. Astonishing! Astounding! The Master and Lord over all creation remembered how much Wingtip had loved the Cubs and baseball in general and had chosen him to defend, protect, and watch over the Cubbies! That day, as Wingtip had shored up his shoulders and stepped through the cement portico, he felt awed God had trusted him with such a weighty responsibility.

Not every lineup was granted a team angel. Ah, but the Cubs! The Lovable Losers. The team with the long-suffering fans. It had been a long, long, long time since anything good had happened for them. Every time they made a run at the pennant, these guys couldn't quite make it happen. They gave it all they had to give, carrying all the past failures and all the past successes and the expectations of four generations to the ballpark; they were just a bunch of kids trying to take it one game at a time. They hadn't won a series for a hundred years.

Which could be quite a challenge for a member of the heavenly realm, if you stopped to think about it.

Not until Wingtip had noticed Mitchell in the bleachers, not until that boy's innocent hope had tugged his heart harder than the rope tugged his arm when he strung up the flags, did Wingtip start to think that, perhaps, the Heavenly Father might be using him for something more as well.

Wingtip had braced his elbow on the ledge and peered over the crowd, doing his best to keep Mitchell in view. Wingtip was so intrigued with him that if someone hadn't hollered, "Top game! National League! Two runs in the seventh!" he might have missed posting the score altogether. Tenderness for this child chose Wingtip instead of the other way around. As he knelt for conversation with the Heavenly Father that night, Wingtip said, "Well, Lord. I guess you expect me to do something about that kid."

"Ah." The Father hadn't seemed surprised in the least. "So you noticed Mitchell Harper."

"I did. And I think he noticed me too."

"Good job at that."

"Thank you."

"I want you to take care of him, Wingtip."

"I will."

"More than that, I want you to care for Mitchell's family."

"You know, Lord, I am always ready to do whatever you want me to do."

"Yes, but this job might be more of a challenge than the Cubs."

"Nothing could be more of a challenge than that, Lord."

Which evoked a hearty laugh from the Heavenly Father, the Creator of heaven and earth, the Creator of laughter, the Creator of humor itself. After which he said, "Oh, I don't know about that." Even now, Wingtip could still remember how the Heavenly Father had smiled.

"I don't want to see anything else. Please," Sarah begged. The glaring lights of the meeting hall faded and in its place appeared a small, dark, melancholy house. How they traveled so quickly from the boardroom so jammed with people to this other place so forlorn and empty, Sarah had no idea. "I feel like I'm in a rendition of *The Christmas Carol*," she said.

Wingtip shrugged. "Hey, it worked for Charles Dickens, didn't it?" Which couldn't help but endear Wingtip to Sarah even more. It felt so nice that God and his angels had a sense of humor.

The angel went to the door and opened it. The door hinges creaked as if they hadn't been oiled in years. Wingtip stood aside with his hand on the knob and gestured for Sarah and Annie to enter.

Inside the front room, an older Jane twisted sideways to inspect her waistline in a cloudy mirror. She scrutinized the belt around her middle and frowned with distaste. She stood taller, sucked in her stomach, jutted her bosom forward, and, yanking with the same single-mindedness as someone tightening a saddle around a horse's girth, successfully cinched the belt one notch tighter. She smoothed the front of her dress with both hands, turned sideways to examine her midriff in the mirror again, and raised her chin higher.

A child, a little girl with dark curly hair and hazel eyes, no more than six years old, came bounding in with a fistful of dandelions, some with dirt still clinging to the roots. "I picked you a bouquet, Mama," came the child's voice, innocent as a chirping sparrow.

Sarah gasped as realization flooded her. With one arm, Annie drew her close, holding her steady. "It's *me*."

"Don't touch!" Jane swatted the child away and did a little dance step to keep from brushing against those filthy little hands. "Take those right back outside where you got them. You'll get my dress all dirty."

"That's *me*," Sarah said again, as if to convince herself as much as anyone.

"For heaven's sake, Sarah, they're just *dandelions*. Go wash up and let's get out of here."

"Dandy lions," the little girl repeated. "They're so pretty, Mama. I could get a jar for them."

But Jane was busy gathering up her car keys and looping her purse over her arm. "Pitch those nasty things out and get in the car. I'd get to work on time if I didn't have to drop you by the babysitter's. I swear, Sarah, you're so much trouble."

And because a girl believes what she hears about herself, because a child at that age takes her mother's messages into her heart as truth, the little girl stood still and thought, *I am. I'm certainly a lot of trouble.*

"You'll be at the babysitter's late tonight." Jane checked her reflection in the mirror. With her pinkie fingernail, she scratched a speck of lipstick from the corner of her mouth. "I have a date."

This was exciting news. The little girl bounced with excitement. "Is he taking you out on the town, Mama?" She touched her mother's skirt, loved the smell of her, loved the way her hair caught the light in colors of September. "Are you going someplace special? Are you wearing a fancy dress?"

Jane stepped away from the child's hands once more. "No. None of that. I'm cooking him a nice dinner at our house."

"Our house?"

"Yes."

This took some consideration. "If it's at our house, why do I have to stay at the babysitter's? Why can't I come too?"

"You? Come too? Of course you can't. Then it wouldn't be a

date. Besides, no guy would be interested in me if he knew about you."

And the little girl thought, *Mama would be better off without me.*

"Now, hurry up and get in the car. When we get to the sitter's, you have to hop on out and march right on up to the front door by yourself because I can't have you holding me up."

As the child meandered her way down the walk with her head hanging and her fists rammed so hard inside her skirt pockets that she'd probably rip the seams, purposefully scuffing the toes of her Buster Brown shoes against the sidewalk ("What did you *do*?" her mama would shout, but it didn't matter—she didn't care), it was the second time that grown-up Sarah wrenched herself away from her grandmother's arm and tried to follow. The child's knobby elbows jutted sideways, her arms thin as kindling sticks.

"Can't I do something to make her hear me, Annie? I've got so many things I need to say."

"If she *could* hear you, what would you say to her?"

"That she isn't responsible for how unhappy her mother feels. That it isn't fair. She's just a little girl."

Sarah stared at her unlikely angel, who had changed numbers in Wrigley by hand ever since the scoreboard had been built. He'd been a huge Cubs fan all the way back to 1908 when they still played at West Side Grounds, the last time Chicago took the series. A hundred years and counting and he'd seen every sacrifice fly, every tag at the plate, every grand slam. And once he'd gotten appointed to the job at Wrigley, he'd accounted on that board for every run batted in since.

"Don't you see?" he asked. "That's what Annie was always

praying for—that you would know it wasn't your fault. That little girl is listening, only she's inside your grown-up body now. You can still tell her what God the Father would like her to hear, that she is valuable and loved. You can still tell her that she isn't responsible for her mother's misery and that she was created in her mother's womb by the hand of God, who created her carefully and who made her very special."

As they watched the child head to the car across the trodden grass, the ancient Oldsmobile loomed tugboat-large in the driveway.

For goodness' sake, Sarah thought, *that car looks bigger than the ship they raised the bridge for this morning in Chicago!* The little girl tried to open the door but, at the age of six, her thumb was much too small to manage the button on the massive chrome handle. She pressed it with both hands and still couldn't get it. The third time, she bit her tongue in concentration. She pushed so hard that she twisted sideways and her feet lifted off the ground.

Here came her mother tramping down the walk, her slingback pumps making little snaps of displeasure on the cement.

"I left the flowers for you in the grass, Mama. You told me to do that, and I did it."

"Why aren't you in the car yet?" Jane looked like she was about to cry. "Why don't you ever do what I tell you to do? Can't you ever do anything right?"

"I can't open it. It's big. It's more than a little girl can do."

The mother punched the button, yanked open the Oldsmobile door ("Nothing to it!"), and pointed inside. When the child hung her head in disgrace, the bone at the nape of her neck protruded like a drawer knob.

"Come *on*. What are you waiting for? Get *in*."

I'll never be good for anything, will I?

The three travelers watched those words hammer their message ever deeper into the little girl's open, innocent heart.

I can't do anything right. No matter how I try, I'm always going to be worth less than everyone else. If I hadn't been born, Mama's life would have been so much better.

When the car bounced out of the driveway and sped off in ripples of chrome, grown-up Sarah, the Sarah who had watched a child's yearning face as it slipped away behind the window, was the one who began to cry.

ᴖᴑ Chapter Sixteen ᴑᴖ

The divers thought it was time to give up, Joe could tell. He could see it in the weary arcs of their arms as they stroked toward the platform, in their plodding climb as they mounted the ladder from the river, in the way their colleagues grabbed them beneath the armpits and hoisted them up, water falling from their sleek bodies like splinters of glass. The uniformed officers, Chicago's Finest, thought so too. Some forty-five minutes into the search, Joe could see it in the way they pressed their radio mikes tight against their lips, fingers cupping their noses as they squeezed the Talk bar, their voices low and their eyes on him as they spoke.

Joe could see it in the rusty crane that stood at the rain-streaked waterfront motionless, its pulleys, cables, and hook dangling at half-mast.

He could see it in the medics' crossed arms and extended legs, the way they talked among themselves with their heads turned sideways. He could see it in the whirling lights atop the city vehicles. Even the pulsing red-and-blue seemed to have slowed down.

Nearby, out of the corner of his eye, he even noticed Pete glancing at his watch. He saw Gail grab the cuff of his best friend's sleeve and yank it down. Pete lowered his wrist.

Across the way where troopers had cordoned off the street, the yellow tape—Police Line. Do Not Cross—hung in sodden ribbons.

"It's okay, Gail," Joe said without turning. "I know how long it's been." He speared his hands through wet hair. Joe couldn't even feel the rain running down his collar anymore.

Joe didn't know what he would have done without them. Gail and Pete had made it to his side in record time. They'd fended off reporters. They'd done their best to answer questions from the police, and when they didn't know the answers, they relayed only the most pressing questions to Joe. Before she even arrived, Gail was the one who phoned Sarah's parents and suggested they pick Mitchell up from school. Pete had kept his rope-of-an-arm snaked behind Joe's shoulders and held him upright. Joe leaned on his best friend, too empty and shocked to speak, his only thought to overcome the dark dizziness that told him he might pass out.

All this time, all this searching, and Joe felt like he was the one drowning.

"Your nanny's number? Do you have it, Joe?" Gail asked. "I think I ought to call again."

Joe shook his head dumbly. He couldn't think of it. Not only the number—he couldn't even think of the woman's *name*. "They're going to stop, aren't they?" he asked. "Any minute now they're going to call off the search."

Pete clenched his friend tightly around the shoulders. "Man, Joe. I'm sorry. This is tough stuff."

For some brain-misfiring reason, while Joe couldn't remember the nanny's name, the date of Gail's party popped into his mind. He sat down hard on a concrete barrier. "It's your birthday, isn't it?"

"I'm calling Sarah's mother again too," Gail said, ignoring him.

"You should do that," Pete said. "They should pick up Kate. The family ought to be together."

"Pavik," Joe blurted as if he'd figured out the *Jeopardy* question just before time ran out. "Her name's Pavik. That's it."

"Let me have your cell phone again," Gail said. "I'll just scroll down to her name."

Joe couldn't stop shuddering. He could hardly make his lips move. He fished in his pocket for his phone.

A shrill signal echoed across the river. What looked like two buoys bobbing in the waves changed into two straggling divers. One waved, his arm raised high overhead.

The other folded his fingers against his teeth and whistled again.

Along the shore, men jumped into action. The crackle of two-way radios seemed to meld into one seamless strand of sound. "They've got something," Joe heard the officer beside him say.

Not until Joe rose did he hear the shriek of sirens again. He realized they'd never been turned off; the wail had simply drifted above him somewhere until it had become so common that it disappeared. Nothing moved in slow-mo anymore. Divers were donning air tanks and racing into the water everywhere.

The crane lurched forward, its pulleys swaying. An EMT notified ER they might have located a victim, they might be coming in, to be on standby. Patrol boats revved from trolling speed to full throttle. From crackling radios, snippets drifted into earshot.

...settled on its...

...no apparent way to...

...dislodged at impact...

Joe staggered toward the closest medic and gripped his arm. "They've found the car, haven't they? That's what they've got. The car. And she'll be in it."

A vise-grip claimed his shoulder. The hand belonged to Pete. "Come on, Joe. Stick with me. Let them do their job."

"That's my wife down there. You've got to help her." But Joe only said it by rote. He said it because he'd been repeating those words like a broken record for three quarters of an hour.

"We're doing everything we can, sir."

Gail anchored her arm around Joe for support, and he let his friends propel him aside. These two had become his lifeline. "Thank you. I don't know what I'd do without you being here. I wouldn't have anyone." And it was true. He would have been alone. His own parents would take hours to get here from Wisconsin. At least he had Harold and Jane to be with the kids.

"You want to know one of the last things I said to her?" Joe said. "I kept complaining to her about her job. I kept finding things she was doing wrong, especially with the kids. I kept telling her and telling her. She was furious with me. She said I didn't see how hard she was *trying.*"

The question hung in the air between them. Maybe Pete took a second too long to say, "Joe. You can't think this is your fault."

"If I hadn't upset her, she might have been driving more carefully. It *is* my fault!"

"No." Pete stood his ground. "This is absolutely not your fault. When it's all over you'll sort it out—" Pete stopped abruptly. He'd been about to say "*together.* You'll sort it out *together.*"

The crane began its task. The gigantic hook ranged out over the water. It reflected in the river, two steel *J*s, one upside down and one right side up, as Joe's throat tightened with dread. "They're just raising the car. Why are they doing that? Why aren't they bringing her up first?"

The man with the Patterson badge, the one introduced as chaplain, started toward Joe. Another officer fell in beside him, their steps synchronized, their movements choreographed with purpose.

Run, Joe told himself. *If you aren't here for them to tell you, then it can't be real.*

But his feet stayed glued to the spot. "You know what's going to happen, don't you?" He gripped Pete's shirtfront. "I've lost her." *I lost her a long time ago*, he thought, only he wouldn't say that.

Something between them had always been missing; he'd tried for years to put his finger on it. Even after they dated, even after they fell in love, he realized there was always something about her that she kept aloof from him.

But was that all it was? Really? It almost seemed she'd been looking for ways to hide her true self from him. To put up barriers between them. Walls to hide behind. She behaved as if she had a dark secret, something she didn't want anyone to know about the real her. Even him. *Especially* him.

And now there'd never be any chance to make it right. Maybe there never had been. "It's taking too long, Pete. You know what they've found."

Not until the officers approached, not until they began to speak and shake their heads in somber confusion, did Joe realize he'd been mistaken. There was the chaplain, of course, and the badge said the other man's name was Hamm. Together, each of them starting where the other left off, they went to great lengths to describe the position of the vehicle. Located forty-three feet below the surface. Front end demolished from colliding with the water. Vehicle resting on its right side. Nothing unusual there.

Patterson crossed himself.

Hamm probed the crevice between his gums and one of his tricuspids with a frayed toothpick. "I'm afraid they found a car but not a body."

All Joe would remember later was the round slowness of the guy's mouth as he pocketed the worn toothpick and tried to explain.

But there wasn't any explanation for it. Although the front end had been mangled, none of the windows had been broken out. They'd found the driver's seat belt fastened.

But the SUV had come up empty.

Sarah Harper wasn't there.

Chapter Seventeen

We're no longer visiting the past," Wingtip warned them as they entered the tiny apartment. "This time, we are visiting the present."

Sarah recognized the place the moment she, Annie, and Wingtip entered. When she and Joe had first gone to inspect this place, they'd found it adequate, although not much larger than a sardine can. "Do you think she has room to turn around in here?" Joe had whispered.

"She's slender," Sarah had quipped. "Let's make sure she doesn't gain weight. Otherwise there won't be room for the baby."

The visit had been a planned inspection arranged by the nanny service at Sarah's request. And although the two-room box appeared undersized, they'd been impressed by the condition of the quarters. The linoleum floor was so clean you could almost skate on it. Although the faucet and the tub looked to be more than fifty years old, the pink tile, the grout, and the chrome looked brand-new. It must have taken hours to clean with a toothbrush.

Sarah remembered Joe shrugging. "Never mind the size of the place. I'm impressed."

"I don't know," Sarah had said. "If she wants to do this as a profession, her surroundings ought to be more important to her. She ought to spend enough to have some sort of play yard." Even though Kate couldn't roll over in her crib yet.

"But isn't she spending most of her time with Kate at our house? And this is right by the park. Plenty of good places here for strollering."

"I want this woman to be willing to bring Kate back and forth. You know I have plenty of days when I bring work home. I can't have a nanny and a baby distracting me."

"Maybe this is all she can afford."

"I doubt it. She's single and hardworking. If you ask me, I think she's a miser."

"Oh?" Joe's eyebrows rose.

"And these surroundings are important because Kate will be spending a lot of time here." Not until Sarah read her ominous prediction reflected in her husband's disapproving eyes did she realize the significance of what she'd said.

If anything appeared out of keeping in this minuscule set of rooms today, it was Annie standing smack-dab in the middle of them wearing her polka-dotted dress and platform peep-toe pumps, with her hair pinned forward in *I Love Lucy* style. Annie's shoes resembled those in the fall display of cute new styles Sarah had noticed the last time she'd darted past Macy's windows.

When Annie poked her head into the bathroom, she gasped in awe. "Oh, I just love this pink! I've always thought pink tile would be the perfect thing for a bathroom counter and a dressing table. I would have installed it in the house right after Jane moved away, but Gordy and I never had money to remodel."

"Grandmother!" Sarah said in great earnestness. "That pink

tile is so bad that it never came back. No one has tried to resurrect that stuff since the 1950s."

The only things out of place in the spick-and-span little kitchen were a high chair, a Tommee Tippee cup, a bowl of baby cereal, and an infant-sized spoon.

Sarah did the same thing she did at home when she felt out of place and uneasy. She stoppered the sink, squirted soap in a pattern vaguely resembling a scribble, and began to rinse off the mess.

"You can't do that." Wingtip lifted his chin, and their glances caught. "She's here."

"Mrs. Pavik's here?" Sarah set the cereal bowl upside down in the dish drainer. One glistening bubble slid down its side and popped. "But she shouldn't be. It's the middle of the day, and she—"

"Not any day," he reminded her. "It's the middle of *today*."

Sarah froze. *The day I'm gone.*

Wingtip made a wide berth around her as if he thought she might slosh suds on him in retaliation. "Guess it wouldn't do her much good to walk in here and think there's an angel doing her dishes."

"Truth is, Sarah, she's so upset right now, she'd think she'd done them herself. She wouldn't even remember."

"She's upset?" Sarah asked. "*She's* upset?" Her arms had gone stiff in the sink. This was different from visiting her past and reliving her mother's blame laid at her feet. It was different from seeing Annie skinning apples over her curvaceous stove or remembering how impossible it had been, trying to tug open that old car door when she was in first grade.

Hadn't she been a great sport up until now with all this traveling? Wingtip couldn't expect so much from her! This journey started out differently because today was...well, it was *today*. This was the morning she untangled herself from the blankets with Kate whimpering in the other room like an abandoned kitten and an empty, lonesome cavern on the other side of the bed where her husband should have been. This was the morning she finally understood that the man who had once loved her wanted more from her than she could ever give.

The thought flashed hot through her before it sprang beyond her grasp, that flicker of astonishment you get when you touch the truth: life will go on *just like this*; everybody will do everything just the same way; nothing will stop; everyone else will be too busy to remember this day for very long. The world will belong to everyone else, you realize, and *you won't exist there anymore*.

"You can't expect me to do this," she argued, feeling like she was trying to outrun some old, nagging fear. "I can't go around looking at my life now that I'm no longer in it."

"You can't afford *not* to, Sarah."

Sarah hadn't known Wingtip all that long. Still, she had never heard him speak with such gravity. Misgiving beat inside her chest like a moth captured under glass. "Wingtip, why are you doing this, really? I've read the story before. Is this like you're the angel of my past and present? I suppose you're going to make me look at my future too." Sarah knew this much: looking at the past and the future could never be as bad as looking at her life the moment she stepped out of it.

"There are plenty of things I could show you, Sarah. I could show you the schnauzer still waiting for you to come home."

And she pictured the dog, waiting where he wasn't supposed to be, curled up for a nap in a nest of her lingerie.

"I could show you the times Joe's called your house just to hear the answering machine, to listen to your voice again."

And she pictured that too as her stomach clenched with sorrow, seeing how grief dulled his eyes like rain dulled the fog-bound sky.

"But I happen to think what I'm going to show you here today is far more important."

"What? What could be more important than how much everybody misses me?"

"I want you to figure it out." He stepped aside. "All your life, you've wanted to be happy. Maybe this is the day you will finally learn how."

Behind him postcards plastered the refrigerator almost to the floor. Had the pictures been there when she and Joe inspected Mrs. Pavik's little home? For if they had, how could Sarah have missed them? How could she have combed over the premises in search of incriminating stains or insects or mold or mouse droppings and never noticed this display?

The pictures must have all been of the same eastern European village; it had to be somewhere in Poland. Some showed a street zigzagging up a hill, its cobbles bleached white by the sun, a domed cathedral, a house with a thatched roof, a close-up of a goat drinking Coca-Cola from a sea-green bottle. There were market scenes and an aerial shot of a lake and a beautiful picture of a girl with ribbons braided through her hair. But the cards that caught Sarah's attention were the ones that hung the other way around, the ones with messages showing.

Sarah couldn't translate any of them from Polish, but she could tell they'd been written in a child's painstaking hand. Each had been signed with the same name. *Elena.*

Sarah scrolled down with her finger. "The same person wrote all of these. Every single one." By the time she reached the bottom of the fridge, several notes proudly included some cryptic, primitive English.

HI MOMI, ELENA.

I LOVE YOU, ELENA.

WILL YOU COME GET MI? ELENA.

Sarah thought, *Mrs. Pavik has a small daughter? How old is she?* She must have lived a hard life. Sarah had always thought she was an older woman. Spotty ink on the foreign stamps made the postmark dates indecipherable. Sarah thought the numbered day came first, the month second, in European style.

Baby Kate's belongings, the extra car seat, one of an enormous tribe of stuffed bears, the foldable stroller—the very best money could buy, everything the Harpers had stockpiled to equip their infant daughter, waited in a row by the front door, each with its "How's my nanny doing? www.nannyrating.com" sticker affixed.

"You remind me of the KGB with your computer," Mrs. Pavik had huffed the last time Sarah spoke to her about the Web site.

Someone had sent an e-mail post about how the nanny tied Kate's shoelaces too tight. Only one problem, Sarah realized later, after she'd complained to Mrs. Pavik about it. The nanny-rating post had been submitted on an afternoon when Sarah herself had tied Kate's sneakers at the play yard. And still, she'd felt too awkward to apologize.

"I will let Kate climb backward up the slide. I will let Kate swim in Buckingham Fountain. Someone will send you a message about that. You want to bug my phones too?" Mrs. Pavik asked in her histrionic manner. "This is not what I have always been told about America."

And suddenly Sarah understood. Sarah would always remind Mrs. Pavik of the wall between herself and her young daughter, half a world away. If Mrs. Pavik ever dared let Sarah see past her melodramatic behavior, she risked revealing that she too had made a desperate, painful choice.

Mrs. Pavik sat in the other room now, jamming the phone against her ear, her face crimson with determination. When Elena's voice sounded, her fingers relaxed on the receiver, her eyes flooded with light.

"Mrs. Pavik is having a hard time today," Wingtip translated. "She's just been called about what happened to you at the bridge. You know how sad things like this can magnify the distance that already exists between two people."

Somewhere across the world, Mrs. Pavik's daughter yearned for her mother to send for her. Money had to be made for Elena to go to school and have what she needed, but most important, money had to be made for Elena's medical expenses. Good, solid American dollars, not zlotys. Elena had been born with a heart condition that required expensive medicine and regular doctor visits. And what Mrs. Pavik longed to do most for her own child, she took pay to do for Kate instead. It broke her heart, but if she wanted Elena to live she had to have the money for her care.

The Father had shown Sarah she'd never been responsible for her mother's unhappiness, but she had always taken the blame for it. Now he was showing her that she'd been so focused on redeeming herself that she'd missed really looking at others—she'd missed a great deal about the people in her life.

"I wanted to know if she had experience handling babies," Sarah said. "She gave me references, other nanny positions here in Chicago. I spoke with one family in Lincoln Park. No one ever told me anything about this. Someone should have found out about it and tried to help her."

Annie said, "It's more blessed to give than to receive, but very few people get around to doing it."

Wingtip said, "Everyone else has been busy just like you have, Sarah. No one's ever bothered to ask Mrs. Pavik anything about her life."

◦⤳

Before today Sarah had been in Tom Roscoe's office only when he invited her. She'd entered only when Rona glanced up from her computer screen, gestured, and said, "He's expecting you." To end up in Tom's office this way, when only she and Annie and Wingtip could see him, and he couldn't see them, made Sarah's heart pound with fear.

"Do we have to do this?" she whispered. "This isn't my place."

"All of it is your place," Wingtip said. "It was your life."

Tom sat in his office chair, swiveled away from his desk. He sat staring at the droplets rolling down the pane, at the vapor smudging the windows. No matter how hard he looked, he couldn't see the street below. "Rona!" he said into the intercom. "Rona!" Still no answer. "Where is she? *Rona?* Where is everybody? All I want is the midday futures prices."

He rocked forward in the chair and stood. "The world still goes on. The trading floor is still open." He stared at the pelting rain, as if it might give him some answer. He stood for a long time, peering down, his expression granite hard. "All we've lost is one employee, not the whole company."

When his phone rang, he grabbed it like a fish he'd banked, something that might get away. He banged it against his ear and winced. "Tom Roscoe here." Then, "Oh. Maribeth." He turned to stare out the window again.

Sarah didn't want to hear what Tom had to say to his wife. She whispered to Wingtip. "Can't we go now? This isn't something I need to be a part of."

"Shhhh," Annie said into her hair. Then, over Sarah's head to their guide, who was a kind man but who kept taking them to places that were harder and harder for her to see, "Wingtip, is it necessary that she see all of this too? She's shaking like a leaf."

"Ah, why are you afraid, child?"

The feeling went too deep for her to put it into words for them. She was desperately trying to outrun the familiar, tormenting fright.

"There's nothing here that actually affects you."

"Yes there is," Sarah pleaded. "It's everything."

"Don't you see? The Father wants you to see how you *made* it everything, Sarah."

Sarah thought she couldn't bear it any longer. She remembered how powerless and worthless she felt most of the time. The pain of it was overwhelming. This had been the place where she knew she could prove her worth. The harder she'd worked, the more she'd found favor. Sarah was admired by peers, complimented, and promoted. The more she'd found favor, the better she'd felt about herself. She felt worthwhile when she accomplished something and was honored for it. As long as she stayed busy working and accomplishing, she felt good. But when she got quiet, when she was home attempting to be a wife and mother, the sickening feeling of shame and worthlessness returned to remind her that she should have never been born.

Panic seized Sarah's throat. "I'm sorry I prayed any prayer,

Wingtip. I'm sorry Annie prayed for me when I was a little girl. Please just let it stop."

"It's too late," he said, his eyes showing how much he cared about her. "There isn't anything I can do."

"I don't want anything to change. I just want to go back to the way things were. I want to go home, and I want to get back to my life."

But there was no possibility of that at all. Things had to change, and for her to go forward she had to deal with the past.

"It's okay," Wingtip said, encouraging her. "Look, Sarah, no matter how difficult it is, you must be courageous. The Heavenly Father wants you to see that things aren't always what they seem. He wants you to know the truth because the truth will make you free."

"I'm upstairs in my office, Maribeth," Roscoe was saying. "Would you please come up? Rona's not answering her intercom. It's like everyone's taken the day off for no good reason. You'll have to let yourself in."

Sarah didn't have any idea how long it took for the woman to find the elevator and ascend twenty-four luxurious floors to burst into her husband's cherry-paneled office.

The woman blurted the words the minute she rushed in the door. "Oh, Tom. Why don't you come home? It's just awful." That's as far as Maribeth moved. She didn't rush across the room and take her husband in her arms. She stood on her side of the office, and he stood on his, his silhouette dark against the massive clouded window that, when the weather was clear, enabled him to see out across his entire domain.

"I wish the weather would clear up," he said, crossing his arms. "I get tired of not being able to see anything on the street down there."

"You know how these early autumn storms are," she reminded him. "They stall over the lake for a few days and then they blow over and it's back to normal again."

"What is normal?" Tom asked with a deep sigh. "Is our life normal? Is it what it should be?" What could be normal when the financial world had turned upside down and no one could guess where the end would be?

Maribeth Roscoe dressed impeccably, in a red two-piece Armani suit and a necklace of gigantic pearls. Her hair had been recently coiffed and her makeup meticulously applied. She looked like she'd spent hours in a movie studio's wardrobe department just to look presentable to visit her husband. One could easily tell that she spent a lot of time and money making the best possible appearance.

Sarah remembered that Tom liked to say, "The way things look can make or break a deal." He made it clear to everyone that appearances were very important to him, and Sarah remembered soberly checking herself in the hallway mirror prior to each time she entered his office after being summoned. She remembered the fear she felt that he might find something to disapprove of, and she couldn't let that happen.

"Tom. I'm so sorry."

"What have you got to be sorry about?"

Her voice pitched a tone higher. "Wasn't Sarah Harper one of your best employees?"

He shook his head. "She was good, but they come and they go, Maribeth. It's always been that way. Someone else will come along that will be even better than she was. Until someone does, I'll take care of things myself, just like I have in the past."

One of the last pieces of Sarah's pride, boulderlike and pendulous, crashed loose and plummeted.

"I will have to get on top of things right away. Heaven only knows what's happening in the trading pits this morning. I could lose my shirt in one day in this company."

"Tom."

"I could lose everything I've worked for to pass down to my sons. I cannot believe Sarah was crazy enough to try to dart across a Chicago bridge after the barricade went down. Now her stupidity has put me in a position where I'm forced to take on an even heavier workload than I already have."

But I did that for you, *Tom!* Sarah wanted to cry out.

Someone spoke into her heart, the voice and its gentle nudge a sense of loving knowledge that didn't come from either Annie or Wingtip. It was a voice that went straight to the core of her heart, her heart alone. *No, you didn't, beloved. You did it for yourself.*

The dark, plush room started to spin. This was the place she'd been most exposed to the danger of failing, the place she'd carried all her pain, where she fought to succeed. She'd paid a high price for every positive word this man had ever spoken to her. She had worked hard for him; she had been loyal to the company and available whenever he needed her. She'd sacrificed everything, even time with her family, just to gain his approval—the approval every child needs, but she had never received growing up. Every raise and commendation he had bestowed upon her had gone toward filling that empty place in a child who had never understood where true love and approval came from.

A child who had never realized she had a heavenly Father she could take refuge in, who would never put her to shame. Her self-esteem needed to come from her Creator, who'd made her exactly how he wanted her to be. Anytime anyone had told her she wasn't worth much, Jesus, the one who had gone to the cross to show her what she was worth to him, had ached the same way she'd ached. His heart hurt along with hers because she'd been told lies and didn't know the truth. She didn't know that she was created in God's image and that he fashioned her in an amazing way. That she was unique, one of a kind, and precious in his sight.

Tom didn't take so much as a breath. He groused about how frustrated he was. He complained about how he'd felt sitting there with an important client while his employee missed such an important meeting. On his return to the corporate offices that bore his name, he grumbled, he'd passed some ruckus at the bridge without any inkling that the commotion might have anything to do with him. And when he'd arrived at his office and found out that it did, the thought never occurred to him that he ought to rush back there and see if he could help.

"You know what I'm thinking, don't you?" he asked his wife.

"Of course I do."

"That's good. I knew you would understand me."

"You're thinking you need to get down there. You're thinking you need to close up this office for the rest of the day and go support the family of someone who did a very good job for you."

He couldn't have looked more disappointed if he'd been a little boy and she'd just told him he couldn't keep a new puppy.

"I'm thinking this is the perfect opportunity for Jonas," Tom said. "This is the time for him to come forward and start his training. One day I plan for him to sit in this office and have his name on the door."

Maribeth visibly flinched. "Oh, Tom. That's what you want to do right now?"

"Think about the internship I've been offering him. Everything will be in disarray. He'll be able to step into the job without interviewing with five different panels and officer boards the way that poor kid Leo did."

"You ought to let this go, Tom. That isn't what he—"

"Isn't what he wants? Of course it's what he wants. He's just a kid; he doesn't know what he wants. If he was my intern, he could walk right into the trading pits and start making a name for himself on the first day, just like I did."

Very carefully Maribeth said, "I'm going to leave now, Tom. I can see you don't really need me for anything."

"And if Jonas would take the internship, Richard would see how it would be—"

Tom glanced up just as the door sighed shut on its heavy, expensive hinges. He was the only one in the room again. Or so he thought.

"Rona!" he shouted into the intercom. "Get my son on the phone, would you? Get Jonas. I don't care what you have to do. Just find him."

No answer.

"Hello? Rona?" He jiggled the button. "*Rona!*"

He rolled his eyes and sat down. Did he have to do everything around here himself? Outside, the clouds seemed to hover just above him. While he scrolled down the contact list in his Black-Berry, looking for his son's telephone number, one of the amoeba-like clouds split apart. A dramatic ray of sunshine speared through. At last he could see the ground.

Beneath him the city shimmered. Which he liked. Maybe he

couldn't hear the sounds from down there, but he enjoyed watching the people swinging their computer cases, dashing around each other, pushing their way past the slow goers, sometimes almost trampling them to get ahead.

Finally. Everything moving along as normal. Tom Roscoe had gotten his bearings again. Perusing his cell phone with squinted brows, he saw he didn't have the kid's number in any of his contact lists. Had he always let Rona make these calls?

He planned to use familiar words when he spoke to his son Jonas about filling Sarah's position at the firm. *It's the chance of a lifetime, son. You couldn't do any better than this.*

Tom had been telling *her* the same thing. So how was it that, now, Sarah felt such emptiness? The chance Tom gave her wasn't doing her any good now. Actually, she was beginning to see just what a waste of time and effort it had been.

Tom finally found Jonas's number in his desk. "Hello?" he roared into the phone. "Hello?"

Tom pulled the phone from his ear and stared at it, his face smoldering with fury. A one-two count and Tom's expression changed to rage. Was it possible? *Maribeth must have called Jonas when she left and told him what I was going to ask him*, Tom thought. Had he heard someone pick up the phone and then hang it up when he started talking? He raised the receiver again. "Jonas? Are you there?" Then one final time, "Jonas!" before he sent the phone skittering across the surface of his desk.

Sarah had visited a place where a Polish nanny to whom she'd never paid much attention clung to a daughter far away through a telephone line.

Next she'd watched a man she had admired offer his son the best thing he knew how to give, and his son had hung up on him. After seeing Tom Roscoe as he truly was, she understood why.

All this time she'd measured herself by what others thought of her. She had spent far too much time in her life trying to gain approval from people. People who had problems of their own, problems they were running from too.

Her work addiction had merely anesthetized the pain of being rejected by her mother; it had not healed her.

It stole her breath, thinking of all she'd let herself give away. All the time she had wasted and how she had devalued the people in her life by the way she treated them.

And when Sarah realized how wrong she had been, although it grieved her, she suddenly felt that the sun had risen on what had been a very long dark night, and she no longer felt afraid.

∽◌ Chapter Eighteen ◌∽

When she and Annie and Wingtip ended up on the fifth level of the Smart Park Tower, Sarah knew exactly what was happening. It didn't surprise her to find them flipping a coin for her parking space.

As Sarah moved closer, she saw the crowd gathered, the guys from the ninth floor standing somberly with their suit coats buttoned and their hands clasped as if they were groomsmen in a wedding. She glanced around the run of faces, Roscoe's entire staff, as well as people wearing trading jackets from rival companies, the whole gang from human resources, all staring at one rectangle of pavement, marked by a curbstone at one end and two stripes painted along the sides, as if this were the most important piece of real estate in all of downtown.

"I don't understand," Rona said. "What's the big deal about a parking place?"

"It's right next to the elevator," someone explained.

"She would have done anything to get it," said someone else.

"She always made that last corner fast to make sure no one took it from her."

"She would have swerved and sent you into a tailspin if you'd tried to steal it away," added another.

"This is what I have to say about Sarah Harper," said one of the ninth-floor guys who sounded ready to launch into a lengthy memorial speech. "She was determined to get what she wanted out of life and that included her special parking place here in the parking tower."

A long pause. At a time like this, perhaps it was best not to correct anyone. But finally a gentleman wearing a jacket from the Reyson and Minor Commodities Firm said, "Not only in the parking tower." They exchanged glances, perhaps remembering that the reason they were having this impromptu memorial was because of something she'd done in her car. "She drove that way *everywhere*, and that's why she isn't here today."

Just when Sarah thought someone would get brave enough to pipe up and say, "You guys are all crazy. Something like a parking space could never have been that important to her," they bowed their heads in silence, staring at the four-sided slab of asphalt, paying homage to it as if it were some holy relic.

It's just a parking place! Sarah wanted to remind them. When she glanced over at Annie, her grandmother's eyes held a tinge of sad amusement.

These people had gone all out. Someone had affixed a wreath of plastic flowers to the concrete curb. An assortment of teddy bears had begun to trickle in, and now they had grown to a pile that would rival the stuffed animals Kate had amassed during her first Christmas. Someone had brought colored ribbon and tied purple, yellow, and pink bows in the chain-link fence lining the upper floors of the parking tower. Someone had laid a Cubs baseball cap right in the center.

"Well, she liked the Cubs, didn't she?" the guy from personnel asked when they all looked askance at him. "She was always trying to get to a game. I wanted to put something she liked up here."

"Yes." Leo said it as snappishly as if he were a bear defending his young. "She liked the Cubs."

A ninth-floor guy tugged a quarter out of his pocket and rubbed it between two fingers. "This is the best way I know to honor her," he said. "She would like the competition. Now who wants to vie for this spot?"

"She would *not* like it done this way," someone else said. "She would like all of us to wait in our vehicles at the ticket booth with our engines revving and then, on your mark, get set, *go*."

"Well, of course she would like that best. But that would be dangerous and we don't need to lose anyone else today, do we?"

"This is the way we're going to have to do it, then," Leo suggested. And it seemed that because he'd been her intern, even though he'd never been paid a penny for his work, they respected him and looked to him for guidance. "No racing. Just a coin flip."

They murmured and nodded their heads in approval.

"But does it have to be a quarter? Can't it be something a little more distinctive? Doesn't anyone have a silver dollar or something?"

Sarah had never seen so many people digging in their pockets and sifting through their coins all at once. Heads shook. Pennies fell to the ground. Finally someone came up with a Kennedy half-dollar—that's the best they could do—and Rose, a woman from bookkeeping, did the honors.

"Call it," she said.

"Heads, I get the space." Ninth-Floor Guy pretended to wave the checkered flag once again.

Rona asked, "If it's tails, who gets it?"

They glanced at each other to see who would be most appropriate. Leo asked, "You want it, Rona? You're Roscoe's assistant. You're the one who should park here."

Rona dabbed at first one eye, then the other, with a tissue. "I've got my own space reserved on the street." Which made everyone peer down their noses at her with suspicion. "Leo should have it. We shouldn't even be flipping."

Leo just stood there, looking a little lost and a lot pitiful.

"Why, Leo did so much to help Sarah, he would have climbed up and carried down the Ceres statue from the top of the Board of Trade if she'd asked him to."

Leo didn't know why everyone had to make such a big deal.

Ninth-Floor Guy, who began to feel the tide of popular opinion turning, said, "Just get it over with, will you? This whole thing seems a bit ridiculous, if you ask me."

So Rose flipped. With her thumb, she tossed the half-dollar high into the air. It tumbled heads over tails over heads, somersaulting in the shaft of sunlight.

"Wingtip." Sarah yanked at his arm. "Can I fix that?"

"We haven't let you fix anything else, have we? We sure can't start now."

Rose caught the half-dollar and slapped it against her wrist. She removed her hand and peered at the coin. "Tails," she said with a small amount of glee. "Leo gets the space."

"No way."

"Way."

"I don't believe you."

"Let me see that," Ninth-Floor complained, teasing. "I think the kid is teacher's pet. I think you're yanking my chain."

Pleasantly, Rose held out her arm so the guy could inspect the results. "I told you so. Take a good look."

Not until the fellow was lumbering off in the direction of the elevator did Leo say, "You can have the space if you really want it. I don't care. I ride the 'L' most of the time anyway."

"Oh, I've got your permission, do I, kid? Who died and gave you all the authority around here, anyway?"

Which gave them both pause because it hit way too close to home.

Leo said, "I'll even have a plaque made with your name on it if you want me to. That's what I was going to do for Mrs. Harper."

"You can stop standing up for her now, Leo. She's gone for good. And we've all seen how she treated you. She ran you around like a slave."

"I wanted to do it," Leo said.

"Why? Because she was giving you your big break? Because you thought she cared about you?" The man pulled a stick of Wrigley's Doublemint from his pocket, unwrapped it, and folded it inside his jaw. "You got a lot to learn, kid. The only thing Sarah Harper cared about was proving her prowess at everyone else's expense. It was just a matter of time. You would have been next."

"You're wrong about Mrs. Harper," Leo said as he followed the man to the elevator. The doors slid open. When the whole group of them loaded and turned to Leo, they were certainly a somber-looking bunch. Ladies dabbed their noses with Kleenexes. Men stood with their shoulders squared, their expressions restrained, their hands crossed.

Leo, feeling very scrawny and young and determined, thought nothing of taking on the entire Roscoe professional staff. "You never gave her a chance to show you what a great lady she was.

She was the best person I ever worked for down here." *She was the* only *person I ever worked for down here*, he thought as the elevator doors began to slide together, *but it will take them a while to figure that out.*

Even though most of the group was well aware of Sarah's determined attitude and didn't like her methods, some of them, especially the ladies, couldn't help but be emotional about her being gone. Although nobody talked about it, this incident made them realize how their own lives could change any minute too. Some of them made jokes just to avoid the thoughts that came to the forefront of their minds when they were quiet.

Could this happen to me?

If it did, am I living the way I really should be living?

Am I ready to die?

What will people say about me when I'm gone?

Throughout his journey with Sarah, Wingtip never once complained about overseeing the Chicago Cubs. He never once launched into any detailed discourse about wishing he had been assigned a team like the Red Sox or the Cards, or even those pesky Philadephia Phillies—any team that stood to win a World Series. He told Sarah he'd learned to trust God with everything and that that made his journey easy rather than hard.

When he turned to her with grief in his eyes and said, "It's time," she hoped he'd gotten some emergency call from Lou Piniella or he was being paged for some desperate duty with the pitchers in the bull pen. But what if it was something much more serious?

"God's not going to call me back to heaven, at least not until my job is over." He spoke as if reassuring himself as Sarah tried to decipher his worried expression.

"What is it, Wingtip? What's wrong?" she asked.

"I'm not sure exactly," he said. "Just a strange sense I've got."

"A sense about what?"

"Just a sense that my job might be almost finished." He shook his head as he thought about it a while. Then his eyes widened. "You don't suppose—"

"I don't suppose . . . what?"

"That this could be the year the Cubbies win it all? That the Lovable Losers might succeed in postseason? That I'm the one who helps the Chicago Cubs bring the commissioners' trophy home to the Friendly Confines of Wrigley Field?"

"It's a tall order," Sarah reminded him, teasing him. Still, she didn't understand his melancholy expression. *It's time.* What did that mean? Was it time to tell him good-bye? She pointed toward the sky. "But I guess there's somebody up there who's very good at filling tall orders."

She tried to smile. But when Wingtip lifted her chin and bent to inspect her face, she turned quickly aside so he wouldn't see her holding back tears.

Sarah inspected her grandmother's face. Maybe their time together was drawing to a close too, because Annie's colors seemed to be gradually fading away. Her lacquered, pin-curled hair, which seemed brighter than a sunflower when Sarah first saw it, now had softened to a color resembling a sparrow's lair. Somewhere along the way even the flamboyant dress had faded and the shoes were a bit down at the heel. When Sarah grasped Annie's hand, she felt knuckles knobby as acorns.

"Wingtip?" Sarah asked him. "What's happening? Does Annie have to leave?"

"Not quite yet."

But Sarah noticed how his enthusiasm about baseball waned, how his expression grew even more pensive. It hinted that her time with both of them was drawing to a close.

"There's one more place your grandmother needs to take you."

"The future?" Sarah asked. "Aren't you going? I thought you were supposed to take us there."

"Relax, Sarah," Wingtip said. "God always has a good plan. He just doesn't always let us in on it."

Wingtip's telling Sarah to relax didn't help one bit. Her knees weakened with fear again. Maybe it was selfish, but she didn't think she could bear to let go of Annie this second time. Each place she had stopped with Annie and Wingtip and the Father's loving guidance had brought her from a place of pain and unhappiness to a place where she felt like she was being made new.

"If I ever get back to my old life, you'll be there. I know you will!" Sarah called after Wingtip. "I'll see you on LaSalle Street picking out a new pair of shoes! I'll see you changing the score by hand at Wrigley just the way Mitchell says you do. This time I will see you, Wingtip. This time I'll believe that angels watch over us every step of the way."

"Ah," Wingtip reminded her. "You won't ever be able to go back to that old life, remember? Sarah, you are on a new journey now, and you must let go of the old one."

She didn't know what she would do without either of them, Sarah thought as she wrapped her arms around herself. She was in uncharted territory, which excited her and frightened her all at once.

As she and Annie made their last journey together, Sarah couldn't tell whether they'd become a part of the clouds or the clouds had become a part of the two of them. She remembered dreams like this from when she was a little girl, like she was dog-paddling across the horizon, swimming through air.

Annie stopped outside an open door. "I think this is it." For the first time in a while, she seemed worried, as if she wasn't certain what Sarah's response would be.

If it could be possible, this room seemed even smaller than Mrs. Pavik's place. *Much* smaller. College dorm small, with strategically placed bookshelves lined with psychology titles and political science volumes and even a gargantuan volume called *Macroeconomics: Understanding Supply and Demand.*

"Freshman year." Sarah ran her fingers along the spines. "I'd recognize these subjects anywhere."

A young woman sat at the desktop computer, her face bowed over its keyboard, her glasses reflecting numbers as she perused data on the screen.

"Do you recognize her?" Annie asked.

"No."

"Are you sure?"

"Should I know this person?"

Annie rolled her eyes. "Perhaps you'd better have another look."

Dark wispy brown hair, not quite as curly as Sarah's own. Highlights shining in streaks of Italian Chianti red. The profile, so different yet so familiar. She could have been a young-girl version of Joe. That's when Sarah finally knew.

She felt like her knees might go out from under her again. "It's Kate. Oh, Annie. It's Kate."

Annie smiled knowingly.

"My daughter. How old is she? What? Eighteen?"

The first thing to be said was, "She looks just the same." The second was, "Of course she doesn't look the same." But the features were there, made more distinct and more unique by time. "Oh, she's so beautiful, isn't she?"

At second look, Sarah could see Kate wasn't happy. As Kate stared at the screen it seemed like her eyes alighted on the same line over and over again. She couldn't take anything in. Every so often, she sniffed and wiped her eyes with the back of her wrist. Sarah lost track of how many times Kate fiddled with her hair, pulling it away from her face, binding it into a messy chignon with a scrunchie, tugging it free until it fell across her face again.

Sarah couldn't take her eyes off this beautiful young woman. There she sat, this child who had so recently nursed at Sarah's breast, the baby who had once felt so weighty, so like an obligation in Sarah's arms. Kate had turned into the most beautiful young woman Sarah had ever seen.

A knock sounded at the door behind them. Another young lady stuck her head in. "Come on, girl. You going to study all night?"

"Yes."

"You're going to give yourself mono."

"Excuse me, April. Studying is not the way to get mono. Who told you that?"

The roommate plopped her books on the bed and held up both hands like a scale, weighing the odds. "I'll never tell."

"Why not study like this? There isn't anything else better to do."

"On Saturday night? Are you kidding me? There's a big group of us going bowling. Hot guys all over the place, Kate. I don't think you should miss it."

"Go have fun. I don't have my hot-guy radar turned on right now. Anybody I'd meet would never measure up to Cooper."

"Anybody you'd meet would take your mind *off* of Cooper Dawson. He's a jerk. You deserve so much better."

"You should never say that to your best friend. What if we get back together again and end up getting married? Then on my twenty-fifth anniversary, when you and I go shopping or something, I'll always look at you and remember you said my husband was a jerk."

"He's a jerk. Read my lips. *Jerk.* Player. Boy toy to the masses. Doesn't respect you. Looking for any girl who is unsure enough about herself that she'll let him have his cake and eat it too."

"Don't they all?"

"Guys like Cooper Dawson have a sixth sense, Kate. They know the girls who'll give them what they want. They prey on the ones who don't have enough self-esteem and are looking for guys to give it to them. You're selling yourself short if you even think about doing this."

Baby Kate, who'd been left so many times at Mrs. Pavik's, who'd smelled like Dreft and lotion and gummed bits of baby cookie. Who, this very morning, had held her mother's face with one tiny, prickly fingernailed hand. Kate, who made every iota of Sarah's motherly instincts kick in.

Some unknown boy was trying to take advantage of her! Some unknown young womanizer was trying to convince Kate she wasn't worth his time if she didn't cave in to his wishes. What if she was looking at this predator to give her self-esteem? Well! Sarah would certainly have something to say about that.

She marched directly toward her daughter's desk before she remembered Kate couldn't see or hear her.

At that precise moment, Kate said to her friend, "I'd give anything if I had a mother I could talk to. I wish so hard that I could talk to her about things like this."

April said, "Honey, I'm so sorry."

"I really miss having someone to share my heart with."

Sarah wheeled toward Annie. "I'm not there for her," she said as the guilt and shame deluged her again. "That's the cost of the choice I made today. She doesn't have a mother to talk to because I'm gone."

Annie was backing away. And Sarah's heart froze because she could see her grandmother almost completely faded now. It seemed like she could see through her, to the shapes of boxes and Kate's storage trunks and the little refrigerator on the other side.

"You don't understand, Sarah. This visit was meant to show you Kate's future if you hadn't driven off the bridge. This is to show you what would be happening to Kate if you were still around."

"No," Sarah whispered, reaching for Annie's hand, feeling like she'd been struck in the chest with a bulldozer.

"I'm not the one you need to reach for anymore, Sarah." At first she'd barely noticed Annie's voice fading, but now Sarah faintly heard her grandmother say, "The one you need is Jesus, not me."

"But where can I find him? Will he help me even after the way I've lived?"

"He's been waiting for you to ask for help all your life." Then, faint as a whisper, "And should you decide to go back—"

"What do you mean, 'Should I decide to go back'?"

Then silence.

"Annie? *Annie?*" When she whispered her grandmother's name again, no one answered.

"I never knew," Sarah wept as she called out to Jesus. "I never knew."

She felt strength, amazing strength, and love like warm liquid pouring into her and all over her. She was too stunned to talk. Whatever happened to her now, it didn't matter. She knew without any doubt that she would be taken care of and loved forever. Someone besides Annie, a Savior who had always yearned for her to call his name, held Sarah close and wouldn't let go.

Chapter Nineteen

The sun slipped from behind a cloud, sending a shaft of gold toward the river. Joe, who'd been rocking on the edge of the concrete barrier, lifted his head. The rain had soaked his shirt clear through.

Joe felt like such a heel. Earlier, while traffic was backed up in every direction, Gail had walked a long way to find him a breakfast bagel. When she'd unwrapped the hard roll with its greasy flaps of ham and cheese, he'd stared at it like it was made of rubber. He shook his head. His eyes felt full of grit. "I don't want that."

Gail rearranged the cheese so it flopped to the other side. As if that would make it better. "Come on. You need to eat something."

"I'm not hungry." He didn't think he'd ever be able to do normal things like eat, sleep, or drink again. "Thanks for getting it, Gail, but I just can't—"

He tried to hand it away but no one would take it from him. Somewhere during the next half hour, while Joe watched the fire department stand down and the hydraulic Jaws of Life get reloaded onto the waiting truck bed, the sandwich disappeared from its paper. Maybe he ate it. He couldn't remember. He didn't know where it had gone.

Police no longer had the bridge cordoned off. They'd removed the vehicle barricades, rolled the plastic tape into monstrous wads, and extinguished flares that had been strewn like jeweled rubies across six lanes. Only a handful of divers still scoured the depths. The remaining rescue boats skimmed the surface, calm as swans.

Slowly the area was returning to normal. Most onlookers had given up and scurried away. Gapers still slowed the pace along the road overhead, but even passersby had speeded up considerably. Tires clicked over seams in the bridge. A golden retriever came bounding down the cement steps not too far from him, plunging in full-speed and sending a duck quacking in panic. Joe watched the dog's masterful swimming as it made its way to shore. Before he could even think about getting out of the way, the dog climbed out of the water. As golden retrievers will do, it shook all over him.

"Oh, gee. Sorry." A woman in a jogging suit came hurrying down the steps too and grabbed the dog's collar. "He got off his leash."

Any other day Joe might have warded off the spray with his hands and laughed. *No problem.* But today he wasn't capable of speaking, much less making small talk with a stranger.

"What's all the excitement about?" she asked innocently. "Do you know what happened here?"

With a perverse sense of satisfaction, he finally spoke. "Yeah. My wife drove off the bridge. They're still searching for her body."

"Oh my goodness." The woman jerked the dog's collar so hard

the dog yelped. "Oh, I'm so sorry." She practically skittered away, but not before the dog shook on him again.

If he'd eaten the sandwich, he shouldn't have done it. His stomach churned in complaint as he listened to radio transmissions snapping with urgent voices. He watched the car being dragged up, water rushing from its open crevices, seaweed dangling from its appendages, the buckled metal and the undercarriage leering at him like something indecent—the thought left him feeling like he'd swallowed metal shavings. Joe already knew the worst. If Sarah hadn't been in or near the car, chances were they'd never find her.

He had to get out of here.

Joe sprang from the curbstone and began to pace, his fingers closing over the cell phone in his pocket. Mitchell had called. Joe had seen the Cattalos' number appear onscreen. He'd checked the message, listened to it twice, the brave, quavering voice of his son asking him to call back.

He couldn't do it. Any good father ought to phone. A good father ought to get his son on the line and offer some comfort to a small boy who had lost his mother. But what was Joe supposed to say? "Everything's going to be all right, son"? It wouldn't be all right. Nothing would be all right ever again.

Then from the depths of his soul came *Oh, God. Would you comfort Mitchell? Would you be with him, even though I'm not?* Joe wondered why he was praying since it didn't seem that God was listening to him. He felt so desperate that he didn't know anything else to do.

"Here," Pete said. "Drink this." He handed Joe a cup of water from the medics' truck. Joe stared into it, skeptical, before he downed it. He winced at the last swallow, handed back the cup.

"Thanks."

"You need coffee or something? They've got that too. You're looking a little green around the gills."

"I'm fine, Pete," he lied.

"At least go over there and let them check you out."

Joe's shoes squished as he walked.

"They can give you something to help you relax, or they might need to treat you for shock—"

"Do I look like I need treatment for shock?"

Pete surveyed Joe's appearance as Joe realized he'd left himself open for rebuttal. "Never mind. Don't answer that question. I'm sure I look like a total wreck."

Pete signaled for Gail to bring a blanket anyway as he fell into step beside his friend. "I'm here for you, Joe, whatever you need and whenever you need it."

As sun spilled through the clouds in a broader circle, downtown Chicago took on a green cast, the same sort of faint glow that came with oxidation of copper. Rows upon rows of office windows glinted, reminding Joe of vacant eyes. The skyscrapers protruding overhead seemed to lean in on each other.

Pete searched the ground at his feet.

"What are you looking for?"

"A skipping rock. Anything I can throw across the water."

There weren't many rocks for throwing in this high-rise district of the city. The river was bound on both sides by concrete walls and tour boats at their moorings, by colonnade arches and lines of lampposts marching farther than the eye could see. Pete's hand darted inside a concrete planter, filled with small stones and dried remains of chrysanthemums, well past their prime.

Gail appeared with the requested blanket and stretched it

across Joe's shoulders. Joe humored her. He gripped the blanket around his arms and held it there for a good ten seconds. As soon as Gail turned away, he let it fall to the ground.

Pete sidearmed the stone across the river and counted. It skipped three times before it sank.

"Is that the only one?" Joe asked.

"There's plenty. Help yourself." Pete pointed toward the planter.

Side by side, they flung stones. Settling into the camaraderie that, for male members of the human species, doesn't require speech. Joe didn't know why throwing the rocks made him feel better, but somehow it did. At least it was something to do.

Joe pitched a rock, and Pete followed its arc with his eyes.

Pete launched one, and Joe shook his head, thinking he could do better.

Joe sorted through the stones remaining in the flowerpot, searching for the perfect shape.

They kept this up for a while. Until Pete finally voiced the question Joe had also been thinking, the one Joe hadn't been brave enough to even ask himself.

"Joe? You don't think she would have meant to do it, do you?"

Joe's arm froze in mid-windup. His arm lowered to his side.

"I hate to bring it up. But you told me the two of you were not getting along. I just want you to get it out in the open if you're thinking that maybe she did it on purpose."

Not until Pete turned did he read Joe's face—haunted, sick, breathing fast with unspent anger. The stone fell at Joe's feet. He locked his fists on his friend's collar and his voice bit: "Don't say it. Don't say that. How dare you?"

There was a crack of static as a nearby officer saw the fight and radioed for backup. He charged in to make a tackle, the badge catching the light on his chest. With legs broad as clubs, with cuffs and nightstick swinging from his belt, he tried to grapple them apart but didn't stand a chance. Joe, every movement magnified by frustration, ground out to Pete, "Go home. Take Gail with you and go. Who said I want you down here? Not if you say things like that. How *dare* you say that?"

Just as the fight grew intense enough for them to start throwing punches, Joe yanked Pete forward by the shirt and began sobbing against Pete's neck with pent-up grief, his tears racked with hopelessness. And there was nothing Pete could do to take it back. Nothing.

Pete clamped his huge forearms around Joe's midsection. He hung on to his buddy and wouldn't let go, as if he could save Joe from drowning, as if he could keep his friend from being tugged into a bottomless place.

By noon, Nona said, coworkers from Lathrop would be bringing casseroles.

Mitchell had heard her on the phone first thing, calling the big steel-pipes company where she'd worked since before he was born, trying to explain that she had to take care of him and that's why she wouldn't be working today. Nona had one of those big phones for the hard of hearing—Harold said it was because he was deafer than a doorpost—and when Nona talked on that thing, it looked like she had a sea creature from *Pirates of the Caribbean* suctioned to her head.

"Jane? Isn't your grandson school-aged? Why isn't he in class? Is he sick today?"

"No. He isn't sick."

"Well then. Why?"

Nona issued a long weary sigh that sounded like air being let out of a tire. "My daughter's been in a car accident."

"Goodness, Jane. You should have said something at the beginning. That's horrible. Is she hurt?"

"We believe so. She's driven off a bridge."

"Oh my."

"And actually, they can't find her..."

"Jane."

"...but there's no need for everyone to be worrying about me."

"Of course we're worrying about you, Jane. What can we do to help?"

"Casseroles would help. I don't feel like cooking. And I know I said Mitchell isn't sick, but actually he *is*."

"I'll let everyone know. Don't worry about anything."

"Actually, we are *all* sick. We're sick at heart."

"Understandable."

"I have to go because I don't want Mitchell to overhear this. We're trying not to upset him." Even though he could have overheard this particular conversation clear over in Wheeling.

Nona had never been one to offer up much in the way of entertainment or juvenile handicrafts. Which is the reason Mitchell was surprised when she pulled apples from the pantry and told him she'd come up with an idea—they would make sour-faced dolls.

"Dolls?" he asked, wrinkling his nose. Mitchell didn't quite know what had inspired Nona's burst of inventiveness.

"Like this." She pushed cloves into the apple skin, one after another. By the time she finished, the apple had a face. "Next, we set them in the window and forget about them. After about three weeks, they get all shriveled up like mean people."

With a hollow feeling in his stomach, Mitchell obeyed her. Nothing could replace his ache to speak to his dad or his distress that something had happened to his mom. And any mention of dolls made a boy Mitchell's age want to run in the opposite direction. Still, Nona offered a diversion that included poking sharp objects into fruit and leaving it to rot. Mitchell straightened his crooked glasses and proceeded to impale the McIntosh, leaving numerous holes.

Not until he carried his creation to the sill and set it beside Nona's did he glance out the window. Mitchell stared, pressed a hand to the glass. On the other side of the pane, there was a sight he'd thought he'd never see again, something that made him realize he wasn't alone.

Nona didn't miss him until the screen door slammed behind him. By the time she turned, Mitchell had already bolted outside.

When it rang, the phone's screen lit up Joe's pocket. He stood leaning against Patterson's cruiser, finally letting the chaplain corral him and offer encouraging words. Beneath the blanket, which someone had managed to wrangle over his shoulders again, Joe slipped his fingers inside his jeans and played them over his vibrating mobile. Didn't people know they shouldn't call at a time like this?

When the shrill signal ended, Joe breathed a sigh of relief. Only to be interrupted by it starting all over again. In desperation he yanked it out and stared it down. Not until the third call did Joe recognize that, each time, it was the same number.

He didn't even have to ask. He rocked forward, stood straight. "It's my son," he said. "It's . . . it's difficult. Will you stay while I talk to him?"

"I'm right here."

Joe triggered the button. "Mitchell. Hello, son. It's good to—"

"Dad!"

"—it's good to talk. I'm sorry I haven't—"

"Dad, listen."

"There isn't anything to say about your mom yet, Mitchell. They still haven't—"

"That's what I'm trying to tell you!"

"—found her. There still isn't any news."

"No, Dad. Listen. He was here."

"Who was there?"

"The man from the scoreboard. Remember? I told you about him at the Cubs game?"

This call was coming from the opposite side of the world. It seemed so out of place that momentarily Joe was completely stumped.

"He came to Nona's house."

"Son. I'm sorry, but those things aren't important right now."

"They *are*. He came to Nona's house to tell me Mom is going to be okay."

"I know you want everything to be okay with your mom, Mitch. I know it's what you wish for."

"I'm not just wishing, Dad. He *said*—"

Icy fear threaded Joe's veins. "Who is this man talking to you about your mom?"

"He's an angel sent by God," Mitchell said. As matter-of-fact as if he'd said, "He's a shoe salesman."

"For the Cubs? That man you saw in the scoreboard?" Joe gripped the chaplain's arm in terror. He hadn't suspected Mitchell might take this so hard. "Mitchell, can you put your grandmother on the phone?"

"That's what he said, Dad. He said they're going to find her. Right now."

"Son, I know that's what you want to *hear*. Please, Mitchell. Tell Nona I want to talk to her."

"He says they're going to find her any minute."

At that precise moment, an earsplitting whistle speared the width of the river. Joe snapped to attention, stood erect. The phone clattered to the ground.

"Joe," Patterson said. "Joe, get off the phone."

The cry went up across the water. Patterson's radio exploded in a celebration of static. "She's down there. They've got her!" Voices twisting against each other made it difficult to decipher the words.

. . . when we cable-lined the car.

. . . got that clean shot.

. . . don't know how we missed her . . .

The diver appeared midriver with a sodden bundle in his arms. It couldn't be Sarah, Joe thought as his whole body buckled. She looked no bigger than the dog that had accosted him.

The swimmer powered his way to the makeshift platform, toting the rag-doll body. Many hands hauled her toward dry land. Joe saw the CPR begin. He felt Pete's grip on his elbow, holding him upright. An ambulance engine started up from what seemed, through the blur, to be a great distance. Its light bar remained dark, bleak with emptiness.

Joe had seen emergency vehicles rush to accidents, lights fencing the sky. He'd seen those same vehicles slink back to dispatch, lights off and sirens silenced—embarrassed to have made such a fuss and not be needed—after a fatality.

The joy of finding Sarah would be short-lived. In the end, they'd say it had been a blessing just to find a body. A gift. "The family should be thankful for closure," mourners would whisper at the memorial service. How could Joe even think about getting everyone—or even just himself—through a funeral?

Joe didn't recognize his own voice when he spoke. The frantic EMTs working over the crumpled silhouette had blurred. "I want to see her. Will they let me see her?"

That's when the ambulance light bar flashed to life like a sparkler on the Fourth of July. That's when a disbelieving voice overrode everything else on the frequency. "Do we have cold-water revival?"

"It doesn't make sense. Water's not that—"

Someone interrupted. "We've got a pulse over here, guys. I kid you not. I repeat: we've got a pulse. It is faint, but we've got one."

Pete gasped at Joe's side.

When she finally coughed and the fluid rushed from Sarah's lungs, she took her first breath since everyone had thought she was dead. Joe felt his chest heave with a jolt of relief. He gasped for air as though, all along, he'd been the one who'd needed to breathe for her. How could it be? How could she be in the water that long and still be alive?

Realization tunneled around him as his fists fell open at his sides. The worst hadn't happened. He hadn't lost his wife yet.

Was it possible that he and Sarah still had a chance? Could they possibly make things work?

Joe vaguely wondered what was ahead. He was grateful to have her back, but he didn't want things to be like they were. He felt deep inside that he had to find a way to love Sarah into wholeness, even if that meant being firm with her. He had to stand behind the words he had spoken to her. He knew he would have to be strong.

⁓ᓚ Chapter Twenty ᓗ⁓

Sarah didn't know what had happened. She didn't know where she was or how she'd gotten here.

Small things began to ply her awake. The sharp smell of disinfectant. The crisp burned scent of laundered bedsheets, which she'd always loved. The cradle of a pillow beneath her head. A blanket tucked so tight around her feet that she felt the need to kick free.

For a moment she suffered from a bout of claustrophobia. She thrashed in the bed, trying to spring herself loose, until she felt the cool touch of a hand calming her, the click of dosage being turned up in an IV overhead. She remembered this from giving birth to Kate; when nurses entered the room on their soundless soles while you were sleeping, their uniforms sounded like rustling angels' wings.

A distant beep called her toward consciousness. Still, she drifted, floating in and out. She was aware, or so she thought, of the passage of time. She couldn't remember ever feeling so odd. And somewhere in her dreams, she thought she might be at Annie's house—a lost, faded memory from when she was a child.

It had been like this, waking up at Annie's when she was a little girl. She'd never wanted to sleep late at Annie's. She'd always wanted to get up and play with the kittens or find out what was happening with Grandpa Gordy in his workshop out in the garage.

She remembered the day of Annie's funeral when she'd walked to the grocery store and bought flowers because her mother didn't have time to take her to the florist. She remembered laying the pale pink roses in the casket around her grandmother's shoulders. She remembered how even light pink had looked garish, how Annie's hair looked an awful blue, the way the funeral home had done it up. For as far back as she could remember, Annie's complexion had always shown like pale crepe, a blush of satin.

The names were on her lips when she slit open her eyes against that blinding light. "Wingtip. Annie." She sprang to life and gripped the coat sleeve of the woman leaning over her. "They were there. I was with them."

Even though the nurse had hurried away, someone was still in the room with her. Sarah sensed it, rather than knowing for sure. A presence lingered at the foot of her bed.

"Annie?" she whispered again.

There wasn't any answer. Only a gasp and a soft shift of fabric as someone stood from a chair.

For reasons she didn't understand, Sarah felt a burst of freedom. She wiggled her toes, realizing someone must have loosened the blankets around them. What an odd dream she'd had! It flittered through her mind the way moonlit clouds flitter unnoticed through a night sky.

Sarah opened her eyes and struggled to sit up. Where was

Kate? She'd seen Kate. She'd been with Annie. And what about the angel that seemed a bit off his rocker? Where had *he* gone?

It *was* a hospital. The beeping came from a monitor, the rhythm of her own chest. The lights splayed down on her face from a deck of fluorescents overhead. As she raised herself on her elbows, she shook her head to clear the fog.

"Joe?" she asked.

But the person she recognized took her back much further than that. She realized who had unfastened all those sheets at the foot of the bed. She'd always made perfectly sure her mama knew how she hated to be confined.

"Mother?"

Jane jumped when Sarah said her name. She looked as guilty as someone who had just been released from the slammer.

"Why am I in the hospital? How did I get here?"

Jane didn't even try to answer her questions. She just started scolding. "Goodness, Sarah. You can't wake up right now. They've all been waiting. I'm not the person you should be seeing first."

Normally Sarah would have thought, *You don't want to see me, Mama? You aren't glad I'm here?* But to her own surprise, she found herself feeling sorry for Jane. She wanted to say, *Mother, I know why you've been so unhappy. I know why you never really liked me, and I forgive you.* But that had all been a dream, hadn't it? Sarah's thoughts were so confused; she didn't understand any of them.

Jane continued: "You got yourself in an accident. That's what you did."

"Is Joe angry at me? We had a terrible argument." Sarah covered her face, at least remembering that much. "And I wrecked the Lincoln."

"Let me go get them," her mother said.

"Would you? Would you get my kids? I want to see them."

Something flickered through Sarah's mind, as evasive as a child hiding among trees—a name, although she didn't know where it had come from. "Ronny," she framed the name in a whisper. "Ronny Lee Perkins." Now what did that name have to do with anything?

"What's that?" Jane asked, thunderstruck.

Sarah shook her head. "I don't really know. Something about—" Sarah frowned. It had been there, but now she couldn't remember.

⌒⌒

Not twenty-four hours later, Sarah had wheedled and cajoled, coaxed and flattered, until her doctor had to admit he couldn't come up with any more reasons for her to take up a hospital bed.

There were only so many tests she could undergo. Only so many MRIs he could reasonably put her through. Only so many MEG scans she could endure. Other than an indistinct ache somewhere in the vicinity of her rib cage, which the doctor deduced had come from CPR, and a deep gouge on her right arm that had taken eleven stitches to close, she appeared unscathed.

Northwestern Memorial touted itself as one of the nation's top teaching hospitals. Sarah held court with an ever-changing array of interns, who queried her about her recovery. ("Recovery from *what*?" she would ask as they laughed on cue.) They came with yellow legal pads and poised pens. They came with laptop computers and nimble fingers, all of them certain they could glean enough information from this patient to use for a case study or research paper.

Joe overheard them in groups in the hallway, comparing notes, lobbing ridiculous words such as *neurocognitive deficit* and *controlled hypothermia* like tennis balls in a match.

Joe was happy to let these medical students dote on his wife. That way he didn't have to face her in a room that felt twice as empty with only husband and wife in it. He didn't have to pretend easy small talk about the car and its insurance policy or last night's record low temperature or the nurses' drawing on the dry-erase board. Most of all, he didn't have to tiptoe around the fact that she'd almost died and that, during their last cherished conversation, he'd told her he couldn't take much more of being married to her.

If a man could be overwhelmed by a swarm of buzzing emotions, well, that was Joe Harper. Every time he tried to sleep, he closed his eyes and saw those emergency lights strung out across the river. Every time he tried to erase the vision of those divers popping out of the water and the firemen shaped like bells in those coats, he could examine the back of his eyelids and count more. Which reminded him how terrified he'd been of losing Sarah. How he'd risked everything giving her the ultimatum, how he wouldn't have been brave enough to be so honest if he didn't care.

If he ever actually found himself able to drift off for a few minutes, he'd jerk awake again, realizing he'd relived yet again the sight of her being rolled onto the diving platform.

And here she sat on a throne of pillows giving details of her ordeal to breathless admirers as easily as if she were giving details about her latest summer cruise.

Joe liked to think, with all the commotion going on, that he could slip in and out of her room unobserved. But it didn't take him long to begin to suspect he was wrong. He felt Sarah's eyes burning into the back of his shirt every time he stood to leave. He saw her glance quickly away from the door every time he returned.

On one of the rare occasions when he entered and found the room empty, he stumbled over his words, saying anything he could think of. "Do you know that the whole hospital is talking about you? You are one of the few people who have ever been underwater that long and lived to tell about it. Everybody was talking about how cold it was that day and how they hated it, but the extremely cold weather actually saved your life."

"Is that what saved me?" She gave a weak smile, as if she wasn't certain what to say to him. "I'm sick of being poked and prodded and having my body run through magnetic fields. I'm so glad I get to go home."

Joe didn't dare say how he felt about the doctor's releasing her so soon. After such a close call, maybe the doctor should keep her longer for observation. Still, Joe's reservations were caused by more than that; he knew it.

He felt uncomfortable bringing her home. He pictured himself measuring his words, trying not to say the wrong thing to make her angry. He knew he'd tiptoe around, feeling like he was walking on eggshells, trying not to upset her.

Joe didn't even want to think about the ultimatum he'd laid down about their marriage. Whenever they were alone together, he knew he'd be weighing his wife's every word, waiting for her to get mad at him again.

"In life," the doctor remarked when he came to check Sarah out, "maybe each person gets one or two miracles. You, Mrs. Harper," he said, smacking her thick medical chart against his leg, "just used one of yours."

When they left the hospital, Joe didn't have much to load in the car. Just one bag of toiletries he'd gathered for her as he raced through the house—toothpaste and toothbrush, shampoo so she could wash her hair, a pair of pajamas so she wouldn't have to spend all day in a hospital gown. Pete and Gail had sent an arrangement of fall-colored chrysanthemums. Sarah's intern, Leo, had sent a vase of carnations and daisies, which Mitchell had agreed to hold in the car between his knees.

A nurse's aide rolled Sarah out the side exit in a wheelchair. Joe held the door open for her as the aide helped her with the seat belt and Mitchell juggled flowers in the back. Joe unfastened Kate's car seat and slipped her in. As Kate kicked her feet in the seat, Joe's blood ran cold. He hadn't even thought about it until now. Kate's other seat had gone down in the accident. What if Sarah had done something like that when she had the kids with her?

As he drove her home, Sarah stared out the window at the passing traffic. He could see her fist bracing her cheek through her tangle of hair. "Sarah?" he asked. When she didn't turn to him, Joe thought it was just as well. He didn't know how he would have asked this question anyway.

Can I trust you, Sarah? After what you've done?

It dawned on him how frightened he was because of everything that had happened to her. She'd risked everything, making the choice she'd made.

As they pulled into the driveway, he couldn't help wondering where they would go from here.

Anyone might have known it. When Sarah said, "It won't be long until I go home," she really meant "It won't be long until I get back to work." No languishing around the house in sweatpants for her. No letting anyone wait on her hand and foot as she took time to build up her strength.

Joe had just finished putting together Mitchell's school lunch on their second morning back—an apple from Harold and Nona's yard, a tub of yogurt, and a bologna sandwich with mustard. He'd just finished folding over the bag and making a crease in it when Sarah came tapping downstairs in her sling-back pumps with her computer bag slung over her shoulder.

He raised his chin a notch, unable to fathom what he was seeing. "You're not driving."

"You're right," she agreed. "I'm not."

"What are you doing then?"

"Leo's coming to get me."

"You asked your intern to drive the Tri-State Tollway?"

"He doesn't mind. He'd do anything for me. I told him I'd pay the toll. And gas."

Joe couldn't believe it. Nothing ever changed. "Did it ever occur to you that you shouldn't take advantage of that kid, even though he's willing to do anything you ask?"

"It's good for his career, Joe."

"Is it?" Joe asked. "Or is it just good for you?"

Joe turned to his wife, ready to do battle. He expected her to come at him with both barrels blazing. Instead he caught her standing in the middle of the room, her computer case dangling from her arm as she stared into space with an undecipherable expression. But before he could ask, *Sarah? What's wrong?* her demeanor returned to normal.

"Look," she said. "I know you're worried. But it's my job, Joe. I had an accident. Yes, it was a close call, but I don't need to stop my life." Then she added in challenge, "No matter what you think I should do."

"What were you thinking about? When you were standing in the middle of the room just now?"

For a moment she seemed startled that he had noticed. "I was thinking about"—she shrugged, as if she didn't know how to put it into words—"about this dream I had."

"A dream you had? Last night?"

"No," she said, "while"—she tripped over the words a little—"while I was gone."

It was the first time either of them had mentioned it. During the short time they'd kept Sarah in the hospital, she had either been undergoing tests or answering her doctor's questions or granting interviews to fascinated med-school students as they scribbled notes. She had wondered if she should tell the doctors about her "dream" or "experience" or "trip to heaven." But during the hours that passed, the details had started to fade. Like most dreams do, the particulars had gone hazy.

The dream had started to dissipate when Sarah awakened to find her mother at her bedside. Now, she had nothing firm to hang on to except the difficult reality of her life before.

"While you were gone," he repeated. "Like you took a trip or something." Then, "Do you know how I felt when I thought you were gone, Sarah?" he asked. "Like a part of me had died too."

She shot a look at him in disbelief. "Is that what you felt? After what you said to me, I would have thought it would be something different."

"Don't," he said. "Let's don't even start."

"We have to talk about it sometime."

"Not right now," he said. "You don't want to hear what I have to say."

"Joe."

"Call Leo and tell him I'm giving you a ride." When Joe switched the subject that was answer enough. "I'd like to be the one to take you downtown."

"You said you felt like a part of yourself had died too. Did you mean it?"

"I wasn't sure I wanted to live anymore when I thought you were dead. But when I finally realized you were alive, I started wondering how we were going to live together if things stayed the same. I don't know what motivates you anymore. I don't even know who you *are*—"

"Maybe," she reminded him, "I don't know who I am either."

"Sarah, I cannot live like we have been living."

"Joe, I had an accident, and I need time to get over it before we start trying to solve our personal problems. I just want to go to the office and get my mind off this whole mess."

"You don't have your head on straight anymore. I can't trust you—don't you see? What if you'd made that stupid move with my kids in the car?"

She looked like she'd been kicked in the teeth. "Joe? What are you saying?"

He stayed quiet for one beat, two beats, too long.

"They're my kids too," she said. "Do you think I could have hurt them? Do you?"

He was furious. Furious because she was hurting the entire family and didn't seem to see it. Furious that she didn't love them enough to get her priorities straight. Furious because he'd grieved like a baby when he'd thought he lost her. Furious because now he might have to grieve her loss again.

Neither spoke again about the distrust and the hurt they had caused one another. It crouched in the center of the room, something they would stumble over, like a trap waiting to spring.

Chapter Twenty-One

Sarah wasn't sure how everyone in the offices of Roscoe Futures Group would react to her return. After all, she had never been presumed dead before and then come back to life. Would they take great pains to avoid her? Would they be thrilled to see her?

Joe dropped her off at the curb on LaSalle Street.

Sarah jumped out of the car and immediately noticed someone on the sidewalk turn and dart the other way. Sarah pushed her way through the gleaming glass revolving door, and before she had a chance to greet the guys at security, one man dropped something and had to bend down to pick it up. On the way up the elevator, a woman she didn't know very well from bookkeeping began an immediate, deep conversation about the latest diet fad with a woman leaning in the opposite corner.

When the door slid open on the ninth floor, three separate colleagues pivoted at the same moment, each murmuring about forgetting something. People seemed to be acting funny. When Sarah disembarked on her own floor, she expected the entire human resources department to ignore her like she thought everyone had done so far. But maybe it was just a wrong perception. Maybe she was just afraid. And as the elevator doors opened again, she knew she'd been wrong. Everyone was welcoming her. Sarah lost count of all the people who rose from their desks and came to greet her.

"We're so glad to have you back, Sarah!"

"Oh my goodness, that's quite the bandage on your arm. But you look *great* for what you've been through."

"We thought we'd lost you. So glad you're still with us."

Rona came prancing along in search of a printout from someone's overloaded flash drive only to see Sarah and embrace her with a squeal. "You should have seen Tom that day," she whispered in Sarah's ear. "Making phone calls. Trying to get things done around this place. He was beside himself without you here."

Sarah straightened and surveyed Rona's face, searching for some clue.

Rona nodded. "You know Tom. He went a little crazy."

"Did he?" she asked with a spark of interest.

"His wife had to come in and calm him down. Even then, she didn't do a very good job of it."

"Maribeth came in?" Sarah asked, her throat tightening.

"I know. She never does that. But you really shook everybody up. And Tom wouldn't come out of his office for a while."

"So sorry I shook everyone up." Sarah wanted to believe that things had been in an uproar without her. But she kept having foggy flashbacks to things she had seen while she was gone. She kept telling herself it was all nonsense, just a silly dream. Or perhaps a nightmare. That might have been a more accurate description.

Sarah kept trying to get back to business as usual in her life, but something didn't seem quite the same and she couldn't figure it out.

"You *should* be sorry." Leo bolted from their joint office and, with a broad grin, offered her an energetic handshake. "Mrs. Harper. I'll bet your family is glad you're okay. And I know I usually ride the 'L,' but I sure wouldn't have minded coming to pick you up today. I could have saved your husband the trip."

"I know you didn't mind, Leo." Sarah looked at the faces around her and, for the first time, saw how they wanted to help her. "I tell you, just knowing you were willing made me feel good." She started toward her office, then stopped, turned back to him. "Leo. Thank you."

"You're welcome." His eyes narrowed. He looked like he might be thinking, *What? Was that Mrs. Harper paying me a compliment?*

As he scurried off to his next duty, Sarah watched his retreating spine. Ordinarily, his eagerness to please drove her a little nuts. But she wanted to do something nice for Leo. Something that would make him understand how much he was worth. Something he wouldn't know had come from her.

Sarah stood in the hallway, watching him go and couldn't describe what was happening in her heart. A gentle welling up of love for these people. How grateful she felt that they were still here.

She turned to see Tom Roscoe stepping out of the elevator. His eyes slid toward Rona, who gave him a slight smile, and then toward Sarah. At first it didn't register that he'd left the confines of his gilded office and descended from his thronelike perch just to have a word with her. He stood in front of Sarah, assessing her with a critical eye. *Why aren't you out there on the trading floor?*

she expected him to ask. *We don't build this company by standing around, do we?*

But Tom surprised her. He smiled. "It's good to have you back in your rightful place, Sarah."

"Thank you, Mr. Roscoe."

"I expect the Cornishes will want to schedule another meeting to discuss trading strategy as soon as possible."

"I expect they will too."

"And you're up for that?"

"Of course I am."

"Very good. I'll have Rona check with you about your schedule."

"Thank you," Sarah repeated as she turned toward Rose from accounting and shot her a disbelieving glance. "I'll let you know when I can fit it in."

"Very good." Tom started across the room. But he turned back. "And Sarah?"

"Yes?"

"I guess it would have been pretty tough on us if you'd really been gone."

Well, yes, Sarah thought. *I guess it would have been tough all right.*

It was one of those comments you don't know exactly how to answer. She shrugged, feeling awkward. "Luckily, you didn't have to find out."

"No." He'd been carrying a pen in his fist. He pitched it in the air and caught it again. "Luckily. Now things can go on just as they were."

After Tom left, Sarah noticed one of the ninth-floor guys headed her way. He nodded in her direction, opened his mouth as if he intended to make some snide comment about her driving prowess. But then he snapped his mouth shut again as if he'd thought better of it.

"You know what?" she asked, suddenly thinking of something. "The weirdest thing happened. I dreamed you guys got together and flipped a coin for my parking space. Isn't that crazy?"

Ninth-Floor Guy froze in his tracks. He glanced in both directions like he was checking to see if anybody would overhear.

"Yeah," he said, "that's crazy all right," his face turning quite red.

"What?" she asked. "What's wrong?"

"Nothing's wrong," he retorted. Before she could ask him anything else, he bolted away.

One particularly endearing trait of Chicagoans is that they think nothing of making noises together. Big noises. Loud, strident noises.

Their collective moan every time the "L" train stops for nightly construction.

Their shared sigh when a bridge opens and they have to wait before crossing over.

Their joint oohs and ahs as lightning scribbles the Cook County sky or their collective *ewww* each time the ump calls a strike a ball.

Now, at the Starbucks on North State Street, a whole chorus moaned as one because everyone had somewhere else to go and some woman was holding up the line.

While the woman dug in her pocket to pay for her double latte and discovered she didn't have her wallet with her, Sarah smoothly took out her billfold. Since she was next in line, it was easy for her to wink at the cashier and slip the dollar bills onto the counter beside the cash register.

The girl smiled, punched the button, and discreetly slipped the money into the register. She even managed to hand Sarah her change. By the time the woman looked up, still trying to sort through the few coins she had found, the girl said, "No need to worry. Someone already paid for your coffee." She motioned to the end of the row where the barista slid the tall cup toward her. The woman just stood there, stunned, and the girl repeated, "It's been taken care of."

"It has?"

The girl nodded.

"By who?"

Because of the winks, the cashier understood this was a secretive deal. She shrugged, but tilted her head toward Sarah.

The woman turned to see who had helped her. She raised her eyebrow gratefully at Sarah, although Sarah never confessed to her good deed. The woman smiled self-consciously at the impatient crowd before she walked away, clutching her cup to keep her hands warm, her eyes alight with happiness.

Sarah couldn't say exactly why she'd done it. Some who'd known her well through the years would tell you she did it just to get the line moving again. She'd stood in that line every morning for the past five years, watching people fumble through their purses or filing through their wallets, and she'd been perfectly willing to complain right alongside everyone else.

The days passed quickly once she returned to work. As she stood in the trading pit one morning that week, as the price of precious metals had begun to rise and she stood on tiptoe to make the hand signal and shouted, "Taking! Leo, we're taking all the way! Taking! Taking!" a gentle, certain voice whispered into her heart: *Is that what you want, Sarah? To take? When you can't be really happy, not the way I intend you to be, without giving?*

And so she did something about it. She realized Leo wasn't able to leave the office until she left first. She glanced at the clock that afternoon, making a mental note to head home at a decent hour so Leo could go home too. Another day, after they'd enjoyed a particularly successful trading session, Sarah said to him, "I've taken you for granted, Leo, and I apologize for that. Your help means so much to me. I'm proud of all we're able to accomplish together."

She watched him straighten his shoulders. "Really?" His voice sounded doubtful. "You are?"

"Absolutely," she said. And Leo stood even taller.

The more Sarah saw how kindness affected people in such a positive way, the more she wanted to be kind. She was beginning to realize that it not only affected the recipient, but it affected her too. She felt different. She had an excitement about ordinary, everyday life that she had never had before, as if in searching for opportunities to give, she was searching for treasure.

On a cold day at the grocery store, she returned her shopping cart to the boy who happened to be stooped into the wind, pushing a snakelike row of carts toward the door.

"I thought I'd bring this to you." Normally she left it propped against someone's car, not caring at all that they would have to deal with it before they could leave.

He stared at her like she was nuts. "I could have just come to get it. It's my job."

"I didn't mind pushing it over here. Thanks for all you do."

Sarah left a pack of gum on Ninth-Floor Guy's chair. She secretly notified the waiter and paid the lunch tab for a young couple who looked like they might not be able to afford to go out very often. She left a potted plant on Rona's desk and didn't sign her name.

She watched a little boy on the sidewalk who'd been left to take care of his little sister and told him she thought he was a very good big brother. She poked her head into a bridal boutique and spent a few minutes admiring the prospective brides. "Oh, how beautiful!" she said, grinning as one of them surveyed herself in the three-way mirror.

In the gift shop that opened off the lobby of her office building, Sarah told the cashier that she should always remember how loved she was by God. She took an extra half hour one afternoon and helped a friend in human resources organize some of her shelves. Rose commented how she liked Sarah's purse, and Sarah emptied it on the spot and gave it to her.

"What *happened* to you?" asked one of her colleagues.

If people at Roscoe had made a wide circle around Sarah Harper before, it was worse than ever now. No one had any idea quite what to expect from her. What had happened to the old Sarah Harper? Who was this new woman?

"She must have taken quite a bump on the head," Rona decided. "She's not acting like herself."

"Watch your back around her," suggested one of the ninth-floor guys. "Today she offered me the parking space by the elevator. The one she always used to race for. She said everyone was leaving it open, and she didn't want it anymore."

They figured the "new Sarah" had come up with some creative scheme to get everyone to help her so she could get another promotion. They couldn't believe she was just being nice. Even if she was, it wouldn't last more than a week or two. Once she got over the trauma of her experience, everyone whispered, everything would go back to normal and she would be the same selfish woman she'd always been.

"I tell you," they commented with wide eyes when they saw her traipsing back from the trading floor with that unusual, broad smile on her face, "there's something drastically strange going on with Sarah."

As the evening grew soft outside the window, Sarah treasured the few moments of peace before Joe came home. These days, the minute Joe walked in, brittle tension permeated the house as a shadow of anger fell over everything. Sarah had changed in other places, but at home, where it mattered most, she was still fighting with her pride. Being vulnerable at home felt especially dangerous to Sarah because she remembered all the times she had tried to be kind to her mother at home and been rejected.

Any minute, the car pool would drop off Mitchell from his weekly Cub Scout meeting. Kate gurgled happily from her high chair. Sarah plopped in the seat across the table from her and, with the schnauzer curled at her feet, started up a conversation. She rambled on about a great many things while Kate listened—politics and fall fashion trends and a client who changed his investment plans every time she phoned him. Finally she talked about the particularly pleasing shape of Cheerios, which was in Kate's department of expertise.

But mostly they sat across the table from each other, examining each other's gazes. Sarah touched her daughter's pulse where it rose and fell in the soft spot atop her head. She gazed at Kate's toes, which resembled a row of tiny butterbeans.

Kate picked up a Cheerio and held it in her mother's direction. Sarah ate it out of her daughter's fingers.

Sarah held back tears as she watched her daughter's innocent face.

She knew deep inside that she needed to have a heart-to-heart talk with Joe, but each time she planned to, she got scared.

A huge chasm still yawned between the two of them. Sarah really, really wanted to cross it, but she didn't know how. Every time she tried to say something kind to Joe, a lump constricted her throat. Her tongue felt like ice. She'd tried with her mother and failed miserably. She couldn't risk failing with Joe. This was the man she loved. It would be too awful.

Oh, Father, she thought. *There are so many walls built up between all of us. Especially between Joe and me. But Mitchell has been hurt too, and I can tell he doesn't trust me when I tell him something. I need your help, Father. How do I go about repairing the damage I've done?*

Joe called and said he would be home after bedtime because something had come up at work that he needed to finish. That had been happening more and more since her accident, and Sarah wondered if he was really busy...or just making excuses not to have to be with her.

Harold invited Sarah to meet him at Daley Plaza. He had business at city hall, he told her, and she owed him a rain check on the coffee date she'd forgotten.

She leaned against one of the cement planters, watching her stepfather approach carrying two paper cups complete with travelers' lids and hot sleeves. "Hey, kid," he said, handing over an Earl Grey tea he'd picked out for her. "How's my girl doing?"

She thought about that. "I'm fine," she said, nodding. "I really am."

"Do you have a few minutes to talk about your mother?"

The question felt like a jab to the pit of Sarah's stomach. *Ah.* So that's what Harold had wanted to meet about. *After all these years of watching Jane and me wound each other, poor Harold is still trying to play peacemaker.*

Sarah sighed. She couldn't help being disappointed. "I guess so." She had hoped he wanted to talk about other things instead.

"What's that face?"

"You know what it is."

"Yes, I guess I do."

It was easy giving things to people she didn't know very well or to people who hadn't hurt her. Surely God couldn't expect her to reach out again to this woman who pushed her away every time she tried. Sarah already knew what would happen. She'd only get shot down.

"Your mother had a lump removed from her breast last month."

"Oh no."

"The lump was benign, but she had a scary week before the results came back. I wanted her to tell you about it, but she wouldn't."

"Wow." Sarah stared at her drink lid. *Why would Jane go through something like that alone?* But she already knew the answer. Her mother would rather face a crisis alone than ask for help from the daughter she'd never wanted.

"A lot of time has passed, Sarah. I thought you might want to try reaching out to her again."

Sarah lifted her cup in a semitoast to the man who had loved them both, who had raised Sarah as his own daughter, who from the beginning of his marriage to Jane had been caught between them. "Have I thanked you lately for stepping in to raise me when no one else would? Have I thanked you for teaching me how to drive on the Ike?"

Harold threw back his head and laughed. "Don't you dare do that to me, Sarah. Don't you dare tell people I'm the one who taught you to drive. I'll never live it down."

She gave him a teasing cuff on the sleeve, but he grew serious again. "Your mother got hurt when she was young, and she never did anything to stop her heart from growing hard."

"Wasn't that her choice, not mine? Why should I have to be the one who keeps trying?"

Harold didn't speak.

"I was a child who felt responsible because my mother didn't accept me. I thought *I* was doing something wrong when it was Mama's job to love me."

She turned her cup in her hand. She didn't raise her eyes from the plastic lid on top.

"People on this earth don't always do the job they're supposed to do; we all have to live with that," he said. "We have to learn to forgive so we can enjoy life as much as possible. If we don't forgive those who have hurt us, then we end up hurting other people who are not responsible for our pain at all."

Sarah thought about that comment and then blurted out, "All I ever wanted was for my mother to love me. Was that too much to ask?"

Harold set his paper cup on the ground and took his step-daughter's face in his hands.

"Was it, Harold?"

"You have to keep trying because if you don't, you'll be the one hanging on to your mother's bitterness, and it will ruin your life."

Chapter Twenty-Two

Jane Cattalo had worked so many years at the Lathrop Steel Casings Company, it was easy for her to hit key sequences on the steno machine, keep a running tab on the expenditure spreadsheet, and carry on a conversation with someone across the counter all at the same time. Her hands tapped the keys as she scowled up at her daughter.

"Come on, Mama," Sarah pleaded. "It won't take long. You can do it over your lunch hour. I've already made the appointment."

"You made the appointment without asking me?"

"I wanted it to be a surprise."

If Jane wanted to say no, she couldn't. The other ladies in the Lathrop front office wouldn't let her. "Oh, go with her, Jane," one of them said. "It's a nice thing, what your daughter is doing. We'll cover if you're late getting back from lunch."

"You know how you like pretty fingernails," Sarah said. "Let me do this for you, Mama, please."

"Well, I'll go," she barked, shooting a look at her associates that said, *This is the last thing I wanted to do with my lunch hour.* "But I'm perfectly capable of paying for my own manicure."

As soon as they arrived at the salon, the receptionist stowed their purses and directed them to the manicurists' stations. Sarah slipped her hands into the hot water to let them soak while the manicurist showed her polish colors to choose from. If Sarah had thought an easy conversation with her mother might start up during this outing together, she was sadly mistaken. Rows of other customers sat with their nails being filed and their cuticles being snipped, their ears perked for any snippets of interesting conversation.

Every time Jane's manicurist removed Jane's hands from the soaking solution, she tapped Jane's knuckles with her cuticle stick. "Will you relax your fingers, please?"

Forty-five minutes later, mother and daughter still hadn't spoken to each other. The only reason Jane let Sarah pay the bill was because her freshly painted nails were still wet and she'd smudge them if she dug inside her purse. Sarah had thought ahead and had the money already out of her purse and lying on the table.

"Do you want to stop for a bite to eat?" Sarah asked as they walked toward the car again.

"You've used up all my time," Jane said. "I'll have to go hungry."

"No. You won't." Sarah steered into the first drive-through she could find and ordered a salad and a turkey sandwich to go. She paid at the window and set the sack in Jane's lap.

When they pulled up in front of Lathrop again, there was no reason for Sarah to go in.

"I don't understand why you did this," Jane said.

"I guess I wanted to thank you for taking such good care of Mitchell. I know you had to miss work and that was hard on you. I know it must have been a really scary day for him, and you made him feel better."

Jane clasped the sack between her thumb and her forefinger, holding it away from her as if it smelled bad.

Sarah finally gave up. She slumped in her seat and hated the impatience that nibbled at the edge of her voice. "And I guess I just thought we could talk, you know? I thought you would open up, and we could just have a conversation. I would like to have a good relationship with you, but you have always seemed to resent me for even being alive." She wondered if Jane would have been happier if she had died in that accident. Sarah tried once more to get through to her. "I had hoped that since I almost died you would open up and let me in, Mama. That's all."

"Well," Jane said, obviously hurt at the criticism. "I don't know why you always expect so much."

Each time Sarah checked www.nannyrating.com, she learned that Mrs. Pavik was taking Kate on trips to the park and other daily escapades. When Sarah returned home each night, she found the dishes washed, the carpet vacuumed, and the living room tidy. Kate's laundry was always done, and there was never a shortage of anything in the cupboards. From both the nanny-rating reports and evidence at the house, Sarah felt confident that Mrs. Pavik kept Kate fed, entertained, and bathed.

Every night before Sarah went to bed she plumped the cushions on the couch and straightened the afghan. The night after she'd taken her mother for a manicure, Sarah picked up one of the pillows, fluffed it, and was just about to arrange it to her liking when something caught her eye. At first glance, she saw it was a plastic ID holder from someone's billfold. Sarah didn't mean to pry. But she thumbed through it, already guessing its owner. This must have fallen out of Sophia Pavik's purse while she was taking care of Kate. In it Sarah found Mrs. Pavik's work visa and her U.S. driver's license. As she hurried to the phone to let the nanny know she'd found her important documents, the sleeve flipped open.

A photograph stared up at Sarah, a picture of a little girl with dark hair and dark eyes. Sarah's heart missed a beat. She'd seen pictures of this child before, but she couldn't quite remember where. In the corner of the plastic, Mrs. Pavik had stuck this note.

I LOVE YOU, MOMI. ELENA

No. It couldn't be.

Sarah sat down hard at the kitchen table while memories flooded her mind.

Mrs. Pavik had a daughter named Elena! A little girl who lived somewhere on the other side of the globe, a child who really did write notes like this!

Sarah stared at the child's beautiful little face. She berated herself. She ought to have asked Mrs. Pavik about her situation the day she'd gotten out of the hospital. Was Kate's nanny saving to bring her own child to Chicago? Because if she was, if that much was true, then there were other things that must be real too.

Sarah had assumed that the memories running through her mind came from some kind of offbeat dream—the kind people must have when they go through something traumatic.

But what if the whole thing wasn't an illusion? What if Wingtip really was an angel for the Cubs? What if God really had let me spend time with my grandmother?

Even though she'd been shown pieces of her own life, even though she'd thought she was dreaming, what if it had really been the Heavenly Father letting her look at herself through his eyes?

What if God really loved her as much as Annie said he did? What if the things about her mother were true? What if Tom Roscoe was as devious as it appeared when God gave her a good look at him?

That night after she phoned Sophia Pavik to let her know her documents and photos were safe, Sarah lay awake trying to figure things out. She stared at the stripe of moonlight where it seeped beneath the bedroom curtain. She lay on her half of the mattress, staring at the ridges and valleys of the man who slept as far on the other side of the bed as he could, turned away from her.

By the time the night had dissolved against the lozenge of a rising sun, Sarah could only come up with one answer. There was only one place she knew to go to find out if what she was thinking could possibly be true.

The traffic along LaSalle Street moved slower than a crawl. With the black trash bag slung over one shoulder, Sarah jaywalked. She darted in front of a taxi, giving the driver a nod of thanks for not running her down. She froze between two lanes, waiting for a garbage truck to rumble past before she bolted across another lane.

She'd filled the garbage bag with an assortment of clothes from her closet. She'd thrown in several good-sized leather purses, four or five pairs of shoes that she thought would go a long way toward keeping someone's feet warm, two jackets, a blouse or two, and several sweaters that still had tags. Hopefully the women who came to the clothing bin would all find something they could use.

The Windy City awakened to life around her. Steam rose from manhole covers. A street sweeper had just trundled past, leaving ribbons of water behind its huge wheel broom. A delivery truck honked in an alley. A man passed, shaking open the latest edition of *The Chicago Tribune*, trailing the scent of fresh newsprint behind him.

Sarah stood beside the clothing bin and looked around. Now that she'd arrived, she began to feel foolish. She yanked open the heavy metal door and began to slide her donations inside the receptacle.

In the back of her mind she was thinking, *Maybe I should have let Mitchell do this. Maybe he would have stood a better chance.* But she didn't dare run the risk of disappointing her son if she was wrong.

She was halfway through when she heard wheels squeaking behind her. Sarah turned to find a woman pushing a shopping cart.

"You going to put that sweater into that bin?" the woman asked.

Sarah nodded.

"You think I could have a look at it before you do?"

"Which one is it you like?" Sarah was holding one in each hand.

"The red one. I think the red one's real pretty."

Ordinarily Sarah wouldn't have done this. And even if she had done it, she would have pitched the sweater toward the woman in fear and hurried away. But today something larger and stronger than herself took over. She unfolded the sweater and held it up to the homeless woman's shoulders. She cocked her head and examined the effect as thoroughly as if she were a salesgirl in a fancy Magnificent Mile store. "You look very pretty," Sarah said. "I think it suits you."

"Do you?"

"Yes," Sarah said. "And it's a good color for your eyes. It makes them sparkle."

If the red yarn of the sweater didn't make the woman's eyes light up, then the compliment surely did.

"You really think so?"

"Yes, I do."

The woman had slipped the sweater on over her head and made it halfway up the block with Sarah smiling after her before Sarah remembered what she'd come for. "Wait!" she called out. "I've got something to ask you."

"What?"

"There's a man who comes to this bin sometimes. He looks for wingtip oxfords; those are the ones he likes best. People call him Wingtip. He's bald but has pieces of hair sticking out all over his head."

The woman shook her head. "Doesn't sound familiar at all."

"He asks people if they're lost and says he'll show them to the 'L' station if they give him a little money."

"There's about fifty of them that do that."

"Are there?" Sarah asked, losing hope.

"Yeah."

"Well, thanks anyway."

"Yeah."

After the woman ambled along, Sarah didn't know what else to do. She emptied the rest of her clothing donation into the bin. She stood on the curb for a long time, watching people pass. She was about to give up when she heard a small snort behind her and turned toward the sound.

She hadn't noticed the deep window well in the building behind her. A man slept there with a dirty canvas jacket shoved beneath his head for a pillow. Here was one of the most odd, telling pictures Sarah had ever seen. The window well, where the man slept hidden from view on limestone bricks as cold and gray as spent cinders, opened upon the display for a dazzling high-end furniture store. A gold brocade couch with overstuffed cushions stood empty between two blazing cut-crystal lamps. A chandelier overhead emitted light and warmth like a tantalizing joke.

This radiant, golden world waited on the other side of the glass—enticing, unreachable. The man had slept on a cold ledge of stone while a sofa of splendid style stood in plain view.

A tight knot formed in Sarah's throat. She'd found him! She touched the slope of the man's shoulder, which seemed familiar. "Wingtip?" she whispered.

He didn't move.

"Wingtip? Is it you?"

The man sputtered and snorted. He squinted into the morning light as he rolled toward the street and readjusted the jacket beneath his ear.

"I'm sorry," she said, her heart plummeting with disappointment. "I thought you were someone else. I'm looking for a friend down here, and I thought you were—"

The street bum sat up and blinked at her anyway.

When he realized he wasn't the friend she was looking for, he looked just as disappointed as Sarah.

"Hey," she said. "Are you hungry this morning?"

"You bet I'm hungry."

"I'll buy you something to eat, if you'd like. Maybe eggs. Hash browns. You want coffee? I'll get you some coffee."

"I'd rather have hot chocolate with whipped cream on top."

She nodded. "Maybe not at the top of the healthy list, but I will get you whatever you want."

"Would you talk to me?" he asked. "Do you want to hear about my family and my life? I haven't had anybody to talk to in a long, long time."

"I want to hear it all."

"I'm really hungry and awfully tired of eating other people's leftovers out of the garbage. Having somebody to talk to is better than a meal, you know." He grinned wildly as he stood up and poked an arm inside his tattered jacket. "I get lonely out here on the streets. Being cold and hungry is bad, but being lonely is the worst."

Sarah stood in the center of the cavernous room, the board dark and silent, its black surface reflecting the paper-littered floor. It was the late-afternoon lull at the Chicago Board of Trade. It had been another stormy day in the pits. Sarah lifted her headphones from where they'd been horseshoed around her neck and began twisting the cable around them.

The text message came on Sarah's phone at five minutes to five: Cornish meeting at 6:30. Drake Hotel lobby. I told them you'd be there. T.

Mitchell's Cub Scout pack was having its annual blue-and-gold banquet tonight. Sarah had helped him make place cards for each member of his family, including Kate.

Although Sarah had started to learn that God controlled time, she also knew that her time with her children wasn't infinite. Sarah stared at the screen, contemplating Tom's message before she hit Delete. *Oh, Father*, she asked. *Help. This is such new territory for me.*

She wasn't asking for the strength to get out of her job, but for the strength to rely on God, who wanted to show her a place of self-esteem in his love. She prayed that she'd be able to talk to Tom and draw a boundary based on respect; this, instead of self-centered needs that hadn't been met in her childhood.

"Hey, Leo," she said when she got back to her desk. "I'm headed up to Roscoe's office. Don't wait on me, okay?"

"I will," he said. "I don't mind."

"Nah," she said. "Thanks again for your hard work. I'll see you tomorrow."

When Sarah arrived on the twenty-fourth floor, she found Rona still typing furiously on her computer. Rona glanced up with a harried expression. "Oh good. There you are. He's been waiting to hear from you."

"Can I talk to him?"

"He's on the phone right now. I'll let him know you're out here if you'd like."

Sarah noticed the deep circles beneath Rona's eyes. "Are you okay?"

"I'm fine," she said. "Fine." And then in a fit of candor, "I'm just really, really tired, that's all. I just need to rest and he"—she indicated Tom's office door—"he's always got another project for me."

No sooner had Rona texted her boss than Tom appeared at the door, still on the phone, and waved Sarah in. Still deep in conversation, he pantomimed for Sarah to take a seat.

Oh, Father. I give you all my fear and resentment and insecurity, everything that made me work without balance in the first place. I give you everything that made me put impressing Tom Roscoe and others like him before Joe and the kids.

At first Sarah's hands were trembling. But by the time her boss hung up the phone, she felt calmer, more certain of herself. She leaned forward and explained that she couldn't make it to the meeting later because she had a previous family commitment.

"It's family," she told Roscoe. "There's nothing more important to me than that."

As Tom Roscoe's face contorted with disbelief, she explained that she was learning what to say yes and no to. "I'm good at this business," she said. "Maybe not the best, but certainly not the worst either. I'd like to be at your meeting, but that means you'll have to reschedule."

"You're asking me to arrange my calendar to fit into your time-table?" he asked.

"I am. I cannot keep putting my job before my family. If I do, I'm going to lose them, and I refuse to do that." Then she got really brave and said, "Tom, I realize God has not been pleased with the choices I've made. I have put myself and what I want to do before anything else. I mistreated people here at the company. I used them to get what I wanted, and I refuse to do it any longer."

"Sarah," Tom said with his face as red as a beet, "I'm sure you are well aware that there are a dozen MBAs waiting in line for every job that opens up in my company. Do you have any idea how easy it would be to fire—"

She interrupted him quickly to make sure she got to say everything that was on her heart. She wasn't going to let him intimidate her. "I like working here, Tom, and I believe I can be a benefit to you, but from now on, if I have made a promise to my family and you need me to work late, they will come before my job." Then she decided to dump everything on him while she had his attention. "Furthermore, I won't do anything even remotely dishonest to get, keep, or take revenge on clients. I really hope I don't have to leave and become your competition, but I have confidence that I can be a success even if I do have to work someplace else. Even if I need to start my own business."

Nobody had ever talked to Tom Roscoe like this, and she might be the last person to try, but Sarah had made up her mind—he could see that on her face. As she looked into his eyes, she thought she saw anger turning into respect.

His tone of voice remained firm. "Why don't you go home for now? We'll see what we can work out."

~◦ Chapter Twenty-Three ◦~

Joe Harper was miserable. Every time he looked at Sarah, he remembered how he'd felt when he thought he'd lost her. He remembered how his heart had clamped up every time the divers appeared on the surface of the water and signaled they hadn't found anything. He lived it in his dreams—the terrible wait as, over and over again, the searchers came up empty.

It seemed impossible that the two of them could be living a regular life now, with Sarah beside him in bed every night. He still felt as if she was separate and missing from him even after all that had happened. *Will it ever end? Will we ever be able to have an honest, open relationship?* he wondered.

It was worse because other things seemed to be going well for Sarah. She'd been arriving home from work on time and she'd made it to Mitchell's Cub Scout banquet last night and she'd even spent time with Kate and Mrs. Pavik. But she made no effort to make things better with *him*.

When he walked in the door from his work at the auto shop, he saw her eyes darken and her chin lift in defiance. When he sat on the edge of the bed and got ready to climb in at night, he saw her whole body go stiff.

On Saturday afternoon, while she stood putting on mascara in the mirror, Joe finally decided he couldn't wait any longer to talk to her. As he stood behind her, watching her reflection, he longed to put his hands on her shoulders. But just in time, he thought better of it.

When her eyes met his in the mirror, they were blazing. "What?" she asked. "What do you want?"

Not until he noticed his own eyes in the glass did he realize they were filled with fear.

I want to not be afraid that I'm going to lose you.

I want to not be afraid of the question Pete asked.

I want you to tell me you didn't do it on purpose.

"I want to know whether you made that split-second choice because you wanted to get away from yourself or because you wanted to get away from me. I have to know if you really had an accident or if you went off that bridge on purpose."

He saw her reaction, saw that his words had shocked her, but he was determined to get an answer. He was not going to live any more days in this cold silence that lingered between them.

"I want," she said very carefully, "for you to stop telling me what you want. Can't you see that I've changed? Can't you see that I'm trying?"

Neither of them saw the little boy listening, crouched in the corner with his baseball cap turned backward, trying to figure out a way to make his mom and dad stop fighting. They remained so consumed with themselves that they couldn't see beyond their own world of pain and hurt. Here at home, with so much at stake, Sarah and Joe found it impossible to stop demanding and start giving.

It was the schnauzer whimpering at the door that finally made Sarah realize something must be wrong. Sarah carried Kate to the front door and looked out, trying to figure out why their dog was standing at the front door whining.

"What's out there, Kate?" she asked her daughter. "Do you see anything? Mitchell? Do you know what's making this dog so crazy to get out in the yard?"

There wasn't an answer from Mitchell.

"Mitchell?" Sarah called, immediately heading toward his room. Then, "Joe, did you give Mitchell permission to play outside? Joe?"

But Joe didn't answer either.

After their heated exchange had ended earlier, Joe must have stormed out, anxious to put distance between them. Sarah opened the door to the attached garage and called his name again. She found him folded under the hood of the car, the place he always went to escape her. He straightened, the socket wrench still in his hand.

"I'm worried," she said. "The dog's going nuts. And I can't find Mitchell."

Joe mopped the grease off his hands with a rag. "I'm sure he's around somewhere."

Sarah's voice started to rise. "He isn't, Joe. I've already looked."

Joe's old television blared the Cubs game from the corner. Joe turned it down and called for his son.

"Did you tell him he could go somewhere?" she asked, her voice breaking.

Joe shook his head. "No. I never told him anything. I haven't seen him in, what?" Joe checked his watch. "An hour maybe?"

Even though Joe had turned down the television, the crowd noise from Wrigley seemed to fill the entire room.

Sarah froze. "The Cubs are playing right now?"

"They are."

"Oh, Joe."

"I don't know where he could— What?" He looked at his wife, uncertain of what she was getting at. He couldn't have been more confused. Then, suddenly, he knew.

"How long has the game been going on?" Mitchell's words raced through Sarah's head. The day he'd said at the clothing bin, "This man is our friend. I saw him at the Cubs game."

"A while."

"Do you remember when Mitchell asked you all those questions about the guy he thought was an angel? That man he told you he thought was helping God?"

Joe nodded.

"Where was he?" Sarah asked. "Where was that man when Mitchell saw him at the ballpark?"

Joe paused. "He was up in the scoreboard where he could look down on everything. That's why Mitchell thought—"

But Sarah interrupted him as she flung her coat over her arm. "Get the car keys, Joe. I know where he is. We have to get to Wrigley."

"What are you talking about?"

"He's gone to find Wingtip."

"Who's Wingtip?"

"I'll tell you on the way," she said, urgency flooding her voice. "Please, Joe. There isn't any time to waste."

⟋⟍

The inside of the scoreboard looked just about the same as it had back when it was finished in 1937. The paint was the same rust red as always, and the shadowed corners were littered with all sorts of junk—folding chairs, coolers, lost-and-found jackets—from years gone by. A three-story steel catwalk stretched across the entire width of the monstrous front wall and could be accessed only by a skinny metal ladder.

If it had been an ordinary day at the ballpark, Wingtip would have been happy standing on the second story of the catwalk, watching hits and runs. He would have made sure all the stats were properly displayed for all to see. But plans could change when the Heavenly Father spoke up.

"Mitchell Harper needs you," said the Creator of the universe. "Are you willing to help the boy?"

"Yes," Wingtip said. "You know how I feel about that kid. I'll do anything."

"Are you sure?"

"Yes, Lord."

"Even leave your post at a crucial moment in the game?"

"Yes, Lord. You know I will."

"Ah," the Heavenly Father said. "You are a good and faithful servant. You are the right person for this job. I knew so from the very beginning."

"For the job with the Cubs?" Wingtip asked.

"For Mitchell *and* the Cubs," the Lord of Hosts told him.

What could make a difference for the team and *for Mitchell?* Wingtip was about to ask. But he never got the chance to finish his own question. At that moment, he spied Mitchell climbing up the steps in the bleacher seats, weaving his way through the rowdy crowd. No matter how many people stood in his way, the little boy managed to shoulder his way through the hordes.

Even from this distance, just as he'd done the first time he'd laid eyes on Mitchell, Wingtip could sense the little boy was troubled. The baseball fans didn't pay him much mind as he shoved his way past and kept climbing to the top of the bleachers.

Suddenly Wingtip knew what Mitchell was doing. *He's coming to find me!* No young boy ought to attempt such a climb. No young child had legs long enough to make those last precarious steps. A friendly gentleman cuffed Mitchell on the sleeve and said something Wingtip couldn't hear. *Stop him. Please!* Wingtip ached to make the man hear him. *Don't let that little guy try the ladder! Ask him where his parents are. Ask if you can help him!*

But the man didn't heed the tug in his heart. He glanced around once, as if he didn't know what to do. "Hey, kid," he asked. "Are you supposed to be going up there?"

"Yep," Mitchell said. "I got a friend up here. I'm going to find him."

Much to Wingtip's distress, the guy shrugged Mitchell off and turned his attention back to the game.

Mitchell snuck beneath the scoreboard and started his assent as Soriano snow-coned a catch against the ivy and hurled it toward second base. It was a tricky climb to make it up the spindly metal ladder, but once Mitchell started, he never looked down, only up. The wind blew in from the lake in a steady gale. Halfway up the rungs, Mitchell lost his baseball cap. It blew off his head and probably landed somewhere on Sheffield Avenue. "Bottom game, top floor, American League," someone shouted to

Wingtip. "One run top of the seventh. The score! Who's changing the score?"

But Wingtip wasn't about to go higher on that catwalk while Mitchell Harper was in danger. The numbers remained unchanged. It was the seventh inning, and everyone was having a good time; no one thought too much of it. Mitchell was intent on his climb.

"Wingtip?" he called. But the wind blew his voice away. "Are you up here?"

Halfway up the ladder, the metal rungs seemed to widen and stretch farther apart. Mitchell grabbed the next rung and pulled himself up, but not before his sneaker slipped and his knee banged against the metal. He steadied himself and, for the first time, he looked down. A pebble had dislodged from the sole of his shoe. He watched as it bounced against metal and sailed out into open air. Mitchell watched it fall and froze in fear.

Sarah and Joe entered the ballpark at that moment, a security officer in tow. "I'm sorry, ma'am," the officer was saying at her elbow. "Security's tight around the scoreboard. They'd never let a kid climb—"

But Sarah gasped and pointed. Beneath the scoreboard, inside a cage of chain-link fencing, Sarah could see a small figure inching his way toward the trap door at the top. "There he is." Joe grabbed his wife's shoulders. Sarah gripped her husband's arm.

He's going to fall. But Sarah didn't dare think it.

"Joe," she whispered. "We've got to do something."

"We will." This he promised his wife. In that one instant before Joe took off running, the rift between them dissolved. There was too much at stake. Too much to think of losing.

"Help him," she whispered.

High atop the ladder, Mitchell forced himself to move. With shaking hands, he pulled himself up three more rungs. He'd almost made it to the top. He stretched as far as he could and, with one fist, pounded on the piece of plywood meant to keep everyone out.

It took precious seconds for someone to move the two-by-four that wedged the door shut. The lumber moved with a terrible grating sound. "I'm looking for Wingtip?" he asked the head scorekeeper the minute a crack appeared.

"Kid! You can't be up here. What do you think you're doing? Why didn't someone stop you?"

"I—I've got to talk to Wingtip."

"There's security down there. Supposed to keep idiots from climbing up here."

Mitchell was crying. "He's up here, he's got to be. He can do anything. He could make them stop fighting."

"Who? There's not anyone named Wingtip that I know of. Just us scorekeepers." The man reached to pull him up. "Good heavens. Kid, grab my hand. Let's get you safe."

Mitchell reached up. Their fingers brushed. But before the man had a good grasp of the boy's knuckles, a wind gust came off Lake Michigan, stronger than most.

The whole scoreboard moved. The huge flags and their lanyards clattered against their poles overhead. The tin walls vibrated.

The numbers shuddered in their windows.

Mitchell lost his balance...and fell.

Wingtip had stayed in his corner of the scoreboard scaffolding, watching, waiting. And in this split second, he finally understood. All these years he'd thought he was here to nurse the Cubbies through a century of losing, to help them make it through the play-offs and, finally, to emerge victorious in the big game. But now he knew he'd been put on this earth for something else entirely. He'd been put on this earth to be a guardian angel for one eight-year-old boy who needed him, for one family that deserved another chance, for one woman who longed to be whole.

Wingtip flew into the Windy City sky without counting the cost to himself. The Heavenly Father might have to do some searching; angels might have a few reservations about overseeing the Lovable Loser Cubs these days. But Wingtip had no doubt that God could assign the Chicago Cubs another angel someday. It *was* time. For him to do the job he'd been called here to do.

And from where she stood across Wrigley, Sarah caught a glimpse of her son falling. At the same time, she thought she saw something else. She saw another silhouette catch up and pause in midair. A flash of motion, and then all went still. The action on the field went silent. All Sarah could hear was the heavy flap of feathered wings, and she could only think that the sound was the seagulls as they dipped and screeched and wheeled over the ballpark, knowing there would be plenty of snacks to scavenge after the game ended.

For a long time the people who saw it would speak in reverent whispers of the day a boy fell from the scoreboard with only a broken arm to show for it. They would talk about how the boy's father came racing up the bleachers, the woman right behind him, only to find their kid sitting up and looking confused and asking what had happened.

Only the Heavenly Father knew why the momentum switched and the Cubs suddenly lost a game they had been winning. Only the Heavenly Father knew that a trustworthy angel had made a choice to forget about his favorite baseball team. Only the Heavenly Father and a grateful mother and a relieved father knew that Wingtip had saved a little boy's life that day.

Sarah stood in the hallway and peeked into her son's room. Joe and Mitchell were reading a chapter book together, each of them taking a page, their heads drifting together as they drifted closer to sleep.

When Joe came to the end of his page, he didn't hand the book over. Instead it fell into his lap, and he began to snore. Mitchell didn't complain because he was already sound asleep.

Sarah watched father and son for a long time before she tiptoed across the room and awakened her husband. "Hey," she whispered when he lifted his head. She spoke in a tone that let him know she wasn't afraid anymore, that she wasn't protecting herself from being hurt, that let Joe know everything was going to be all right. "We need to have a long talk."

He smiled back sleepily. "I think so too."

"Are you going to stay in here all night, or are you going to come with me?"

Joe smiled again. "What do you think?"

She asked Joe to come downstairs and sit on the couch with her. They both got comfortable, and as Sarah started to talk, tears filled her eyes. "Joe," she said, "I have an amazing story to tell you."

She told him in vivid detail everything she had seen during

the time she was gone. She told him that she now realized she had been living all wrong and that all of her motivation for what she had done was selfish. She tried as best she could to help him understand how fearful and insecure she had felt all that time. When she finished, Joe was visibly moved.

Their eyes locked.

At that moment, Sarah felt free. Taking responsibility for her behavior, being completely honest with Joe about everything, lifted a weight from her that had made her more miserable than she could have ever imagined. Sarah knew, at that precise moment, that no matter how difficult it might be, she would always be completely honest. No more pretending for Sarah Harper. She was going to be real and genuine with everyone, especially with her husband.

∽෮ Chapter Twenty-Four ෮∿

Just past four o'clock, Sarah logged onto her computer and entered the Web site for www.nannyrating.com. It had been far too long since she'd checked how Mrs. Pavik and Kate were doing. But these days she found herself not checking into the Web site nearly as often as she used to. She punched in her ID number, and new data began to load. The site appeared, and Sarah scrolled down the page.

"Your nanny has one new post," the screen announced after completing its search. Sarah clicked and found the message. It surprised her that this one came with a phone number attached. She read through it. And read through it again.

"Your nanny is doing a terrific job," the post said. "You should know that your baby appears totally happy. She eats well, and it's no wonder that she appears quite chubby. She loves to watch the polar bears. If you decide you don't need your nanny anymore, I'd like to have him. And actually, I don't even have a child. But this guy is just so cute with the baby."

That's when Sarah remembered Joe had closed the shop for the day. He'd regally invited Kate to accompany him on a father/daughter date to the Lincoln Park Zoo to celebrate the completion of his latest engine transplant in his latest Miata. And Kate, in her fist-chewing, toothless way, had shot him a grin that meant she, as princess of the household, royally accepted.

Sarah glanced at the time on her real-time commodities tracker. She could either panic and partake in a mad dash to the trading floor, or she could take a deep breath and realize how well Leo had it covered here. She grinned. Just let them do without her for five minutes. They were talented people and knew how to do a great job.

Sarah perched on the edge of her fancy swivel office chair and placed her calves side by side, her feet flat on the floor in the desk's kneehole. She retrieved a pile of financial reports and tamped their edges even.

Since she was about to pay homage to Joe's role as husband and father, she wanted everything strictly in order. She aligned the pencils and pens inside the trough of her drawer. She swept rubber bands together in the corner so none of them could escape. Then she began typing on her computer keyboard with the same finesse a pianist would use in Orchestra Hall.

"Thank you so much for your thorough report on my nanny," she pounded out. She leaned back, surveyed her work from a distance, and liked what she saw. Her fingers tripped over the keys again. "I am pleased to hear of his exemplary performance." Then, "My nanny is wearing a wedding ring, in case you hadn't noticed. He is married to me, and I wouldn't give him up for anything in the world."

She left the cursor there for a time, just watching it blink before she signed her name. She typed *Sarah Harper* with a flourish and then printed a copy.

Joe was going to love this.

She swiveled in the chair, just thinking about it. She couldn't help it; she laughed herself silly.

⁓

Sarah sat on the edge of her mother's table, watching Jane peel apples. Harold told her that Jane was making jelly, so Sarah had stopped over to help.

The recipe in Annie's handwriting, faded and spotted, stood propped against the sugar bowl. Jane was peeling apples in the same round curls Annie had made.

"Mama," Sarah said. "We have to talk."

Jane dropped apple slices into the kettle with a soft *kerplunk*. "We have nothing to talk about."

"Mama, we do."

And even though Jane stood as stiff as a rake handle, even though her jaw stayed set in a stubborn square, Sarah knew she had to try to make a start somewhere. She knew telling Jane her whole experience with Annie and Wingtip would be too much for her right now. So she simply and softly said, "Mother, I know that somewhere in your life you were terribly hurt and disappointed. Someone stole your dreams, and I am sorry about that."

Jane stared at her.

"I am really sorry, but it wasn't my fault, and it's time you stopped blaming me. God loves you, Mama, and he wants you to be happy and enjoy the rest of your life." Sarah waited in silence, hoping her mother would say something. "I've been praying for you, Mama, and I know that God is going to change your heart."

She waited for a reaction, but Jane didn't respond.

"You were hurt, and you hurt me because of it. I want you to know that I forgive you, and if you ever need me, all you have to do is call."

Sarah was prepared to leave and just trust that God would someday make things right. She headed for the door. She stopped, though, when she heard footsteps behind her.

She turned to look. Even though Jane's jaw was still set with stubbornness, she managed to say, "Sarah, thank you for coming today," and they both knew that was a beginning.

Sarah knew her own heart when it came to her mother. Someday she would have the joy of seeing Jane completely healed from her past. She knew that God wanted to do that. And if the Heavenly Father wanted to use her in the process, Sarah prayed for the grace to be whatever he needed her to be, ready to do Jesus' bidding, so she could help Jane make her own journey toward understanding how much she was worth.

The best thing about having a broken arm, Mitchell told his dad, was how everyone in Mrs. Georges's class at school (Kyle, Ryan, even Lydia—*especially* Lydia) used the coolest Sharpie colors they could find to decorate his cast. "2 nice 2 B 4gotten," Mrs. Georges had written with a shy smile. "Way to go, dude!!!!" wrote Kyle Grimes, and beside that he drew a picture of a swimming shark. Ryan had added in green marker, "Don't ever break your arm." Add to that, people everywhere he went, even in the aisles at the grocery store, stopped him, gave him sympathy, and asked how he'd done it. When he told them he'd done it trying to climb inside the scoreboard at Wrigley, that an angel he'd once met had rescued him, that everything had ended up just the way it was supposed to end up, they usually set the jar of mayo or the bag of chips—whatever they happened to be holding at the time—inside their basket and glanced over his head at his mother with an *Ah, the imagination of a child* look, expecting to see a conspiratorial twinkle in her eye. But his mother would nod her agreement every time and shoot them a small tilt of a smile.

"That's the story, just the way Mitchell tells it. What do you think? We're so grateful." Which would make them look a little askance at him and find something fascinating to read about on a cereal box before they wished him well, gave him one more dubious glance, and pushed their carts along up the aisle.

The worst thing about having a broken arm, Mitchell told his dad, was trying to get the sleeve of his Cubs jacket over his cast. Which is the reason he stood at the door this minute with his cap sideways on his head and his jacket dangling halfway off his shoulder.

"Let's see what we can do about this," Joe said. And as Sarah watched him kneel in front of their son, as she rested in the peace and joy she had, she knew she wanted to spend the remainder of her life helping others find what she had found through Jesus. She and Joe had already agreed that they, along with Mitchell and Kate, would spend one evening a week visiting homeless shelters and helping in whatever way they could.

Forehead to forehead, Joe helped Mitchell slip his arm through the sleeve and do up his coat. "How's that?" Joe fastened a few snaps. "You okay?"

Never mind Mitchell's blond hair and Joe's dark locks. Never mind one being young and the other, well, middle-aged. As Mitchell nodded, the eyes, the jaw, the jut of noses, gave perfect reflections of each other.

"Honey?" Joe called. "You two ready?"

Sarah slung the diaper bag over a shoulder, lifted Kate from her high chair, and held her overhead. "Hello," she said to the clear, sun-struck blue eyes of her daughter as Kate thrust a drool-covered fist toward Sarah's nose. "What are you thinking?" For a moment, the tiny, open face was the only thing in Sarah's range of vision. When she kissed the baby's cheek, smelled the milk on her breath, the entire world paused, became beautiful. "Are you ready for this?"

She would have taken Kate to the Cubs game tonight even if Mrs. Pavik had been available for babysitting. The last pitch of the regular season had been thrown. It just seemed like something the Harpers needed to do, being there together for a post-season play-off in honor of Wingtip, as the Cubbies contended for a shot at the series.

Sarah had encouraged Mrs. Pavik to take time off. She and Joe wanted to pay for her trip home to Poland so she could drink in the details of her own daughter's face and hopefully jump-start proceedings to bring her child to America. Even though Sarah and Kate would make do with someone else for a while, the nanny position would be available when Mrs. Pavik returned. Sarah promised. And Sarah also offered to accompany Sophia to the imposing glass tower of the Federal Building when it came time to file Elena's visa petition, not because Sarah had pull at government offices but because her presence could offer a healthy dose of moral support. She and Joe would also point Mrs. Pavik to a social-service agency that could help with the little girl's medical expenses.

It was a new way of living for Sarah Harper. Offering to help people. Encouraging them and offering what she knew could assist them or make them feel better about things. She noticed that finding opportunities to give joy away was the main thing that released joy into her own life. It still amazed her…this principle of sowing and reaping that she had discovered in the Bible. It absolutely worked. When she had sown misery into the lives of others, she was miserable herself. Now that she was sowing joy, she was joyful.

Joe and Mitchell wanted to ride the "L" train to the game. So they wouldn't have to worry about parking, Joe urged. So they loaded the car with the foldable stroller and other baby paraphernalia, drove the new hybrid to the Park & Ride lot, and boarded the Purple Line at Linden, headed south.

By the time they made the connection to the Red Line at Howard, the train was standing room only. Everyone wore red and pinstripe blue. They were all in this together. Fraternity brothers heading in from Loyola struck up baseball chatter with families from Wilmette and businessmen from Bryn Mawr. "Think Zambrano can pitch another no-hitter?" "Think Aramis Ramirez can tag another pinch runner?" "Think Cedeno's batting average stands a chance?"

The elevated train ground to a stop with a shrill screech of brakes, propelling everyone forward. Sarah and Joe, Mitchell and Kate spilled out the sliding doors with the crowd. In the distance they could see the familiar red marquee. WRIGLEY FIELD. HOME OF CHICAGO CUBS.

Hot-dog stands and pizza parlors did a brisk business. Hawkers held up unofficial programs for an exorbitant price. On the corner of Waveland, an elderly lady sold necklaces she'd strung by hand, made of red and blue beads. Directly beside the entrance, a harried clerk sold Cubs jerseys, pencils, pennants, and bobblehead dolls.

Mitchell led the way with his foam claw while Joe pushed the stroller. Sarah followed with one finger crooked through the belt loop of Joe's jeans. When they wove their way through the throngs and stepped through the tunnel and came out beneath the banks of spotlights, Joe heard Sarah's breath catch.

"Dad," Mitchell whispered, "there it is."

"I know, son." Joe rumpled his son's hair. He slid his arm around Sarah's shoulders and pulled his wife tightly against him.

There were the endless stretch of emerald grass and the rumpled curtains of ivy and the red brick wall. Joe said, "There are plenty of nice houses here in Chicago, but nothing that makes so many people feel at home as Wrigley."

Sarah laid her head against his shoulder. She wiped her eyes behind her sunglasses. He knew she was starting to cry.

On the opposite side of the field, the scoreboard gleamed. Its gigantic clock, which read 6:55, smiled down at them like an old friend. The team-standings pennants, strung in order along a sturdy rope, clanged and snapped against the flagpole. The name of each team playing tonight had already been set in slots facing the field. Soon the scoreboard would be posting the triple-crown stats of each batter. For now, each game—including this one—sported a long string of empty panels. A few tiny squares stood open, through which you could see the movement of someone sorting numbers, getting panels ready to set in place after a big play. But no matter that the regular scoreboard manager had been doing this job for years now, no matter that he'd been trained by another guy who'd worked forty years before *him*.

It wasn't so long ago that Wingtip waited with an elbow draped over the sill, his head inclined toward their seats in the bleachers. Mitchell couldn't take his eyes from the scoreboard, thinking of his friend with a starched white shirt, eyes as sparkly as stars, brows as tufted as nettle bunches.

Joe happened to glance in the same direction. He sensed his son's melancholy. "You know that you may not see him anymore, don't you, son?"

Mitchell didn't know how he knew, but deep down in his heart he knew his father was right.

"He can still see you, and the Father might even have him help you at another time in life, but he's finished his job with this family for now. He's probably helping someone else that he met here at Wrigley Field. There are lots of needy people in the world who could use some help from heaven."

Mitchell leaned against Joe's broad arm. "Dad, do you think Wingtip is still in the scoreboard just like before, only now we just can't see him?" Joe thought carefully before answering, but he finally said, "You know son, I'm not sure, but one thing I am sure of is that our Father in heaven is everywhere and he is with us, watching us and taking care of us all the time."

Rounds of cheers went up from the sections above them as the Cubbies took the field. A catcher donned a helmet, stooped behind home plate, and made a target of his glove to help the pitcher warm up. A father hugged his son against his chest. A mother settled her baby daughter in her lap. A husband draped his arm across his wife's shoulders, drew her close while her heart repeated the new lessons she'd learned from her Heavenly Father.

Any minute you might get the chance to make someone else

happy. Any minute you might get your chance to be a giver. So be watchful at all times and don't let any opportunity to do good pass you by.

"Ball's in!" the ump shouted.

The pitcher stood just this side of the mound. He stepped onto the rise and stared straight down the pike toward his catcher. He touched the brim of his cap and spit in the dirt and started his windup.

On the scoreboard, the clock's hand ticked another notch forward; another minute had just gone by. There came the lovely *crack* of bat against ball. As the baseball sailed far against the night, Sarah laid her hand on Joe's knee. He covered her hand with his own, their wedding bands almost touching. Neither of them, ever again, would think of letting go.

Discussion Questions

by Tinsley Spessard

1. Sarah lived at a frantic pace, one that is common and often admired in our culture. Why do you think that hyperscheduled, multitasking lifestyle is revered in America? Why was Sarah driven to stay so busy? Compare that striving mentality with "Be still, and know that I am God" (Ps. 46:10). Why is it so hard for us to "be still"?

2. "Unless you change and become like little children, you will never enter the kingdom of heaven" (Matt. 18:3). In what ways did Mitchell's innocent faith help him see more clearly than the adults around him? Can you think of gifts God has given you that you might have missed if you had been too busy with your adult-sized worries?

3. Sarah wondered, "Wasn't that what being alive was all about, about being *happy*?" (p. 70), and during a fight with Joe, she asked, "What about me being happy?" (p. 108). Is happiness a right—something we deserve? Do you think God promises us happiness? Why or why not?

4. Joe said to Sarah, "If I depended on how you treat me to determine my value, Sarah, I wouldn't think very highly of myself" (p. 108). What should determine your value? If you

believed your worth comes from God alone and lived from a secure belief in how much he loves you, how would that affect your relationships? Would it change what you feel you need from other people?

5. In the story, the characters continually let each other down: Sarah was disappointed by her mother, Joe was disappointed by Sarah, and Mitchell's hopes were dashed by one adult after another. Describe how each one tried to earn the love and attention he or she craved. Did it ever work? Is this what we do with God—try to earn a love he has already given? Explain your answer.

6. After a fight, can the next day ever be "any other day"? Reconciliation or bitterness hangs in the balance. Describe the power "I'm sorry" and "I forgive you" can have. Sarah wanted to put the blame on Joe. Does there always have to be blame in a disagreement? When you feel accused, when is it the right time to let it go? When should you stand up for yourself? Discuss times when Jesus acted assertively and times he chose to remain passive.

7. While rescuers searched for Sarah, Joe thought, *"What does a person do at a time like this…when you really don't know how to pray?"* (p. 146). Do you think prayer is something you have to get right? Are you comfortable praying? Describe ways people can pray without even thinking.

8. During that same moment at the river, Joe thought "he should have let the chaplain stay. That would have been better than phoning the pastor at the church they'd attended a few times. It would have been easier and better and *guilt free*. How did you say, 'You don't know me, but I need you'?"

(p. 146). Why would calling his pastor make him feel guilty? Is that how people sometimes feel with God? Why?

9. Eugene Peterson paraphrases Matthew 5:3 in *The Message*: "You're blessed when you're at the end of your rope." Describe how that beatitude proved true for Joe and Sarah.

10. Joe and Sarah's story had a happy ending, but many times life does not provide those. The car crash is fatal, or the marriage breaks up. Those hard times can bring us to the end of ourselves and draw us closer to God, or they can leave us feeling abandoned because as Joe said, God "didn't fix their lives the way [he] wanted them fixed" (p. 152). How do you think Joe would have ultimately responded to God if Sarah had not survived, and why? What is your response to God when things do not go your way?

11. What do you think of Sarah's "dream" after she drove off the bridge? During the dream, Annie said, "God didn't send you here to change things, child. He sent you here so you'd ask him to help change things that you can't" (p. 160). Discuss ways you might be trying to control parts of your life instead of giving those areas to God. Do you have certain ways to identify these problem issues? Share your techniques for "letting go."

12. Was Wingtip what you would expect an angel to be? Why or why not? Talk about his role in Mitchell's life and in Sarah's.

13. Most of us won't experience the brink of death as Sarah did, but how can we live as if we had? What can we do on a daily basis to keep our focus on the truly important things? Talk about what living with "Christ in you" (Col. 1:27) means to you. For the next few weeks, ask the Heavenly Father to

bring someone specific into your life each day, someone you can help. Schedule a time to meet again and, keeping the ones you've helped anonymous, discuss how you feel after this exercise. Is it something you want to continue? Why or why not?

About the Authors

JOYCE MEYER is one of the world's leading practical Bible teachers. A #1 *New York Times* bestselling author, she has written more than eighty inspirational books, including *The Secret to True Happiness, 100 Ways to Simplify Your Life*, the entire Battlefield of the Mind family of books, her first venture into fiction with *The Penny*, and many others. She has also released thousands of audio teachings, as well as a complete video library. Joyce's *Enjoying Everyday Life*® radio and television programs are broadcast around the world, and she travels extensively conducting conferences. Joyce and her husband, Dave, are the parents of four grown children and make their home in St. Louis, Missouri.

DEBORAH BEDFORD is an award-winning author whose novels have been published in eighteen different countries and in a dozen different languages. She and her husband, Jack, have two college-aged children and two dogs. They live in Jackson Hole, Wyoming, where they enjoy fly-fishing, horseback riding, and kayaking in the Tetons. Deborah began her career by writing romance novels. As the years passed, she began to understand a calling to write books that reflected spiritual overtones, communicating the message that following the Father can bring a healed life and a glorious adventure. She's never looked back. Look for other inspirational novels by Deborah, including *A Morning Like This, A Rose by the Door, Remember Me,* and *When You Believe.* You can reach Deborah by visiting her Web site at www.deborahbedfordbooks.com. She invites you to be a friend on Facebook: Go to www.facebook.com, Deborah Bedford.

If you liked *Any Minute,*
you'll love the *New York Times*
bestselling novel *The Penny*!

Jenny Blake has a theory about life: big decisions often don't amount to much, but little decisions sometimes transform everything. Her theory proves true the summer of 1955, when fourteen-year-old Jenny makes the decision to pick up a penny imbedded in asphalt, and consequently ends up stopping a robbery, getting a job, and meeting a friend who changes her life forever.

Jenny and Miss Shaw form a friendship that dares both of them to confront secrets in their pasts—secrets that threaten to destroy them. Jenny helps Miss Shaw open up to the community around her, while Miss Shaw teaches Jenny to meet even life's most painful challenges with confidence and faith. This unexpected relationship transforms both characters in ways neither could have anticipated, and the ripple effect that begins in the summer of the penny goes on to bring new life to the people around them, showing how God works in the smallest details. Even in something as small as a penny.

Available now wherever books are sold.